CRAB CAKE
&
PEPPER

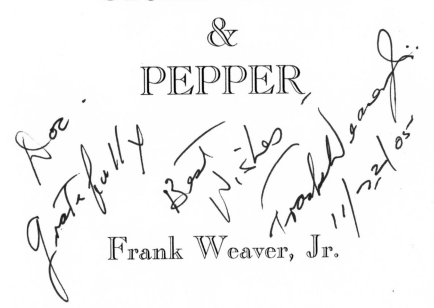

Frank Weaver, Jr.

PublishAmerica

Baltimore

ISBN: 1-4137-3140-6
PUBLISHED BY PUBLISHAMERICA, LLLP
www.publishamerica.com
Baltimore

For Peggy, Jimmy and Wendy, who have always encouraged me to follow my dreams; and for my faithful companion, 'Tego, a Golden Retriever, who, with unconditional love and a deep sense of loyalty, graciously curbs her vivid and creative imagination while lying patiently by my side guarding, but mostly watching, as I write.

This early first edition copy
of CrabCake & Pepper
is number ___ of
the first 500.

Acknowledgments

Whenever novels are written, there's always more than one person involved in the project. Unfortunately, it's impossible to include all those names along with the author's on the byline. Fortunately, we have this method to acknowledge their assistance in helping to bring fruition to *Crab Cake & Pepper*. I am deeply indebted to these wonderful folks, regardless of how small their role may have been. Their task was certainly a labor of love, not for me, you understand, nor for the story of *Crab Cake & Pepper*, but most importantly, to promote reading.

Without my daughter Wendy, this book would still be in the manuscript stage. It was she, asking frequently if the book was finished, standing proudly by, cheering me on, and who first volunteered to proof it in its entirety. She expected its finale. If I had never finished it, her disappointment would've been evident. Unaware, she was that secret force that kept me writing.

Others who have lent their advice are Steve Kyer and his wife, Trixie, both English teachers in the Ohio School system; my 1950-51 Hametown one room schoolhouse teacher, Mr. Claude P. Swartzbaugh, now retired, who taught me in my fourth year of school; my sister and a retired schoolteacher herself, Shirley Indictor of Philadelphia and our long time family friend, Allen Ziegler from Mt. Wolfe, Pennsylvania.

I am also most grateful to my mother, Dorothy M. Weaver of The Courtyards in Shrewsbury, Pennsylvania, for reading the manuscript and offering me words of encouragement along the way, and for the input offered by my younger sister, Jeanne DiLorenzo, of Gap, Pennsylvania, who graciously supported me with words of optimism.

Two others must be mentioned or this list would be incomplete. Former newspaper editor and college composition teacher, Jim Sewell offered help as a literary manager, in writing tips and critiquing chapter by chapter as I wrote. It was Jim who first suggested writing the narration in proper English, but quoting the characters with a dialect. Jim believed that it added a certain dimension when read, that it raised the story to a new level.

The other is Tamara Proctor, an associate editor of our local newspaper here in Ohio's Portage Lakes. Her perpetual confidence and strong belief in my writing ability, along with her daily subtle reminders to finish it, helped in driving me to complete the work in a time frame I never thought was possible.

I must also thank the Editorial Director at PublishAmerica, Ms. Miranda Prather, whose diplomacy alone would be considered by many to be an asset to the publishing industry. It was she who displayed the patience of Job with my persistent questions during most, if not all, of the contract negotiations.

Finally, without the solid support from my wife, Peggy, I would never have started this project. Many were the nights I'd awaken with a thought, an idea, regardless of time, and I'd sit at the computer putting down those thoughts, lest I forgot. She never questioned this nocturnal obsession. She understood the creative juices flowing from the brain, down the arm, out the fingertips and onto the keyboard. She understood. She was a godsend with her skilled knowledge of proper grammatical usage. I relied on her more than any other and to her, I am most grateful.

Frank Weaver, Jr.
Portage Lakes, Ohio
www.FrankWeaverJr.com
March, 2004

"Heaven goes by favor. If it went by merit you would stay out and your dog would go in!"
- Mark Twain

Prologue

Twigs snapped. Dead leaves crackled. Waist high foliage, brown and still lifeless from last fall, bristled as the two sleazy ex-cons, lanky Angus "Tattoo" MacGrew and his heavyweight companion, Isadore "Crazy Eyes" Zitoulleo, cautiously inched their way south under the cover of heavy brush along the high eastern fence row.

The very top ridge bordering last autumn's harvested cornfield overlooked Sawmill Road and separated the hamlet of Potosi from the entrance to White Oak Valley. The spring evening's cold rain poured down upon their uncovered heads, chilling them to the bones. Nevertheless, these two longtime villains were determined neither to be seen doing dastardly deeds nor to be caught ever again.

Serving time in the state prison was enough to mellow any hard nosed convict. After fifteen years, the recently released duo had their fill of incarceration. Both felt they had done more than enough time for their crimes and were exhausted from lack of freedom. This is not to say they were softies. On the contrary. Both were considered to have been dangerous criminals and were still considered as such by many. They got their kicks from living dangerously day to day and from the adventurous rush of successfully escaping the strong arm of the law. So strong was this felonious desire that shortly after being released from the pen the two crooks returned to the only profession they had ever known, armed robbery.

In desperate need of the necessary pocket money most people require to sustain themselves in the business of day to day living, they knocked off a mom-and-pop grocery store along Pennsylvania's State Route 94 just south of York Springs in Adams County and were on the lam once again. But this time it was different. Something went wrong. This time there were people seriously injured in that armed robbery. And while their immediate mission was to stay three steps ahead of the law, their original long range goal still remained unchanged.

9

Upon gaining freedom from prison, their initial plans were to act swiftly upon certain information Tattoo had overheard while he was still doing time. His elder brother, Ian 'Whispers' MacGrew, very softly, but inadvertently, revealed the location to another inmate of a metal box filled with loot from a robbery which had been hidden more than ten years earlier. The stolen money was the result of a bank holdup which had landed Whispers in the slammer with a 25 year sentence.

By this time, both jailbirds had hoped to have retrieved that loot, but lacking a good sense of direction, they were still on the run. "I tell ya, Crazy Eyes, I think we's headin' the wrong way," Tattoo insisted for the third time.

"Then make up yer pea brained, 'tater pickin' mind, Angus "Tattoo" MacGrew," Crazy Eyes lectured. Whenever he was called by his full name, it was a clear and ominous signal that Crazy Eyes was nearing the end of his patience. "'Twas you who said this was the way ta go, not me," Crazy Eyes insisted. "Ain't nobody else around here that I can see. Now 'zactly how far ya think we gonna hafta go 'fore getting there, anyways? This rain's cold, damp an' gettin' to me."

"Not too far, buddy," Tattoo answered calmly, patronizingly and, at the same time, trying his best at a little diplomacy. "Another mile or so in this direction," he said pointing south, "then a mile or two east," his hand moved to the left, "an' maybe a little farther north," he added as he pointed behind him. "Then I think we's gonna be right smack dab in the middle o' the ol' neighborhood, right where we juss might find that stolen loot!"

"Well I ain't gonna last 'nuther mile or two east, west, north, south or whatever pea pickin' direction youse is plannin' on takin' me, let alone four or five miles," Crazy Eyes griped, his arms sarcastically moving here, there and all around as direction indicators. So wet, cold and upset was Crazy Eyes, that he missed his partner's patronization altogether.

"Why can't it rain a warm rain in early spring? Why does April always hafta start out wit' cold rains? It feels like I's frozen ta death wit' all these wet clothes juss a clingin' ta my cold, damp body," he grumbled through chattering teeth while his body shivered.

"Ah quit cher bellyaching," Tattoo scolded. He finally understood diplomacy meant nothing to his partner and was tired of hearing all of his crabbiness. "If you was standing right here in the cold rain," he said, pointing to the very spot on which they were standing, "with that big ol' metal box filled up to the top full o' loot, holdin' it in yer hands, you'd be warmer than a slice o' freshly buttered hot toast on a cold winter's day."

10

"Yeah, maybe ya gots a point, there," Crazy Eyes shot back. "Maybe ya does at that, ol' buddy," he added caustically. Then he started yelling, emphasizing each word, "'Cept we ain't there, partner!" Crazy Eyes was now becoming quite cynical and very cranky. "You ain't sure how ta git there from where we is here, an' we ain't got no loot in our hot little hands. An' that, my genius navigator, makes this rain all the more colder. Now either git us there an' I'll foller, or step aside, I'll lead and you foller."

"How ya gonna lead when ya don't even know where we's at?" Tattoo barked, returning the fire. And then suddenly, as if he had just seen a brilliant light flash before his very eyes, he quickly changed his demeanor and whispered, "Crazy Eyes, ol' buddy? Take a look down there. Ya see that back door to the second floor of that there barn down there in back of that clump o' trees? Huh? Ya see it, don'tcha?"

Crazy Eyes squinted, straining his eyes in the pouring night rain. He never could figure out how Tattoo could see the things he saw, especially in the dark of night. His eyes weren't nearly as good as Tattoo's and he knew it. Still, even though he couldn't quite make out what it was his partner saw, Crazy Eyes nodded in the affirmative.

"The house is up there ina front, off to the side," Tattoo continued, pointing to the farmhouse barely visible behind another clump of trees to the right. "Don't know if it's empty, but even if someone is home, they ain't gonna see us enterin' from the back. If we can juss slip into that barn, unnoticed, we'd be outta the rain, dry and with all the animals downstairs, we'd be warm enough for a good night's sleep, or at least until this here rain lets up. But we gotta be quiet, buddy. C'mon, Crazy Eyes, let's try it."

Crazy Eyes surveyed the situation, and even though he was struggling to see everything, he still agreed with Tattoo that this indeed could be the solution to their cold, wet dilemma. He had no other choice but to trust his partner. After all, Tattoo's cleverness and crafty moves had gotten them this far. In the early hours of the morning they'd simply slip out the back of the barn, climb the fence row hill to the woods and continue south along their way. Before the day was over, they'd be two rich hoodlums, and, they figured, no one would be the wiser.

"One more thing," Tattoo reminded his partner. "No matter what happens, no more violence. I'm wit' ya when it comes to the robbin' an' the stealin' an' all that there illegal pilfering. I'm willin' ta go along wit' ya takin' from others what ain't ours, ol' buddy. But I gotta hafta draw that line ina dirt there when our life's chosen work turns to downright violence," he insisted.

"Now I tell ya what we gonna do. Tonight I's gonna stand guard while you gits ya some shuteye, then you watch whilst I git some," he told Crazy Eyes. "An' if anybody does come our way, we juss gonna quietly and quickly slip out the back, nice an' easy like. No trouble, no more violence and juss walk away. Agreed?"

After lowering his head, Crazy Eyes shuffled his feet nervously before shifting his weight from one leg to the other as he reluctantly agreed. "Yeah," he muttered, but still had to swallow his pride. Forcing himself, he finally sealed this unwritten covenant by shaking his partner's outstretched, waiting hand. "Had no other choice but to knock 'em two old geezers upside their heads with that there two by four that was a layin' on the floor over by the cooler," he said, trying to justify his actions from the robbery earlier in the week. "I figgered the noise from shooting her might attract attention from outside. 'Sides, that there old lady wit' the gun had it pointin' right smack dab on ya, Tattoo. An' the old man was probably going for one, too."

"How was she gonna shoot me, ol' buddy? Huh? That gun 'twasn't loaded. You knowd that," Tattoo reminded his partner.

"Not at that very time, I didn't," Crazy Eyes said quickly, defending himself. "How was I supposed ta knowd it? 'Sides, who in their ever lovin', livin', 'tater pickin' right mind carries an unloaded gun around fer pertection, 'cept people wit' pea brains?

"Ya think ya killed 'em dead, huh, Crazy Eyes? Ya think they's good an' dead?" Tattoo queried with an element of hope hidden deep in his voice that the two old folks might still be alive.

"Don't see how they's not, my friend, but I just don't rightly know. I tell ya sumpin' though. It's been layin' right here in the back o' my mind bodderin' me," he said, pointing to the rear right side of his head. "I been thinking 'bout it an awful lot, ever since it up an' happened. Kinda wisht it never did," he pondered aloud to Tattoo. "Like I could juss go on back and undo it all. Then I wouldn't feel so dang bad, an' the cops wouldn't be all over our case like I suppose they is at this very moment." It was one of the few times Tattoo ever saw his partner feel apologetic or even show the slightest signs of remorse.

"Well, good buddy, relax 'cause I ain't seen no flatfoots out there fer the pass three days. So maybe they's either gived up or we just shooked 'em off wit' the cool way we's been coverin' up our trail," Tattoo said, hoping to assure his partner not to worry, that everything would be okay and they'd soon be two rich dudes.

"Coverin' up our trail?" Crazy Eyes questioned, looking at him in disbelief. "Where'd ya ever come up wit' that harebrained idea, ya misguided nitwit? Let me tell ya sumpin' partner. The only reason our trail's got all covered up is 'cause it's been a pourin' down rainin' so hard our tracks just up an' got themselves all warshed away. No matter where we was, the fields, the hard roads, the dirt roads, the rains juss up an' warshed 'em away. An' that was 'cause of Ol' Mudder Nature being on our side an' helpin' us out, not 'cause of any great brilliance on our part. An' don't you fergit it!"

"Alright, ol' buddy," Tattoo whispered, using his pointer finger to cross his lips, "just calm down an' stay quiet." Occasionally Crazy Eyes would get into his periodic uproars over nothing and Tattoo could never understand why. "We's almost at the barn's back door. It's right up there ahead of them there trees. Ya see it? Don't wanna cause no noise that's gonna get all 'em chickens a cluckin' or stir up them there cattle or even wake up a sleepin' hound they might have. Here, you go in first an' make sure all's clear. I'll watch from out here."

When it was all clear and the two ex-cons were safely inside, they removed their clothes to dry, and then wrapped themselves with clean, cloth feed bags they found hanging over a rafter near a horse drawn reaper. Within minutes, hunger gnawed at Crazy Eyes.

"Where ya goin'?" Tattoo asked when he saw his buddy descending the steps to the lower barn floor. Without waiting for an answer, he continued, "Fergit 'em chicken eggs an' that cow's warm milk, Crazy Eyes. Stay up here and get some sleep. Don't always be a pushin' yer luck, man," he ordered, knowing his partner was hungry. "Start milkin' them cows and stirrin' up them hens an' we's gonna be in a whole lotta trouble. 'Sides, we can always eat tomorrow."

Crazy Eyes returned to the barn's second floor tired but mostly hungry. Hoping to ease his mind of hunger pangs, he switched subjects, asking for the umpteenth time, "You shore ya know where this here loot's at? I wanna git it an' git outta here pronto 'afore trout season opens Monday. With all 'em goofy farmers and screwy fishermen sitting out there along the banks, we'd never find it. Don't know 'bout you, but I wanna head fer some warm, dry country an' fergit this cold, damp weather."

"Deep ina bottom o' that there crick what runs through Rehmeyer's Holler on the other side o' White Oak Valley," he assured Crazy Eyes. "I heared Whispers let it slip to his jailbird buddy, juss as clear as I can hear you," he added. "Then I let him know what I heared him sayin', an' Whispers juss up an' confessed. He tole me everything, 'cept that I wasn't suppose to say nuttin' to no one."

13

"Not to worry, Tattoo," Crazy Eyes assured him facetiously as he tried going to sleep. "Yer brudder'll be the last one I ever let know you up an' broke yer promise."

With a saddle for a pillow and a horse blanket for covering, he slept for four hours while Tattoo sat and watched. And then they switched. But much needed sleep got the best of Crazy Eyes and his time standing guard soon turned into a joint snooze with his partner, as he and Tattoo snored away on the top floor of the barn.

Outside, as dawn broke, Pennsylvania Game Wardens permeated the area by either hiding low in their unmarked cars or on foot while surreptitiously watching the many trout streams. They were simply making sure the Commonwealth's fishing laws weren't being violated by poachers who may have been sneaking their lines in the waters earlier than the start of trout season.

All around the two sleeping felons, farm houses in the hamlets of Hametown and Potosi, as well as White Oak Valley and Rehmeyer's Hollow were awakening to another morning as parents were feeding and preparing their children for one more day of school.

Inside one farmhouse across the hill and down the valley from the barn where the two criminals slept, Jack Whelan called his children the second time to wake up or they'd miss the school bus. There were daily chores to do before their mother, Doris, finished cooking the breakfast meal. Nevertheless, their four school age children were keyed up. It was the last school day before the big spring holiday the following Monday. A three day weekend was in store and every kid in the area was excited.

The first day of the trout fishing season would be Monday. That meant the woods and stream banks would be filled with good, hard working men and mischievous, carefree, happy-go-lucky, school kids, some just watching with their dogs, while others would try their angling luck for a big rainbow trout.

Little did they know of the imminent danger lurking from somewhere within their immediate neighborhood. Two hard nosed criminals would soon be pressing their luck as they began their search for a metal box filled to the brim with stolen loot from a bank robbery and hidden deep in the bottom of a stocked trout stream more than ten years earlier. The same trout stream many of these school kids and adults would be fishing.

14

Chapter 1

Crab Cake's right eye opened. Both ears twitched and then perked straight up. The bright sun of early spring shone warmly on the Border Collie, a medium size dog, as he lay near the front of the steps on the back farm house porch. On the first Friday of April the family pet finally opened both eyes, lifted his head from a peaceful mid-afternoon slumber and surveyed his domain.

The black and white canine with several splotches of light brown coloring on his coat looked about inquisitively. Then, as if hearing a high pitched alarm, he ended his mid-day snooze and left the warmth of the sunshiny spot to professionally handle the responsibilities which were expected of him.

Instinctively Crab Cake headed down the long and narrow dirt lane. Before reaching the end of the private road, as he had done so many times in the past, the Border Collie cut across a meadow on the right. From there he reached the main dirt road and continued his southbound journey.

Here and there along the fence rows of the freshly plowed fields, a woodchuck, famous and somewhat revered as a groundhog in the Keystone State, and months past from the annual encounter it has with its shadow, would test the waters. Poking its head high above the hole that serves as an entrance to his underground home, it would cautiously look this way and that before venturing out.

Normally, Crab Cake would pursue the woodchuck at a furious rate of speed, either chasing him back and forth across the freshly plowed fields or right back into his earthly home. As small as he was for a medium size dog, the Border Collie still loved the challenge and in some instances, managed to catch a woodchuck or two. But this time the feisty natured dog ignored the tease. It's not that he didn't prefer to chase the brown furry rodent, but rather this faithful, family pet fully understood the importance his five day a week mission took.

Now moving at a quick pace, the canine abandoned the dusty road and cut across one field after another, reaching an old gray and weathered one room schoolhouse building—one of several that remained in the area. The unpainted White Oak School House wasn't abandoned. It was merely closed for educational purposes. After purchasing the building and surrounding property, Mr. and Mrs. Wertz and their two children had converted it into a home. Since both of their children rode the bus, and their schoolhouse home served as a gathering, it was also used as the school bus stop for the remaining neighborhood students.

Here is where Crab Cake would wait. It was the last stop for the bus. It's where he'd meet the Whelan children and accompany them home. For this canine, it was an everyday ritual. In the morning, regardless of inclement weather or whatever the season, he'd escort them a mile and a half down the dirt country roads to the bus stop and remain there until it arrived.

The old one room schoolhouses found here and there across the countryside in that section of South-central Pennsylvania, particularly in the Pennsylvania Dutch country of Adams, Berks, Cumberland, Dauphin, Franklin, Lancaster, Lebanon, and York counties, were once a common sight in the small villages. From a bygone era, they were currently in the process of closing. Only two, Hogtown and Hametown Schools, remained open in Southern York County and, in fact, were still in use.

Four of Jack and Doris Whelan's five children started the school year in early September 1950 at Hogtown, transferring to Hametown School one week later. The former was closed due to the lack of students. The latter absorbed what few students were left. The following year all the one room schoolhouses would be closed forever by the Southern York County School District, removing the students to multi-room schools and starting construction on the new one-floor high school, named Susquehannock after a tribe of local Indians.

Built before the Civil War, the 1950-51 Hametown School classes had 37 students. More than ten percent of the student body were from the Whelan family. Five students each made up the first, third, fifth and seventh grades. The second grade had seven, the fourth, four and the sixth, six. There were no students for the eighth grade. Even with the small student body, the one room school still had its class clowns, but then again, what school didn't?

A large potbelly stove stood in the middle near the rear of the room. In the winter, those who sat close to the stove nearly roasted from too much heat. The unfortunate few whose desks were on the outer perimeter of the room were constantly cold. Only those who were lucky enough to be seated midway between the two extremes were comfortable.

Mr. Rohrbaugh, a first year teacher from north of the county seat of York, drove the 25 miles south daily and arrived very early each morning in order to start the stove fire. Welcoming the students to a warm classroom, Carl Packard Rohrbaugh was a handsome gentleman who stood five feet ten inches, of average weight, dark hair and blue eyes. He was well refined and had a compassionate disposition. Rarely did he ever lose his cool.

This rookie teacher's patience with students was very close to being on a level with Job. His nearly impossible task was to instruct all seven grades every subject, including English. His pupils, farmers' children whose minds were on fishing, domestics, gardening and other farm chores more than they were on studies, were, for the most part, well behaved. Occasionally a student would get out of line, but swift and immediate punishment taught them to think twice before repeating their offense.

Located on top of the rear schoolyard hill, outhouse toilets, one for each gender, were separated by fifty feet of school yard. To say the least, students tending to their most basic needs in the middle of a bleak cold winter day were forever challenged.

Drinking water was hand hauled in a ten gallon container from an outside pump at a nearby farmhouse some 500 yards away and sat on a wooden stand in the cloak room just inside the front entranceway. There was no cafeteria. Those who rode the school bus either brought their lunches in a small tin lunch pail or a brown paper bag. Those who lived within walking distance returned home for lunch.

Crab Cake knew his job well. It was to shepherd the four Whelan children, Sarah, Paula, Jack, Jr. and Tyrone, safely home. While he remained a family dog, his real master was the oldest boy, Jack, who went by the nickname of Pepper. The two got along quite well. It was Pepper who first spotted the abandoned dog one cold winter's morning sleeping at the bottom of the farmhouse steps. His father, Jack Whelan, Sr. was given the dog, free, by Charlie Stabler, the proprietor, chief cook and bottle washer and innkeeper at Stabler's Cabins & Restaurant, one of the local tourist stops between Baltimore and York along the old Susquehanna Trail.

On snowy days when Pepper would slide down hills on a coaster, Crab Cake rode along on his back. Whenever Pepper went into the woods to fetch wood for fuel, Crab Cake was with him. If Pepper went fishing at the many fresh brooks that run their courses through the White Oak Valley, Crab Cake was by his side. If it was possible to sneak his dog inside the school house each day successfully, Pepper would have done so. Regardless of what Jack 'Pepper' Whelan, Jr. did or wherever he went, Crab Cake was with him. The two looked out for each other. They were inseparable.

A favorite trick Pepper taught Crab Cake was to have him climb the sloping roof of the small smokehouse, a distance of four feet from the ground. From ground level the dog would make a running jump, land on the lower edge and then work his way to the roof peak. Pepper had a unique way of whistling. Without the aid of grass reeds or using any fingers, he'd simply place the tip of his tongue on his lower lip and very gently press down with his upper teeth. Blowing through the small opening which this created allowed him to let out a high pitched whistling shrill, the likes of which could be heard for up to a quarter of a mile on a good day.

Serving as a signal for Crab Cake, whenever the dog heard the whistle, he'd jump from the smokehouse roof to Pepper standing below and, without failure, land in his arms every time. When they were out and about in the fields and woods, the whistle merely served as notice for the dog to return to his master. It was time for them to head for home.

It was the first Friday of April, 1951. The school kids, especially the boys, looked forward to a long three day weekend. Trout season would open on Monday, and all of York County's country schools were closed for this annual event. It happened every year, making the first weekend of April an extended one. Except for a few local tomboys, most of the girls considered it to be exactly what it was, nothing more than a long weekend.

School authorities knew better than to try keeping the schools open on such an important day. If they had, the only ones who would have been in attendance would have been the teachers and a few book worms who, no matter how long it might have taken to explain, would never have been able to fully comprehend the thrill of trout fishing on the first day of the season. For the average farm boy in the early 1950s, fishing was one of his top priorities. It certainly was much better than going to school, and almost every kid in the area looked forward to it.

Even though Pepper and his dog, Crab Cake, loved to fish, he was still further ahead in his education than the average student. Coupled with a high degree of intelligence and some good old fashion common sense, Jack 'Pepper' Whelan, Jr. was considered an academic star... that is, of course, for the caliber of student attending the one room schoolhouse. With the exception of English, his grade marks in other subjects were remarkably high and because he showed such a high degree of hope, Mr. Rohrbaugh worked harder encouraging him in his studies.

Pepper was a low keyed, easy going, but nevertheless, smart young lad. His below average English marks may have been related directly to the fact that for 16 hours every day he was exposed to various dialects from the Pennsylvania Dutch families who populated the area. Each weekend it became two full days and then annually, three solid months during summer vacation. Certainly Pepper's teacher had his work cut out for him. If Pepper Whelan had been raised anywhere else in the country, such as the mid-west, he could very well have been speaking with neither a dialect nor a fractured sentence structure.

Of average height for a ten-year-old, Pepper's strawberry blond locks were neatly trimmed in a short cropped hair cut which was the style of the day. At first glance, the 57 pounds of weight the boy carried on his thin frame would have one believing he was a weakling. On the contrary. Farm work toughened a lad his age. Not being overweight, he was slender but still all muscle. And having very little body fat, Pepper was fast. Considered to be one of the fastest runners in the area in a foot race, he could easily have kept up with Crab Cake. His deep-set blue eyes had him favoring his father more than his mother, and the gait to his walk was smooth and steady.

Pepper worked on his long, homemade, bamboo-like fishing pole that evening. Crab Cake sat quietly by his side, watching his every move. Made from a green sassafras branch, the pole was nearly seven and a half feet long. It had no reel. Instead, the line was wrapped around the thin end at the top, with just enough to drape down to the handle area. At the end was a steel nut, used for a sinker and a cork for a bobber. The Eagle Claw hook was located on a ten inch leader line, strategically placed between the sinker and bobber. It was one his maternal grandfather, Curt Chronister, had given him from their many fishing trips to the Yellow Breeches Creek in the northern part of the county.

Whether Pepper was using the correct bait or tackle to land trout, was immaterial to him. Regardless of what specie of fish he intended to catch, the bait of choice was always the same, earthworms. Wiggly and willowy, those wild, wonderful worms were always freshly dug. For the young lads and frugal anglers in this part of the country, the price was certainly right. They were free for the digging. And in the rich, Pennsylvania Dutch topsoil of the black, damp, spring earth, earthworms were plentiful.

A small tin can with ample holes punched into the sides for air and a thin leather strap served as a homemade bait container. By slinging the bait can over his shoulder, much like a pioneer would have carried his powder horn, Pepper tested the strength of the knots on the leather strap.

Used to attract earthworms, his mother saved the after supper, warm, soapy dishwater for Pepper. "Word has it Roy Haney's mare is 'bout ready to foal, Pepper," his mother, Doris, said as she handed him the dishpan full of water. "Ya hear anything 'bout it?" Being raised on a farm, farm children were exposed to the facts of life early. In the absence of television, word of mouth was the medium used mostly for local news.

Pepper's mind was on fish bait. "Not really, Ma," he politely answered. Grabbing a spade and, along with the dish water, his bait container and a flashlight, he headed for the garden. Crab Cake followed. Since it was spring, the garden needed spaded and he needed bait. By digging for worms in the garden, he'd be killing two birds with one stone. Crab Cake watched.

"Heard it could be any day, now," Doris Whelan said, hoping to keep the conversation going with her oldest son. Then changing to the caring, loving mother she was, added, "You be careful out there, Pepper. I saw a copperhead 'mong them rocks over there along the fence row yesterday. They come out this time o' year; take in the warm sunshine." She then looked off to the garden where Pepper and Crab Cake had gone. Even though Pepper hated snakes with a passion, he didn't give it a second thought. His mind was on the first day of trout fishing.

"Maybe ya ought to take an umbrella, Pepper." His mother was beginning to mother him. "Heard on the radio, might rain. As a matter of fact, honey, been callin' for rain most o' the week."

"Ma! Please," Pepper pled. "Fishermen don't carry umbrellas. 'Sides, that weatherman's never right." Pepper knew everyone would have a good laugh at his expense if they saw him walking up with a fishing pole in one hand, a can of worms slung across his shoulder and an umbrella in the other.

"If it rains, ya gonna get soaking wet," argued his mother. "Whata ya gonna do, Pepper, if it suddenly downpours, like's so common fer this time of year?"

"Run 'tween the raindrops, Ma," joked Pepper. But seeing his mother's hands firmly resting on her hips with a stern look plastered across her face told him this was no time for funny business. His mother was not about to relent. "Ma, a cave's nearby," he assured her. "Me 'n' Crab Cake'll wait it out there."

"Make sure ya do, Jack 'Pepper' Whelan, Jr." his mother said. "Make sure ya do!" Whenever she used her children's full names they knew she meant business. Still watching him as he prepared the ground for the gathering of bait, she reminded her son not to track any mud into her clean house. "Ya know how I hate muddy tracks on my floor. Be sure 'n' take off yer shoes 'fore comin' in."

Pepper began his bait gathering ritual exactly as his maternal grandfather had taught him. First he soaked the earth with the warm soapy dishwater. Then he waited. After being sure the spot was thoroughly soaked, he started digging. With each turn of the spade, the earthworms would scurry to the top of the dirt mound or try to avoid capture altogether by finding a different opening in the earth. In many cases they made their own tunnels, slithering their slimy, elongated bodies through the nimble fingers of the ten-year-old.

Pepper turned on the light. "Here's one, Crab Cake," he told his dog. "There's 'nother one. C'mon, Crab Cake. Help me, boy. Wow, what a night crawler. That's a big un, Crab Cake."

The Border Collie just barked in agreement at Pepper's every word, wagging his tail enthusiastically and watching diligently, making sure none escaped the fast fingers of his master. The two were having a ball. Whenever Crab Cake noticed a worm slipping away, he'd growl, signaling Pepper to get a move on. The boy would respond and then pet Crab Cake on the head. "Good doggie, Crab Cake! Good boy!" The dog loved it and acknowledged the compliment by wagging his tail even faster.

When he thought he had enough, Pepper filled a five gallon pail with soft moist topsoil and into it he emptied his bait. Then he covered it, making sure the cover had holes and plenty of air was circulating. He set the pail next to his fishing rod on the floor of the out-kitchen, just off the back porch. The damp chilliness had turned warm for an early spring evening. Crab Cake would be sleeping next to the worms that night, guarding Pepper's treasures.

Come early Monday morning, Pepper and Crab Cake would be ready to catch the elusive Ol' Uncle Louie, a moniker the kids gave to a rainbow trout that was so old and big, he had become a living legend in the valley.

Chapter 2

Early Saturday morning found Pepper and Crab Cake doing their regular morning chores before breakfast. The opening of trout season was still two days away. For Pepper, it seemed like two years. He could hardly wait. Thankfully, there were enough farm chores to keep him busy and his mind occupied.

The horses, cows, chickens and hogs needed to be fed, watered and their stalls cleaned. The cows had to be milked and the chicken eggs gathered. Firewood was brought in and set in a wooden box near the kitchen range. This was a daily ritual for all farm boys. Their day started very early. Because of that, their bedtime also arrived early. By 9 p.m. at the very latest, all lights were out. This, of course, only seemed to make the time go by much faster.

By six a.m., after the early morning chores were finished, Pepper sat on the end of the bench that ran the length of the long kitchen dining table. His mother had always fixed a homemade Pennsylvania Dutch breakfast consisting of eggs, home fried potatoes, bacon, ham, panhaus, sausages, fried corn mush, flapjacks, warm King Syrup, oatmeal, toast and hot chocolate. The family chose from the table whatever it was they wanted and ate until they were full. Up early and busily doing chores on a farm works up quite an appetite. To maintain adequate energy, his fuel level needed to be replenished a minimum of four times daily. Pepper was a growing boy.

After breakfast, Pepper fed Crab Cake before continuing his busy morning work schedule. The rest of the day would be spent helping out wherever he was needed throughout the farm with various tasks. He may end up helping his father throw straw down to the cows for fresh bedding from the upper part of the barn. Or his mother may need him to help spade her truck garden. Whatever was asked of him, rarely did he ever refuse.

With the exception of church, Sunday morning was no different than the other days of the week. Cows needed to be milked, fed and watered, chickens had eggs which were to be collected and the horses and hogs needed to be cared for. Like the other six days of the week, animals still ate and drank on Sundays.

When breakfast was finished, the family started preparing for services at the local St. Paul's Lutheran Church in Hametown. Besides the church, the

23

unincorporated village consisted of about a dozen homes, the Candlelight Inn Restaurant, Saubel's grocery store, White's Sinclair Garage and the one room schoolhouse. Nine a.m. worship services always filled the sanctuary with farmers and their families from the surrounding areas. For as long as Pepper could remember, after church there was the traditional Whelan Sunday chicken dinner at home, served promptly at twelve noon.

Besides fresh roasted chickens (*rarely were they ever fried*), the Sunday dinner consisted of mashed potatoes, green beans, noodles, creamed corn, peas and carrots, red beets, hot rice pudding, apple sauce with cinnamon, biscuits, filling (*a term used in the Pennsylvania Dutch country meaning stuffing or dressing*), the seven sweets and seven sours, homemade bread, butter, jams and apple butter, and, of course, Doris Whelan's homemade chicken gravy.

Because the table was filled with so many different dishes didn't mean a child had to eat some of each. It was merely there for anyone to try. Otherwise they passed it by and went on to a dish they preferred. One standing rule in the Whelan household was that no prepared food would ever be wasted. If you put it on your plate, you ate it. And if you couldn't, you sat there 'til you did.

Desserts were usually pies, cakes and/or fresh fruit salad. Ninety-five percent of everything used in the meals was either grown on the farm or freshly made from scratch. For the Sunday six p.m. supper meal, rarely was it ever freshly prepared. Instead, it consisted of leftovers warmed up from the noon dinner meal.

After clearing the table and helping with the dishes, once the Sunday dinner was finished there was always free time. Usually the family members rested, went for leisure walks or in the case of the boys, got together with neighbor friends and played a game of baseball in the meadow below the house.

Crab Cake followed Pepper and watched whatever he did. On this warm Sunday afternoon, Pepper traveled across the hill, through the woods and down into the valley to case Rehmeyer's Run, a stream where he would begin his trout fishing early in the morning. It was really a nice-sized creek but for some unexplained reason, the local population referred to it as a 'Run.'

Arriving early, he had planned to find a good spot near his favorite fishing hole; a deep watery aperture on a wide bend in the creek with fast moving rapids, the kind trout love to bask in. Pepper had been watching the area for weeks. Ever since the spring thaw he noticed an increase of action in the rapidly moving waters below. An early arrival would assure him of a favorable position.

On the way, he passed Pete Patterson's home, one of the few with telephones. Whenever calls needed to be made, neighbors usually walked to their home or the Barnes farm in the opposite direction to use the phone. Or they drove the three miles to Stabler's Cabins to use a pay phone. Otherwise calls remained unmade.

The Patterson's had two boys and a girl. George was the oldest. The girl, Cora, was younger. Thurston, the middle child, was one year older than Pepper, and while the Patterson boy considered himself to be a 'friend,' Pepper never considered him to be a 'best friend.' At least he wasn't as good and as loyal a one as Crab Cake. Nevertheless, he was a neighbor, schoolmate, somewhat of a pal and close to Pepper's age. However, Thurston could be headstrong and troublesome. And that's what always bothered Pepper. But for the most part, Thurston was more devilish than bad.

Thurston was outside working on the family swimming pool that Sunday afternoon as Pepper and Crab Cake walked along the road in front of their log cabin home. Their pool was the only one in the area. Naturally, once warmer weather arrived, all the kids in the community, including Pepper and his family, had an open invitation to use the pool whenever they wished. The problem with the water was it was so cold, record-size goose bumps grew the minute you entered. Fresh frigid spring water was used to fill the pool and, after ten minutes in, your skin usually started turning blue.

Due to the heavy leaf coverage from the many white oaks on their property, the sun never got a timely chance to do its thing by warming the water. It was always during the waning days of summer vacation, in late August, when the water finally warmed up to temperatures that might have been considered normal for outdoor swimming. Nevertheless, on hot summer days after a long hard day of picking tomatoes, green beans or potatoes in Roy Haney's fields, a quick dip in Patterson's pool felt good.

Thurston spotted Pepper and Crab Cake and waved. Pepper returned the wave and then stopped briefly to hold, what he had hoped to be, a short conversation. Pepper was never much of a chatterbox, keeping things mostly to himself, but Thurston always seemed to make up for Pepper's lack of conversation. "Where ya headed?" Thurston asked. "Over ta see if Haney's horse had her foal?"

"Naw. Only be ina way over there," Pepper answered, hoping to keep his intentions to himself. "Me 'n' Crab Cake juss walking off a big dinner."

"Heard it's due any day now," Thurston volunteered. "Sure would like ta see it, first day it gets here."

"Yeah," said Pepper as casually as he could. "Mom mentioned sumpin 'bout it. Guess it's the talk o' the whole valley." Pepper was eager to end this small talk and move on, but Thurston continued.

"Goin' fishin' tomorrow?" Thurston queried, eyeing Pepper as though whatever answer he gave, Thurston would still doubt him.

"That'd be nice," Pepper replied with a sigh and then added, "long as I get my chores done 'n time. Udderwise I daresn't go."

"Let's go case the streams," suggested Thurston. He was inviting himself to be Pepper's company for the afternoon. "We got time and 'sides, I got a whole week or so ta finish cleanin' the pool."

Pepper really wanted to be alone. He had planned to keep his destination secret so others wouldn't be attracted to his special fishing spot. When it came to fishing, Pepper didn't trust Thurston. The two were always competitive and more times than Pepper would care to remember, Thurston used questionable moves to pilfer victory from competitors, including Pepper. The young lad despised cheating. He preferred playing fair. The last thing Pepper needed was to show Thurston his favorite fishing hole.

"Don't know, Thursy," Pepper said, shaking his head. It was a nickname everyone called Thurston and he didn't mind. "Really shouldn't be gone too long t'day. Promised the rest o' the family I'd help 'em play a game o' ball when I got back."

"Sounds great," replied Thursy. "I'll join ya after we scout the creek. We'll have us a ball!"

Pepper felt backed into a corner. On one hand, he didn't want Thursy along. But on the other, he didn't want to shun his pal. And even though he had a certain element of distrust for Thursy, he still recognized his neighbor's need for friends. His boyhood pal had very few.

It looked as if he was stuck with Thursy and Pepper knew it. Crab Cake also sensed it. The dog, lying down on the road next to his master, lowered his head parallel with the ground and covered his eyes with his front paws.

"Okay. Let's go," ordered Pepper. "But we can't mess 'round none. We gotta keep movin'. If I ain't back 'fore the game ends, I may not be 'llowed to go fishin' tomorrow," he exaggerated.

"Let's fish together," suggested Thursy, not hearing a word Pepper said. "It's more fun if ya fish wit' a buddy. Ya could meet me here on yer way down 'n' we could be in place 'fore the season 'ficially opens at dawn."

"Gotta think 'bout that," replied Pepper. "Wit' all my morning chores I gotta do, may not be able ta make it 'fore dawn. That'd hold ya up 'n' wouldn't be

26

very fair to ya."

Pepper was starting to feel bad for embellishing. He felt as though he was walking a thin line between telling the truth and a lie. To ease his conscience, in an effort to keep from going fishing with Thursy, Pepper decided he was merely exercising diplomacy by laying it on thick.

"Oh, c'mon, Pepper. Stop ferhoodling me. Ya can certainly get outta chores for one day o' the year, can't ya?" asked Thursy. "Yer cows, horses, pigs 'n' chickens won't die from hunger."

"We'll see," said Pepper. And off the three went; Pepper, Crab Cake and Thursy, down the dirt road towards the old White Oak School House and onwards to Rehmeyer's Run. The afternoon was still young when they reached the babbling brook.

Chapter 3

Pepper knew where the deep hole was located on the wide bend of the stream. But he purposely stayed clear of that upstream area. Instead, when they reached the bridge, he led Thursy downstream, far away from the opposite direction of his favorite hole.

The two boys and dog walked the creek's nearby bank for perhaps an eighth of a mile before fording it on the moss-covered wet, slippery rocks at a narrow, shallow bend just before a series of rapids. While each stepped cautiously, holding their outstretched arms for balance, Crab Cake made the crossing easily.

On the far side, they traced their route backwards, returning to the point of departure. Along the way the two young lads eyed every interesting hole that could possibly hold the key to landing that elusive monster trout, Ol' Uncle Louie. Upon spotting a potential candidate, the boys stuck sticks in the water, checking the depth at various spots.

More than once, Thursy decided a certain hole was home to the humongous fish. Upon declaring so, he'd announce that was where he'd start fishing. That is until he'd run into a different deep hole. Then he'd make another announcement. That's where he'd begin fishing in the wee hours of the morning. Of course, this delighted Pepper to no end. At least he'd be keeping him away from his secret spot upstream.

"Whatta ya gonna do, Thursy, when ya get down here tomorrow mornin' 'n' someone else gots the spot?" asked Pepper, in an attempt to rattle his chains. "Ya just can't go hornin' in on 'em, ya know. Ya gotta respect udder fishermen if they're there first." Pepper was always thinking about the other guy. It was how his parents, especially his mother, taught him.

"Don't you juss worry 'bout that, my friend," Thursy shot back. "I got ways o' getting what I want. If they don't move, then they juss don't move. It's a free country. What can they do if I juss sit down next ta 'em 'n' cast my line in next ta theirs?"

"Well, if they hook a fish 'n' lose it 'cause you tangled their line, ya could be riskin' trouble for yerself," warned Pepper. "In which case, ya'd end up wit' nothin' ta show for yer efforts, 'cept maybe a lot of pain from a sore body."

"Oh yeah!" Thursy became defensive. "Well what would you do?" he asked, trying to pick the mind of his friend and at the same time thinking of where he'd be in the morning. Thursy knew Pepper Whelan would be out fishing early with his dog, Crab Cake. He also knew that so far, Pepper hadn't taken him to the fishing spot where he'd be at dawn. And he wondered if he'd show him the spot at all.

Pepper stopped and sat on a rock on the bank of the fast running waters of Rehmeyer's Run. All around him was evidence of the woods breaking out from its winter slumber. Remnants of tiny green vegetation started appearing everywhere. Skunk cabbage, a ground plant, gently poked its tips through the brown, crisp, dead leaves of last fall. Here and there in opened areas, wild daffodils and crocuses opened their soft colorful petals to the warm sun of spring.

Birds chirped about merrily, chattering to potential mates in their native language. Squirrels scampered nearly everywhere looking for nuts they might have missed during their annual fall roundup. Rabbits hopped to and fro as they left the safety of their underground nests seeking nutrition from the lush foliage of isolated vegetation. Chipmunks could be spotted busily admonishing each other on a makeshift bridge created from a fallen log lying across the creek. Half way across the world in an unfamiliar country known as Korea, a violent war raged on. But here in White Oak Valley, all seemed peaceful with the world.

To Crab Cake, it was a dream come true. What fun he'd have if Pepper would allow him to chase a squirrel or a rabbit or even flush out a ring-necked pheasant from the brush in the clearing. But Pepper was in deep thought. And he needed Crab Cake close by for comfort and companionship. Looking down and softly petting his dog on the head, Pepper thought for quite a while on Thursy's question. What *would* he do in a situation like that?

"Not so sure if that's such a fair question, Thursy," he answered after much deliberation. "First of all, I doubt if I'm ever gonna put m'self in any kind of a sitchiatshun like that. I come ta fish, not ta fight. I think the real question should be, 'What would Thursy do?' Only you can answer that, my friend, no one else."

Thursy knew better than to ask Pepper any questions that had the potential of having an answer in which he didn't want to hear. If Pepper was nothing else, the one thing he was, was honest. If you didn't like Pepper's answers, you soon learned quickly enough not to ask him questions. Pepper never pulled punches. He always told it as he saw it.

Thursy shot Pepper a glare that spelled trouble. If there was one thing

Thursy hated, it was to be shown up. Whether he was with a group or just alone with a pal, Thursy always wanted to feel accepted. Whenever he wasn't he'd become defensive. This was one of those times. Minus the diplomacy, it was a method similar to which his father had always used on him, and Thursy resented it. No one ever tries to make a fool of Thursy Patterson.

The problem with Thursy's interpretation was that Pepper wasn't making a fool of him. He wasn't even trying. But Thursy didn't see it that way. Pepper was simply being honest. By helping Thursy solve the problem himself, he was actually helping the lad. Pepper was simply doing the very same thing his father had always done for him. Instead of solving it for the boy, Jack Whelan taught him to solve dilemmas for himself. In teaching him with kindness and diplomacy, the lad was taught it would make him a better person and a self-sufficient one.

Of course, Thursy never had the discipline and love in his life which Pepper had. This made a world of difference in how he reacted to situations in his young life. Like most people, he was a product of his own environment. Thursy's parents had divorced at an early age and some years later his father remarried. All three of the children lived with their father and step-mother.

Whatever had happened between their natural parents was never known, but throughout the White Oak Valley, whispers could be heard and when they made their rounds back to the children, they hurt deeply. Most of the valley's gossipers claimed their natural mother, rumored to be a loose floozy, was unfit to raise children. That's why the courts decided to put all three children in the custody of their father. No proof was ever established that such rumors were true. Of course this never stopped the gossipers. The less they knew about a situation, the more they talked. The more they knew, the less they talked.

Thursy was an inch smaller than Pepper and weighed about five more pounds. He had a bulky crop of dark wavy hair and wore glasses as thick as coke bottom bottles. Freckles dotted his face, concentrating mostly across the bridge of his pug nose. He was funny at times and for the most part enjoyed his time spent with Pepper. But, alone, he was much more aggressive in nature and prone to either starting or finding trouble. Nevertheless, for whatever reason, Thursy felt offended. "Trying ta make a fool outta me?" Thursy asked Pepper in a threatening tone.

"Ya know me better than that, Thursy Patterson." Pepper Whelan maintained his cool and held his ground. It takes two to fight, he thought. Alone, one person cannot succeed. "You asked a question and after thinkin' 'bout it, I answered ya. If ya want me ta answer only what you wanna hear, then don't ask me. Ya should know by now I either answer questions honestly or keep my mouth shut."

Thursy moved closer to Pepper. He was an inch away from his face. "Don't test me, Pepper Whelan," he threatened. "I'm this close ta layin' ya out flat." His temper flared and his face reddened as he gritted through closed teeth while showing Pepper a narrow gap between his thumb and second finger. With both arms raised waist length, Thursy rolled his hands into fists.

Crab Cake sensed imminent danger. Quickly the dog raced to where the boys were standing inches apart. Moving quickly between their legs and facing Thursy, he looked up into the lad's face and growled deeply. Any strike by Thursy onto Pepper and Crab Cake would be all over him. Thursy knew it, Pepper knew it and Thursy knew Pepper knew it. Slowly, Thursy lowered his arms and released his fists. Staring at the dog, he took a deep breath, slowly backed off, turned and walked away. Spotting a different rock farther away along the bank, he sat down, perhaps to cool off. Pepper and Crab Cake never moved and inch, instead, standing their ground.

Ten minutes later, as the sun started its descent behind the wooded mountainous ridge in the western sky, Pepper walked slowly over to Thursy. "Never 'tended ta make a fool outta ya, Thursy," he reiterated. "Ya misread me, pal. C'mon, let's head fer home. Before long, night's gonna be here 'n' we need ta get some rest if we plan on bein' up early ta land Ol' Uncle Louie."

Pepper held out his hand in friendship. Thursy looked up, not knowing whether he was ready to shake or not. But like the child he still was, he soon realized the hilarity of the situation and laughed. Pepper joined him. In accepting Pepper's hand in friendship, Thursy attempted at a half hearted apology for losing his temper, one that Pepper gladly and quickly accepted.

"F'get 'bout it, Thursy. It never happened. Everyone makes mistakes," Pepper assured him. "Dad says that's why we're human." The two boys walked back towards the bridge. Crab Cake followed.

Pepper feared Thursy would suggest walking upstream from the bridge. If he had, he'd find the fishing spot for sure that Pepper favored and still wanted to keep secret. Instead, he did something completely out of character. Without uttering a sound, Pepper automatically took the lead and upon reaching the bridge, and as if by second nature, turned on the road that headed back towards the old White Oak School House.

Glancing out of the corner of his eye, Pepper noticed Thursy following and breathed a sigh of relief. The secret fishing hole still remained just that, a secret, at least for now. Down the road towards home they continued, just two all-

American boys and a dog, kicking stones here and there, seemingly with no cares, worries or grudges in the world to distract them from their trouble-free lives.

From the looks of the two, it appeared as if no confrontation had ever happened between them that day. Crab Cake, in his effort to keep them separated, continued walking between them. Occasionally, the dog would eye Thursy, guardedly, just to be sure.

"See ya 'n the early mornin'," Thursy cheerfully hollered back at Pepper as he ran towards his house and up the back steps. Already having nearly forgotten the earlier confrontation between them and assuming everything was fine, he didn't bother waiting for Pepper's answer.

"I'd rather not go fishin' with 'im," Pepper said softly to Crab Cake as he stopped on the road to sit down on a fallen tree by the side and contemplate. "He's a hot head. Never 'njoyed any time spent wit' 'im. Ain't gonna have a good time, juss me 'n' you, first day of trout season wit'out offendin' him?" Pepper continued looking out for the other person's feelings, even at the expense of injuring his own.

Crab Cake looked up at the young lad with soulful eyes and whined. The dog seemed to understand what Pepper was going through. Crab Cake didn't care much for Thursy either.

Pepper was lucky he had Crab Cake. Without him, there'd be no one to talk to. Oh there would be others, but with Crab Cake, Pepper felt he could talk to the dog uninhibitedly, without the fear of repercussions. With Crab Cake, whatever Pepper said was always special between a boy and his dog. Anything ever said in confidence was never repeated; at least not by Crab Cake.

The unwritten bond between them was privilege. To them, it was no different than the privilege between a priest and penitent, a doctor and patient or an attorney and client. Pepper once asked Crab Cake if he'd promise to take whatever secret conversations they've had between the two to his grave. That promise was agreed upon by Crab Cake licking Pepper's face and furiously wagging his tail. Pepper responded by hugging his dog lovingly. The bond was forever sealed.

Pepper knew Thursy thought he had morning chores to do, but what he didn't know was that he had agreed to pay his younger brother, Tyrone, and older sister, Paula, to do them for him. He discussed this plan with his father, explaining as his reasoning his desire to be sitting on the bank by the creek at sunrise, signaling the start of trout season.

His father knew his son's passion for wanting to hook Ol' Uncle Louie. So famous had the legendary fish become that a local bait company had offered $100 cash to any angler who could successfully hook the monster trout. From everything that was ever said about the big fish, when caught, he'd break all state fishing records. So the rules were, it not only had to come from Rehmeyer's Run of Southern York County, or any stream it flows into, but it also must set a new state record for rainbow trout.

Pepper, his father, Tyrone and Paula agreed to all conditions. They would rise early to share in the morning chores which Pepper had usually done. From money earned at Roy Haney's farm, picking fresh produce, Pepper had agreed to pay them a dollar each. Naturally, they were thrilled and jumped at the chance to earn this extra money.

Paula had done the morning chores for two years when she was Pepper's age. Before that, her oldest sister Sarah handled them. This was Pepper's second year. Pepper referred to his little brother as Ty, instead of Tyrone, and because Ty was three years younger, Pepper would have another two years of morning chores before handing the duties over to him. While Pepper started at age eight, his parents had set the age limit for Ty to start doing the morning chores at nine.

Crab Cake looked up at Pepper again. His loyal companion licked Pepper's face. Pepper rubbed the sides of his dog's head and softly whispered, "C'mon, Crab Cake, let's head for home. I'm gonna come up wit' some kind of a solution 'tween now and mornin'." The two started back down the dirt road toward the family homestead.

In the distance, Pepper could hear the rest of the family as they enjoyed playing their Sunday game of baseball in the freshly mowed meadow by the house. Breaking into a run, he hoped to get in at least an inning or two before darkness set in. "C'mon, boy," he called to Crab Cake. And immediately the dog kicked it into high gear, ever so slightly outracing his master to the baseball field finish line.

No one mentioned that Pepper was late for the start of the game. The entire family knew of his passion for fishing. Upon arriving, Pepper noticed his brother Ty leading off first base with his sister Paula at bat. His father, Jack, was pitching. On the next pitch, Paula hit a slow roller to Sarah playing shortstop. Before she could reach for the ball, Crab Cake intercepted, picked it up with his mouth, and raced off toward the outfield, thinking surely someone would chase him and he'd have a little fun himself.

Instead, Ty called time out, left the field and went to his father's old workshop building near the top of the lane. When he returned, he had in his hand a brand new baseball and tossed it into play. Jack Whelan, who also doubled as the umpire, hollered "Play ball" and immediately play resumed.

Crab Cake was mortified. He dropped the ball in the grass and, disgusted with the entire Whelan family, went tromping off toward the house. Lying down pouting on the front porch at the top of the steps, he reluctantly watched as the rest of the family enjoyed the all-American pastime, playing out the last inning of the game.

With darkness settling in and the game tied, Pepper's father, Jack, called time and had it postponed until the following Sunday, weather permitting, of course. This was par for the course. Many times games extended over weeks, sometimes months, before victory could be declared for either one side or the other.

From the makeshift baseball field, Pepper walked back to the front porch where Crab Cake lay. The pet had already forgiven his family, and particularly Pepper, for not playing ball his way. He followed the young lad to the back porch. "Get a good night's sleep ol' boy," Pepper said to his dog. "We gotta big, big day ahead of us tomorrow, Crab Cake."

Retiring for the night, it didn't take long for Pepper Whelan to enter into a deep, deep sleep. It was sometime during the middle of the night when his dreams drifted easily to the freshwater stream known as Rehmeyer's Run and of winning for himself a cool one hundred dollars by hooking the record-sized trout known to all as Ol' Uncle Louie.

Chapter 4

Long before the rooster crowed Monday morning, Pepper was up and dressed. First he woke Ty and Paula to start the morning chores. Then he picked up the apple, banana and sandwiches which his mother had packed for him in a brown bag and the tall quart container of sweetened, home-brewed ice tea she had prepared.

The morning air was chilly. Soon the sun's rays would spill its warmth across the fields and onto the banks of Rehmeyer's Run. Until then, Pepper needed help. He slipped on a lightweight, long-sleeve jacket and covered his head with a Brooklyn Dodger baseball cap. Picking up his fishing pole which had been leaning against the outside back porch wall, he slung his tin can full of worms across his shoulder and called Crab Cake. With his pole in one hand, his ice tea in the other and his lunch safely tucked inside his jacket, the boy and his dog started out across the fields for a long first day of trout fishing.

Across the meadow Pepper walked with Crab Cake by his side. Far in the distant western horizon he could make out the darkness of clouds, but in the dark early morning hours of the clear eastern sky, the young lad could plainly see a myriad of heavenly stars twinkling their tiny lights down upon the earth. Coupled with the light of a full moon, it was easy for Pepper to see the way. He would avoid Thursy's house at all costs for fear of meeting up and then being stuck with him for the remainder of the day. Walking a different route to his favorite fishing spot, he was also able to avoid him at the bridge.

Pepper worked his way upstream to his secret fishing hole by walking the high wooded route instead of traveling the dirt road that ran through the valley. That route crossed the top of the hills, giving Pepper the advantage of always being able to look down. He needed to make sure Crab Cake stayed with him and didn't wander off. If Thursy saw Crab Cake, he'd surely know Pepper was nearby and come looking. Then his day would be ruined.

Over the hills and through the woods Pepper and Crab Cake traveled, past Chet Cline's house and then past old Amos Springler's home. From his vantage point high in the woods, Pepper could see both homes clearly.

Chet was a classmate of the Whelan kids at Hametown's one room school and had had a crush on Pepper's sister Paula for as long as Pepper could remember. Both usually sat together on the school bus going to and coming

37

home from school each day. Whenever Chet was absent, Pepper always sat next to his closest sister and, walking home from the bus stop, stayed by her side.

A retired sign and barn painter, Amos Springler favored keeping a pint bottle of alcoholic spirits in his back pocket, the purpose of which was imbibing any time of the day or night, whenever the urge struck. He lived alone in a one floor log cabin with his old Collie dog named Shep. Nailed to trees along the dirt road approaching his house from both ends in an attempt to slow down traffic were two feet by four feet wooden signs. Shep, who was well on in years, was crippled with arthritis, almost deaf and nearly blind. On the signs Springler had painted, *"DRIVE CAREFULLY – SAVE OL' SHEP."*

Some say the dog had been dead for years and the only reason Springler left the signs up was to slow down young drivers who drove the back dirt roads faster than he thought they should. Leaving a cloud of dust in their wake, Springler, whose small front yard abutted the road, ended up eating that dust any hour of the day or night.

However, Pepper, himself, knew the rumors were false. He had seen old Shep alive and had actually petted him one time along the road that ran in front of the Springler house not very long ago. Springler had been passed out on the front porch of his home, soused from taking one too many sips from the flask he always kept in his hip pocket. The dog was old, no doubt about it, but he was also gentle. Pepper sensed the only thing old Shep craved was for some love and attention in his waning years, something Springler was always too inebriated to give.

Three hundred yards below Springler's house the road branches off in a 'Y' shape. Although still a dirt road, it was a main one, an artery that cut through the wooded valley passing Rehmeyer's Run, and that meant heavier traffic than usual this first day of trout season. To avoid that, Pepper stayed high in the wooded hills away from that traffic.

As he approached the bridge that crossed the creek, he could see down below. The accumulation of trout fishermen, starting to vie for position as the morning sky approached dawn, was extraordinary. Pepper continued along the trail until he found the small path that led downward and close to the spot he had selected. Down the slope he cautiously walked with Crab Cake by his side.

Twigs crackling underfoot had a way of giving away his location. Not wanting to stir up a commotion, he walked quietly as he approached the creek. Gradually he made his way along the bank and followed the running stream backward to the bend which held the deep hole he had sought.

Suddenly Crab Cake spotted a squirrel. Turning away from Pepper and moving out at breakneck speed, he chased the wild game. The Border Collie was having the time of his life. For him, this was fun. This was living. This was what it was all about.

Pepper whistled loudly for Crab Cake to halt, but this time the dog kept running. The young lad was left with no other choice but to take off after his dog. By the time he reached the canine, the squirrel was treed. "No, Crab Cake," commanded Pepper. "Whenever I whistle, you gotta stop 'n' come back. Unnerstand? That's a bad doggy ta keep running."

The dog lowered his head and tucked his tail between his legs. Slowly he circled his master and, as a peace offering, moseyed up to kiss him. Pepper took the dog's face gently in his hands and spoke. "We don't want to alarm others, Crab Cake. Ya need to be a good doggy for a while. We both hafta be quiet. C'mon." And with those words of understanding, Crab Cake licked Pepper's face gently as if he was apologizing, wagged his tail in agreement and the two continued their journey toward the secret fishing hole.

Since the deep end was on his side, Pepper needed to cross over and fish from the shallow end. To do this, he'd have to walk farther upstream and ford the water near a narrow shallow crossing. Fortunately, just as there were many downstream the day before, exposed rocks enabled him to cross, using them as a natural foot bridge.

Once again, Crab Cake had no problem crossing, but with everything Pepper was carrying, coupled with the slipperiness of the wet, mossy rocks, the young lad proceeded with caution. The spring water was far too cold for him to get wet this early in the day. If he had slipped and fallen in, he would've had to cancel his day fishing, return home, remove his wet clothes and with dry ones, dress again. By the time he'd return, the day would have been lost.

Across the rocks Pepper gingerly stepped. Balancing his precious cargo in both hands, he finally made it to the other side. Once there, he started his journey downstream to the spot across from where his secret fishing hole was located. Crab Cake remained at his side.

As Pepper approached the site, Crab Cake let out a low guttural growl. The dog stopped in his tracks, looking straight ahead. There on the bank were two fishermen, sitting exactly at the same spot from where Pepper had intended to fish. A deep feeling of loss swept across the young lad's mind. "Easy boy," Pepper said to his dog, trying to calm him. "It's okay."

"Mornin' gennelmen," Pepper greeted them as he approached the creek, trying desperately to remain cheerful. "Is there room here fer one more?"

"Juss stay outta our way and there won't be no trouble," the one guy ordered. Pepper noticed his size. To the lad's eyes he was a big heavy-set burley man in his early fifties. Crab Cake growled. "And keep that mangy mutt away from here if ya know what's good fer him," he barked, picking up a wooden branch and holding it straight out.

The second guy said nothing but shot a mean glare their way. He looked to be about the same age, somewhat taller than, but not as heavy as the first man. He remained quiet, just looking on, watching cautiously and listening to the first guy do all the talking.

Both looked as if they hadn't shaved for days and smelled as if they hadn't bathed in weeks. Their clothes were dirty, and in some places torn. Their breath smelled, and what few teeth remained were stained from the constant use of chewing tobacco. Knees in their jeans were patched more than once and their shoe soles were loose and flapping.

The fat one had an eye that remained in one position while the other eye moved. The taller one had his hair trimmed as if some one slipped a bowl over his head and cut what little hair remained. On his right arm was the tattoo of a coiled snake that extended from the top of his shoulder all the way down to his elbow. It showed its tongue wagging from its mouth and appeared ready to strike.

They were a motley couple and both gave the young lad the willies. "My name's Pepper," the ten-year-old said, holding out his hand in friendship and trying to make the best of a disappointing moment. "This here's my dog, Crab Cake." The canine wasn't nearly as cordial as his master. Crab Cake lowered his head near the ground and emitted a low growl.

Ignoring Pepper's offering of a handshake, the big guy with the crazy eyes again issued his warning, this time shouting loudly while waving the stick at Crab Cake. "Juss keep dat flea bitten hound 'way from me. Ya hear? Beat it! Go fine yer own spot 'n' no one'll git hurt." The one with the tattoo still said nothing.

Pepper slowly moved on, calling for Crab Cake to tag along. Walking downstream he thought of how, after planning so well for weeks, the first day of trout fishing was starting off badly. "That's okay, Crab Cake," he said to his faithful companion. "There're a lot more good spots here 'long Rehmeyer's Run we can fish from. 'Sides, we still have time. Not even dawn yet."

But as they walked away, Pepper felt more depressed than before. Suddenly he realized he had not seen a fishing license on either one of those shady characters. Surely the game wardens will be out in full force the first day of trout season, especially down here where some of the best trout angling in the county exists. If he finds a warden, he'll report them. That way, if they're in violation of the law, they could be removed from the area, leaving the fishing hole to him. Crab Cake listened to Pepper's theory as the boy discussed his plans with him. The dog wagged his tail gently as if he understood.

Around the bend he noticed more fishermen getting ready to cast. Looking at his new $4.95 wrist watch and then glancing at the sky, Pepper figured he had another 15 to 20 minutes left before dawn. As he approached the road, cars were parked along the berm here, there and everywhere. It was beginning to fill up faster than he could have ever imagined. Everywhere he looked, there were fishermen. Some with expensive fly rods, others with casting rods and still others, like Pepper, with homemade poles.

Vehicles were pulling up and parking. Mostly men were exiting their automobiles, trucks, station wagons and even motorcycles and lining up all along the banks with their fishing gear. Periodically you'd see a woman sitting next to her husband, trying her luck with a pole.

Looking up the road Pepper noticed some men being stopped by others. Short conversations were being held and then others were being stopped. Suddenly he realized what was happening. He was watching the game warden checking on fishing licenses and making sure no one dropped their line in the water before dawn.

Deciding to report the actions of the two undesirables who refused to share with him his "secret" fishing hole, Pepper hurried up to where the warden was standing. Crab Cake followed him. "Sir," he said politely, "may I speak with you for a moment?"

"Not now, son," came the reply from the game warden. "I'm too busy. Wait a while and I'll be with you as soon as dawn breaks."

Pepper moved back, giving the law enforcement officer plenty of room to do his job. He heard him tell one guy to go buy a license or he'd be arrested if he tried throwing in his line. Incredibly, the man started to argue, but fortunately common sense won out, and he left in a fury.

Another, who stood there with a pole in one hand and a tackle box in the other, said he had just come to learn how to fish by watching others catch trout. The game warden didn't buy his story either and like the one before, he also left in a hurry.

Even the man who had reeked of alcohol from drinking the night before lost his argument when the Game Warden threatened to take away his keys if he didn't leave. With a cup of hot black coffee in his hand, he staggered back to his car and drove off.

Finally the dawn broke. The sun had peeked up over the wooded hill, shining its rays from across the eastern horizon. As the men spotted those first rays of sunlight, each began throwing their lines into the rapidly flowing waters of Rehmeyer's Run. And each man hoped against all hope that he would be the lucky one to successfully hook Ol' Uncle Louie. Pepper just stood on the sidelines and watched. Crab Cake lowered his head and pouted.

Chapter 5

Pepper and Crab Cake stood watching as others landed fish. Some were small, some medium size and still others were quite large. But all were within the size limit requirements set forth by the Pennsylvania State Fishing and Game Commission and so far, none broke the state record for either length or weight.

Men, boys and every now and then a girl were seen baiting, casting, setting hooks and landing beautifully colorful rainbow, brook and brown trout. Baiting those hooks again, they'd recast in hopes of landing more. Within eyesight, at any point along the creek, someone was landing a fish. The Commission did a commendable job stocking Rehmeyer's Run with fingerlings. To many, it was considered to be one of the best trout streams in the county.

"Hopefully," Pepper confided in Crab Cake, watching the fury of activity shortly after dawn, "there'll still be plenty of trout left in this creek for the rest of the season." Crab Cake sat down along the bank, his head pointed upward, blinked both eyes simultaneously and just stared at Pepper.

"Hey, Pepper?" A voice from the crowd called loud and clear. It was one Pepper had heard before. For a brief moment he froze. Who could possibly know him among all these strangers, he thought. He looked upstream and not recognizing anyone turned to the opposite direction. "Pepper? Over here," the voice directed, "behind ya."

Pepper turned toward downstream and still noticed no familiar face. He walked closer to the area from where the voice originated and noticed a big burley guy with a full length beard chomping on a lit cigar. Behind him, he heard the voice again. "C'mon, Pepper, buddy. If ya don't git your line in, ya gonna miss all the fish."

There, along the bank of Rehmeyer's Run, in the shadow of the big, bearded, burley guy, sat Thursy. "Figured you'd be late with all them there chores ya gotta do first," he said authoritatively. "Saved ya a spot. Sit down. I got plenty o' room."

Not saying a word, but glaring dirty looks that might possibly cause harm to anyone to which they were directed, the big, burley bearded guy with the cigar gave a quick puff, then huffed and swiftly moved on to another location. His departure left even more room along the bank for the two boys. Crab Cake

43

stopped pouting long enough to join them.

"Had two hooked," Thursy said, "but they dropped off when I tried landin' 'em. I gotta buy me a net, Pepper."

"Here, Thursy," said Pepper. "Use this next time." And he removed his blue Brooklyn Dodger baseball cap. "Juss hold it by its bill, slip it unner the broadest part o' the fish an' lift it up to the land. Those five holes in the cap's gonna act juss like holes in a net." Pepper handed it to Thursy. "Don't worry 'bout getting' it dirty or full o' smelly fish," he said. "Them caps wash up real good in soapy water."

Pepper unwound his line and baited the hook with the biggest, juiciest night crawler he could find. Across the bank was a portion of the stream which was void of fishing lines. Pepper decided to try that area first. Into the water he cast his line. Crab Cake wagged his tail in approval.

"Pepper, you shoulda seen the fish they already hauled outta here," said Thursy. "And big uns, too. Course, no un's caught Ol' Uncle Louie, yet, but 'twouldn't surprise me none if he comes outta this hole; or from somewheres in this crick!"

"I caught a glimpse o' all the fish they was catching, standing on the bridge," Pepper said, nodding his head toward the bridge in the distance. "As many people as there are here, I sure didn't figure I'd run into you. Guess it's just my luck," he said, facetiously. That last part was way over Thursy's head. He was much too busy concentrating on his line.

Suddenly Thursy's fishing line went under. It happened so fast the strength of the jerk almost pulled the rod from his hand. Gathering his wits about him, he stood up to reel in the fish. "Not yet, Thursy," yelled Pepper. "Ya gotta set the hook first. Hold the rod tight, jerk it quickly and set the hook or ya gonna lose him, Thursy."

The fish took the line and ran. Out of the water he jumped. The early morning sunshine gleamed off the sides. "Bee-a-u-yoo-tee-ful rain-bow," Pepper said excitingly while pronouncing every syllable and then some. "Looks to be 'bout a 14 to 16 incher. She's a beauty, Thursy." Crab Cake barked approvingly.

Thursy decided now was the time to set the hook, but before he could, the great rainbow spit the bait and swam away to freedom. Into the water went Crab Cake, chasing downstream after the fish. As he raced through the shallow rapids, the lines of other fishermen became disturbed. Before you could say 'good luck fishing,' a hoard of anglers was shouting at Crab Cake. "Get that dog 'way from here," yelled one old guy, shaking his fist and obviously mad as a hornet.

"That dog's a menace," shrieked another. "Get 'im outta the wooder."

"He's scaring 'way the fish. They're scattering," screamed still another. "They'll never return now. Whose dog is that, anyways?"

The last thing Pepper needed was an angry mob of anglers chasing him. He called for Crab Cake but to no avail. The dog was in his glory, chasing the huge rainbow through the shallow rapids in the middle of Rehmeyer's Run. With each jump of the canine landing back in the water, his splash hit the banks of the creek, spraying all who were sitting there. Crab Cake barked enthusiastically every time he thought he had the great trout cornered. But like the veteran fish it was, the rainbow played the dog for all he was worth before giving him the slip. Still, Crab Cake was in his glory. The dog was loving every minute of the chase.

Pepper whistled, but again Crab Cake ignored his command. Pepper knew he needed to do something and do it fast. If he didn't, he'd soon have an angry mob ready to tear his dog to smithereens.

Pepper looked downstream. As far as he could see, fishermen were pulling their lines out of the water in an attempt to untangle them. Words of frustration they were using, and in some cases, sheer anger, could only be described as expletives deleted long before that euphemism entered our lexicon. Their home-spun dialogue could not have been printed in a 1950's family newspaper. As a matter of fact, some of the language they were using to describe the Border Collie's unorthodox behavior may not have legally been able to make the printed word of any publication, period.

Crab Cake continued chasing the big rainbow downstream, or so he thought. Finally Pepper had seen enough. Reaching into his jacket pocket, he found it empty. Pepper had forgotten to bring along a leash. Nevertheless, he took off after Crab Cake. Running along the bank he finally caught up with his dog. Closing in, Pepper whistled, catching Crab Cake's attention. "Crab Cake, get up here, now," he yelled at his pet, his voice filled with authority.

Crab Cake stopped in mid-stream. He looked at Pepper then back into the water where he thought the great fish waited to resume the chase. "Crab Cake, you're a bad dog. Get up here this very minute. Now!" Pepper yelled at him. Their eyes met. Crab Cake knew he was in trouble. As his tail tucked between his back legs once again, he lowered his head. His eyes were looking upward from the top of the sockets. Slowly he made his way to shore and stood by his master. He was ready to accept his punishment.

"You a bad, bad doggie," Pepper scolded. "No, no, no. Ya don't chase fish like that. It's different when we go hunting. You know better'n that."

As if in shame, Crab Cake still held his head low. The dog knew he had done wrong but what invigorating fun it was chasing that trout in the clear cold water. Suddenly Crab Cake arched his back and with all the energy he could muster, shook his fur with great gusto. In the process, Pepper tried to step back but was much too slow. The dog's extra curricular activity sprayed his master with a full shower of fresh, cold, crystal clear mountain spring water, soaking him to the skin.

Pepper was drenched. He walked back upstream with Crab Cake while others watched cautiously. Most gave up hope that the dog would ever leave, and so they themselves left. Hoping to find another spot far away from the kid with the crazy dog, they still felt there was time to land that trophy trout. Thursy greeted them with a belly laugh and handed Pepper a dry towel he always kept with him as part of his tackle. "Next time ya two decide ta go swimming' in a trout stream," he said, jokingly, "wait 'til high noon when the sun at least has a chance o' warmin' up the wooder."

As Thursy handed Pepper his dry jacket, he noticed the Game Warden. Looking up, Pepper noticed him, too. Slowly the Warden approached the two boys, looking first at Pepper and then down at his dog. "Oh boy," whispered Pepper to Thursy. "Now we gonna be in trouble. Big trouble. One o' 'em angry fishermen probably r'ported Crab Cake."

"Now then, young man," the State Game Warden addressed the lad, still staring at the wet mutt. "Thank you for your patience. I have a few free minutes. What was it you wanted to tell me?"

Pepper couldn't believe his ears. He looked at Thursy in astonishment. Thursy turned his head and just chuckled to himself. Crab Cake received a much needed reprieve. "There's a cupala guys upstream, Officer. They ain't got no fishing license showin' on their clothes," Pepper told the Game Warden. "An' they was fishing long 'fore dawn. Threatened my dog 'n' chased me away from where they was sittin' juss as if they owned the crick."

"From where exactly were they fishing and how long ago did this happen?" the officer asked, using impeccably perfect English without the hint of an accent. "Can you describe them?"

Pepper described the two dirty looking characters. He then told the Game Warden where they were and all about how scroungy looking the two men were. Finally he related how they threatened him if he didn't keep his dog away. "They's nasty and nasty looking, Officer," said Pepper. "I sure wouldn't wanna run inta 'em on a dark night wit'out my dog by my side."

"I'll check it out, son," the Game Warden assured Pepper. "Don't worry about a thing. If they're violating the law, they'll pay the price." As he started to leave, he turned back to Pepper and quietly said, "By the way, the next time you want to take your dog along fishing with you on a busy stream, it may be a good idea to bring a leash along to tie him. Helps keep the peace much better among the other anglers. I'm sure you understand, son."

Pepper smiled at Thursy, then looked back towards the Game Warden as he walked away upstream. Calling to him, Pepper thanked him for his kind consideration.

"Had 'nough 'citement for one day?" asked Thursy, sitting on the bank, his line in the water waiting for a strike.

"He's right, ya know," said Pepper. "I shoulda brought a rope along ta tie up Crab Cake. Either that or not bring 'im along at all."

"That's ridiculous, Pepper," Thursy countered. "Ya know's well as me that Crab Cake'd find ya no matter how far ya went wit'out 'im. Why, it's happened time and time again. An' what's the sense o' havin' yer dog along when you go fishing if ya hafta tie him up."

Thursy had a reputation of nearly always putting his foot in his mouth whenever he spoke. Rarely did it ever happen, but this time Thursy was right and Pepper knew it. He also knew the officer was right, too. It just wasn't very fair to the other fishermen to have a dog run loose, chasing away the fish. Pepper was having second thoughts about having Crab Cake with him. Something had to be done before Crab Cake got himself into more trouble than what he could get out of. But what?

A strike hit Pepper's line but his mind was too occupied with the shenanigans of his pet to notice. "Pepper, ya gotta hit, Buddy," Thursy yelled. "Set the hook."

By the time Jack 'Pepper' Whelan, Jr. pulled the pole in an attempt to set the hook, there was nothing on the end of the hook... not even a worm. Crab Cake laid his head on the ground, looked up at his master, and whimpered. For both boy and dog, the day was truly going badly.

The morning sun was slowly inching its way towards high noon. Its rays were beaming warmth down upon the two boys and dog as Pepper reached into his can and baited his hook one more time with another juicy night crawler. Closing his eyes, Crab Cake lay down along side his master, resting his head on his lap. Perhaps there was still hope. After all, the day was young.

47

Chapter 6

The Game Warden approached the two seedy characters who had been using the secret fishing hole that Pepper and Crab Cake had cased much earlier in the closing days of winter. Both had their lines cast into the water. The heavier of the two, Crazy Eyes, had his line farther away across the bank. The taller one, Tattoo, had his cast more toward downstream. As the officer entered their field of view, both appeared startled for a moment, and then regained their composure. Neither had seen the Game Warden approaching.

"How's the fishing, gentlemen?" the warden asked in an attempt to make small talk, reducing the risk of appearing as a threat. Lying in the back of the Game Warden's mind was the fact he was alone. After all, he was only one; they were two. "Have you had any luck since dawn?" he asked. Steadily approaching the noon hour, the sun was finally beginning to succeed in warming the banks along the meandering stream.

"Unless ya got some 'ficial business, don't bodder us," snapped the heavy set man, his one eye on his line and the bad eye pointing in the direction of the warden. "Git lost 'fore you wishtd ya hadn't. An' ya better make it snappy," he added.

For Crazy Eyes and Tattoo, saying these words to a Game Warden was certainly not very bright. But then, of course, these two never would have been accused of being among the most brilliant stars in the night sky.

They were the wrong words to say to a peace officer, especially one who carries a loaded weapon. Certainly, it was not the best example of diplomacy. But then these two characters never understood that you don't challenge persons of authority who hold within them the power and influence to enforce the peace without running the risk of repercussions. Common sense dictates otherwise. That's why the number one rule of thumb is, never do you ever threaten Game Wardens.

Seemingly forever, the Game Warden stood there staring at the two goofy looking anglers, wishing he had with him his assistant. While it's true his gun was loaded, it was nevertheless secured safely in his hip holster with a snap on the end of a leather restraining strap. Rarely was there ever a need for any Game Warden to draw a firearm on as gentle a segment of the population as were fishermen. And most assuredly, he did not wish to reduce the odds of

49

survival by antagonizing two mean looking characters who, although older, were also bigger.

Without saying a word, the game warden retreated. With his right hand resting on the snapped strap of his secured side holster, he slowly backtracked down the bank of the stream, keeping both eyes on the two until they were no longer within his sight. When he had reached the point of personal safety, he turned, and walked swiftly back downstream from where he came. Passing the two boys and dog, he continued walking at a swift pace straight to his radio equipped car.

The two criminals were relieved. "That's telling him, Crazy Eyes," Tattoo said in praising his buddy. "Bet they don't ever mess around wit' us again, huh?"

But near the bridge, close to the warden's car, Pepper thought otherwise. "Sumpin's up!" he said to Thursy in a hushed voice. Even Crab Cake sensed a mysterious difference in the air. Perking his ears and alertly raising his head, the small Border Collie cocked it to one side and then to the other. Suddenly he sprang to his feet and rushed to Pepper's side. His tail was neither drooped between his legs nor was it wagging. Instead it remained straight as an arrow, pointing outwards. Crab Cake looked inquisitively at his master and gave a low keyed whimper as if to say, "C'mom. Let's go see what's up."

Pepper dropped his fishing line. Knowing there's always safety in numbers wherever danger abounds, he asked Thursy to join him. "Naw, Pepper," answered his fishing buddy, "you go on ahead. I wanna stay an' fish."

"Sumpin's wrong, Thursy," Pepper insisted. "What if the Game Warden's in danger? We should at least follow at a safe pace behind so to be close by if help's needed. After all, he was nice 'nough not ta arrest Crab Cake, or me. Maybe we owe it to him. It's the least we can do, pal. 'Sides," he added, "I don't trust those two guys any fardder than I could throw 'em."

"Gimme a break, Pepper! I come ta fish, not chase after weirdoes. That Warden can take care o' hisself," Thursy insisted. "That's why they gib 'im months and months o' training. Ya go on 'head. I'll juss stay here an' fish."

"If he can take care o' himself," Pepper argued, "then why'd he come back so fast? An' why'd he have that look o' deep concern on his face? An' why'd he rush right ta his car ta use the two way radio? I think he got troubles, Thursy. An' I think those troubles start right where I 'spect they do, wit' those two goofballs. The ones who chased me away earlier today."

Pepper's questions came at him fast and furiously. Thursy finally tired from trying to win a losing argument. "Okay, Pepper, we'll do it yer way," he conceded in a disgusted voice. "But yer gonna end up owin' me one, ya know that, Pepper? Yer gonna owe me big time!"

Pepper just looked at Thursy and nodded his head. Why his friend had to be so stubborn when it came time to helping others remained a mystery to Pepper. "Someday you might be in a sitchiashun yourself, juss like that, Thursy," he told him. "Then, if needed, you juss might wish somebody was nearby to help you."

The two boys and dog started toward the spot where the Warden's car was parked. Slowly and nonchalantly, they passed the car as if taking their good ol' time trying to find another fishing spot. Crab Cake, keeping pace, stayed between them.

"... it's very possible. Yes, Angus "Tattoo" MacGrew and Isadore "Crazy Eyes" Zitoulleo. Yes, it could be them. That's why I'm asking for backup as soon as possible." The boys heard the end part of what the officer was saying over his two way radio as they approached the car. Before hearing more, the noise of a passing car took them out of earshot as they moved to the side of the road to prevent being hit. "Both look troublesome and have already spoken in threatening tones," the boys heard the warden relate to headquarters after moving back within earshot. "The possibility of both being wanted strongly exists," the Fishing and Game officer added. Then, while waiting for confirmation on backup, he described the two strange looking characters to his superiors.

The boys and Crab Cake turned to their left and walked slowly toward the creek as it meanders through the wooded valley and into a clearing. Past the clearing the stream turns back and wanders aimlessly, turning here and there before returning into the woods. Once there, it leads back to the spot where the two sloppily dressed felons were fishing.

Suddenly a strange feeling, one of deep loss overcame Pepper. A chill ran down his spine as he sensed within him what was about to transpire. Once Thursy Patterson saw the spot where the two undesirable characters were fishing, Jack 'Pepper' Whelan, Jr. was about to lose his favorite and most "secret" fishing hole.

With Thursy by his side, and intent on helping the officer if needed, Pepper understood the price he'd be paying by exposing his "secret" spot to his friend. The place would never be the same again. Long gone would be the days when he and his dog could sit on the bank by the rapidly flowing waters, leisurely fishing in a tranquil and peaceful setting without risking the chance of others, especially Thursy horning in. Nevertheless, it was a price he was willing to pay.

As they approached the top of the wooded hill overlooking the fishing hole, they saw the two seedy men jawing back and forth about something or another. From their vantage point high atop the wooded hill, it looked very much to the boys as if they were arguing. Their arms were flailing close to each other, and the look of meanness enveloped their faces.

Out of hearing range, the boys never heard the conversation as Crazy Eyes, pointing to the deep water hole, asked Tattoo, "Why'd yer brother hafta throw it in there to hide it?"

"I don't know," answered Tattoo. "Ya want me ta go back ta prison an' ask 'im?"

Crazy Eyes just stared at Tattoo. "I could think of a lot better places to hide the loot than in the bottom of a deep mountain stream."

"Hey, it's in a weighted, waterproof metal container. It'll be all right," Tattoo said, trying to calm down his partner. "C'mon, let's throw our lines in again and see if we can snag it."

"I'm tired of fishing for something I don't know where it is," answered Crazy Eyes. "This isn't working. You go in and dive deep. Maybe we'll have better luck that way."

"You want me ta go inta ice cold 35 degree mountain spring water because you ain't got no patience with the hook and line system?" Tattoo shot back. "Sorry, Buddy. But I didn't bring my wet suit 'long this time. Ya wanna go diving, you go in. I'm sticking wit' the hook and line."

Unexpectedly, Crazy Eyes pushed Tattoo to the ground. The boys lay close to the edge of the hill with Crab Cake lying between them and listened, but being too far out of earshot, they struggled to hear.

Suddenly they couldn't believe what appeared from out of the far left peripheral vision of their eyes. Out of the blue the Game Warden stepped. Instead of waiting for backup, he returned alone. With his gun drawn, he approached the two men. As they stood up, it appeared to the boys as if the warden had asked to see their licenses.

Both men removed their hats and looked at them quizzically. It was as if they couldn't understand why their hats no longer had their fishing license badges attached. The boys watched as they soon saw the two fidgeting and fooling with their hip pockets as though they were trying to reach for their wallets, perhaps to offer the warden a bribe.

In the blink of an eye, Tattoo dropped his wallet and in an uncontrolled reaction, the Game Warden looked down. When he did, Crazy Eyes instantly dropped the peace officer with a quick and solid round house right. It was as if the two had rehearsed these moves for years. Grabbing the warden's gun, Crazy Eyes ordered Tattoo to tie him up with rope he had in his pocket that was found in the barn the night before. It had been leftover after making a belt for his pants. Once more he walloped him over the head, this time with a heavy piece of wood, and together, they picked him up, Crazy Eyes his feet and Tattoo his hands, as they swung him back and forth before tossing him into the deep fishing hole.

What the boys had just seen astonished them. They were witnesses to a crime, very possibly a murder. A feeling of fear swept over their young bodies and for an instant they were frozen in thought. Now what are we gonna do, they privately questioned themselves.

Crab Cake was ready to spring, but Pepper wisely held onto the dog. The two sleazy men left in a hurry, scampering up over the hill, straight in the direction of where the boys lay. "Stay still," whispered Pepper to Crab Cake. "Shhh! Stay still, boy."

The perpetrators moved within ten feet of the two young frightened lads and their brave dog. Fully covered with the dead leaves of last fall, a thousand thoughts ran through their minds as Crazy Eyes and Tattoo were passing.

Suddenly Thursy felt a sneeze coming on. With every ounce of energy the young lad could muster, he forced his face deep into the fallen leaves and hard against the earth. Pepper took his hand and held it tightly against Thursy's head. His other outstretched arm held down the dog and, with his free hand, compressed the snout of his faithful companion.

Crab Cake was just itching to bark. More than once he tried but, Pepper, with his hand over his mouth, refused to release him as he watched through natural peep holes created between the fallen leaves. Swiftly the two creeps made their way past the boys and their dog and onto the path that led to the main road and freedom.

Once they were out of sight, Pepper whispered to Thursy, "The warden! We've got to help the warden." And in the split of a second the two boys and Crab Cake ran down the hill toward their "secret" fishing hole at breakneck speed.

Chapter 7

Crab Cake ran even faster, as if he knew he was on a mission of mercy. The dog immediately sensed the danger at hand and broke for the edge of the water. Within the flash of a millisecond, the canine sized up the grim situation at hand and, without delay, did the job Pepper never expected of him.

Into the water jumped the dog. The body of the warden was in the deepest part of the stream. The boys watched apprehensively as Crab Cake moved toward the spot where they could see the warden's body submerged. Suddenly the warden surfaced and floating face down in the water, his body caught the rapids and drifted in the direction of the little dog.

Crab Cake took advantage of this good fortune by grabbing a piece of the clothing with his mouth and, swimming swiftly toward the boys who were standing on shore encouraging their hero, pulled the warden to the nearby bank where they were waiting.

"Crab Cake, over here," called Pepper as he tried to steer his dog to the shallow end of the stream. Crab Cake responded. "Good boy," encouraged Pepper. "That's a good doggy," he repeated as the canine wagged his tail enthusiastically after obeying his commands.

The average size dog managed to keep his head above water as he rescued the much heavier Game Warden from the depths of the "secret" water hole. If it hadn't crossed their minds before, the boys knew those two guys were criminals now.

Pepper and Thursy had no knowledge of any hidden loot. They thought the only reason the two strangers were there was to catch the elusive Ol' Uncle Louie and collect the $100 reward. By trying to do away with the Warden, the two ex-cons thought for sure they had everyone fooled. Everyone, that is, except the two boys and, of course, Crab Cake.

As the Warden drifted slowly toward land in the grasp of the dog's soft bite, Pepper reached out and grabbed one arm while Thursy grabbed hold of the other. Together, the two boys mustered every bit of strength they had to pull the Game Warden onto shore.

Suddenly Crab Cake took off, running downstream along the bank and around the bend. "Let 'im go," Pepper said, holding Thursy back from chasing him. "We got enough on our hands now. He's gonna be back. 'Sides, he

55

probably juss spotted a rabbit or squirrel."

Once on shore, Pepper proceeded to make sure they would not lose the warden. "Help me here, Thursy," ordered Pepper. "He's not breathin'. We gotta get the wooder outta his lungs."

Again, with all their energy, the two grunted and struggled, finally turning the Game Warden over and placing him face down. From back issues of Boy's Life, Pepper remembered reading something about a man who had received some form of artificial respiration. But it was so long ago, he couldn't quite recall everything there was to do in order to perform it properly. What he did remember, he applied.

Sitting on the Game Warden's back, the ten-year-old faced the front with his knees by the victim's side. With both hands on one side, Pepper pushed down on the middle of the warden's back, just behind his lungs. Thursy did the same to the other side. The two young boys would push, wait a moment, then push some more. This went on for what seemed to be forever. Then, when all hope for reviving the warden seemed lost, he suddenly regurgitated water. Coughing, the warden continued, with Pepper and Thursy patting him on the back. As he lay there on the ground, the warden soon realized what had happened.

From around the corner appeared a second Game Warden following Crab Cake. As the backup, he was sent to the scene by headquarters and arrived only minutes earlier. After Crab Cake had left the boys, he returned to the road where the warden's car was parked and, finding the second Warden, led him to the scene. Quickly, the backup Warden took over the work the two boys were doing. Once he was assured of his colleague's survival, he helped him to his feet and assisted in walking him to his car. There he called headquarters for medical assistance.

"Officer Helfrich," the second warden finally said, holding out his hand in gratitude and friendship and introducing himself to the boys. "I'm mighty grateful for your help."

"My name's Pepper. Jack 'Pepper' Whelan, Jr," Pepper said. "This is Thurston Patterson. Everyone calls him Thursy. And this is my dog, Crab Cake," he added, petting the canine on the head approvingly.

Officer Helfrich smiled. "That's a fine name for a dog living in the Chesapeake Bay region," he said to the boys while giving Crab Cake a pat of approval on the head. Crab Cake gave a bark of acknowledgment, then, without warning, shook his long wet coat of its excess water, spraying both wardens and the boys.

"That's okay, son," Officer Helfrich laughed, assuring them no action would be taken against their dog. "What happened to Officer Stambaugh?" The boys never knew the injured Game Warden's name. In their brief conversation with him, it was never mentioned.

Slowly and deliberately, Pepper related the story to Officer Helfrich. He emphasized the two out-of-kilter eyes of the heavier guy and the snake tattoo on the taller one's arm.

When the lad finished, he breathed a deep sigh of relief. "Divine Providence, in His infinite wisdom, decided to spare the life of this good man," Officer Helfrich told Pepper. "Thankfully, you two and your dog were there for a reason," he continued. "Perhaps to act as some form of Guardian Angel sent to assure that all went according to His plan."

Thirty minutes later medical help arrived. With emergency lights flashing on the ambulance and both Game Warden cars, the scene more closely resembled that of a big inner city emergency instead of the tranquility of a wooded country setting. Officer Stambaugh was transferred to the hospital twenty-five miles to the north in the City of York.

"Is he gonna be okay?" Pepper asked. "Is he gonna be able to return to his job?"

"I'm sure he's in good hands now," the officer told the boys. "And I'm sure he will be back. But without your help, and Crab Cake's, he would not have made it. You three are heroes." It mattered little to Pepper, but Thursy smiled at the mention of his name being associated with the word hero. It felt pretty good for a change, receiving recognition for unselfishly helping others. Crab Cake just wagged his tail and gave a bark of approval.

"I need both of your full names, ages, addresses, phone numbers, your school and what grade you're in," Officer Helfrich told the boys. "You can print the information on this paper," he said, handing Pepper a tablet. "Oh yes, better include the names of your parents in that, too. Also, write down the dog's name, his breed and his age," he added.

"We ain't got no phone at our house," Pepper told the officer. "I'll just give ya Thursy's phone number." The officer agreed that would be fine.

"Don't be surprised if you read about your heroics in the *Gazette and Daily*," Officer Helfich said. "People love reading about heroes in their local paper." In 1951 the *Gazette and Daily* was York County's morning newspaper. "And you'll probably receive some form of oral or written recognition from either local or state officials." Then, as an afterthought, he added, "You'll be needed to identify those two criminals once we catch them,

57

so keep yourselves available, boys."

In the excitement of the moment, the boys had almost forgotten about those two seedy characters. Then it dawned on them. They're out there in the fields and woods lurking about. They could very well be hiding. Maybe they're waiting for the officers to leave before attacking the only witnesses to their crime and doing them in. In their excitable imaginations, they had completely forgotten that they had been hiding deep under a pile of fallen leaves and were unseen by the criminals.

Pepper suddenly remembered and laughed. He breathed a deep sigh of relief, then realized it may have been premature. "Oh no," Pepper whispered to Thursy, "that's not such a good idea to publish our names in the paper." At least not until after Crazy Eyes and Tattoo are caught.

He returned to voice his concerns with Officer Helfrich. "We've already thought of that, Pepper," he said, "that's why nothing will be turned into the news media about you two witnessing any crime. Only that you came upon the warden and saved his life. Besides, those guys are long gone from here. They're not going to come back to the scene of their crime and hunt all over these woods for two young kids they've never seen before."

"Makes sense to me," whispered Thursy as they walked back to their special fishing hole. "Can you imagine if the papers said we witnessed a crime and we'd have to run day and night to keep those two from finding us?" Pepper knew Thursy had a habit of exaggerating everything.

"If the papers said we saw what they did to the warden, we'd hafta have 24 hour pertection," Thursy said, his imagination starting to take over his sense of reason. "We'd hafta walk the straight and narrow until they were caught. Think of what'd happen, Pepper, if it took weeks, maybe months or maybe even years? I'm not sure I'd be able to behave myself that long."

"Yeah, Thursy," Pepper joked, "maybe you're right for a change. For you, that'd be giant strides. That'd be a major accomplishment. Probably even make national news." Both boys had a hearty laugh over that one.

"Dateline, White Oak Valley, April 1958..." Pepper started, imitating a news broadcaster by holding his closed hand near his mouth and the other cupping his ear. "... Unidentified sources confirmed Tuesday that Thurston Patterson, also known as Thursy and now 19 years of age, has just entered his 97th month of perfect behavior.

"A House Sub-Committee on un-American activities will soon begin a congressional investigation in order to discover why this previously troublesome teenager no longer has been experiencing extreme cases of the heebee jeebees and isn't driving the Pennsylvania State Police crazy with his usual shenanigans like all other red blooded American kids. Penalties for acting like an adult too early in life could result in an 18 hour a day job, seven days a week, inside one of York's many wire cloth factories, cleaning rest rooms, with all fishing privileges permanently revoked." Again they laughed heartily as they dwelt on the silliness of what Pepper was saying.

Heading back to the secret fishing hole where Crazy Eyes and Tattoo were last seen, they glanced over their shoulders periodically, making sure they weren't being followed. Fortunately, Crazy Eyes and Tattoo were no where in sight. Even Crab Cake watched cautiously as the boys headed toward the fishing hole. If the dog had seen anything, a bark would have been sufficient warning for the boys to run. Crab Cake was really all the security they needed.

Approaching their no longer "secret" fishing hole, they looked down the hill at the creek below, only to discover once again they were too late. A father and his two sons had wandered onto the spot and decided to try their luck.

Realizing the high sun signaled the noon hour, Pepper checked his watch for verification. "It's 12:30, Thursy," Pepper mentioned casually. "What say we take a break 'n' have us a bite ta eat?"

"Sounds good ta me, Pepper," answered Thursy, "but what 'bout Crab Cake?"

"No problem, Buddy. Already thought o' my dog." Out of the brown, paper lunch bag Pepper pulled a long, thick, juicy beef bone wrapped in wax paper. Talking softly, he unwrapped it and handed it to his dog. Crab Cake was thrilled and quietly took the bone in his mouth, walked about ten feet away, lay down on the leaves facing the two boys and started gnawing away.

From the bag, Pepper removed two sandwiches. "Help y'rself, pal," said Pepper, handing a sandwich to Thursy. "Mom packed more'n I could ever eat." Pepper lifted two folding metal Boy Scout cups from the bag, removed the lids, pulled them into position and filled them with ice cold tea from the quart container. Handing it to Thursy, he said, "Enjoy. Mom makes a good homemade ice tea. The best in the neighborhood!"

"How comes he got a name like that?" asked Thursy, suddenly changing subjects.

"Who? And like what?" answered Pepper with two questions of his own.

"Like Ol' Uncle Louie," replied Thursy, laughing at the hilarity of it. "How'd anyone ever come up wit' a name like that fer a fish?"

"Well, Thursy," started Pepper, "I don't rightly know fer sure, but stories I heard, tole by an ol' Italian fisherman by the name o' Lou Passarelli who lived somewheres near St. Mary's Catholic Church in York, say he hooked the fish some years back. When he couldn't land it, he went in the crick an' he tried grabbin' it wit' his hands but the fish got away," Pepper continued.

"More'n once this happened, an' each time he'd come ta that corner bait shop over in Shrewsbury, the one where the bus stops, he'd end up tellin' a new version 'bout the same fish that got away. Got to the point the fellows there could tell the story long 'fore old Lou got his latest version out. Well, sum o' the guys started believin' ol' Lou 'cause all the time he'd be tellin' 'em, he'd be doin' it wit' a straight face," he said.

"For years he kept comin' back, tellin' 'bout how he was still trying to land this one special trout, which he claimed, o' course, was a monster. Late every winter, just 'fore the opening of trout season, he'd tell his fishin' buddies 'bout this same fish that kept spitting his hooks, bitin' his line in half or doin' whatever had to be done to shake the hook. It was almost like the fish had a high level o' intelligence all its own. An' o' course each time he'd tell it, that darn fish would juss grow by leaps and bounds," Pepper added.

"One year ol' Lou Passarelli didn't show up. Never havin had the thrill o' catchin' the fish, he passed away. That winter, sittin' 'round the bait shop's warm potbelly stove, his fishin' buddies started referring to this fish that no one else had ever seen 'cept the late ol' Lou, as *Louie*. From there it grew to *Uncle Louie* and from that to *Ol' Uncle Louie*," he continued telling Thursy.

"Dad said he s'poses they named it that in his memory, but still that fish was nuttin' more'na figment o' the lonely old man's imagination,'" Pepper said. "But ya know, Thursy, I heard udders swear that fish actually exists. I s'pose that's why the bait company offered $100 ta anyone who can catch it. Dad said 'they were probably sick o' hearin' all them stories 'n' wanted to prove once 'n' fer all it wasn't real.'"

"What 'bout him?" asked Thursy, laughing and pointing to Crab Cake. "How in the world did a good looking dog like him get such a ridiculous name like Crab Cake?"

"Right after we got 'im cuppala years ago," Pepper said, munching on his sandwich, "no one knew his name. He was abandoned. Someone dropped him off at Stabler's Cabins on the old Susquehanna Trail. I was helping Mom make crab cakes fer supper that night an' I accidentally dropped a cooked one on the floor. Before I could pick it up, the dog got it with his mouth. I yelled fer him ta drop it but 'twas too late. Guess the poor thing was hungry," he said, swallowing a bite of sandwich.

"'Drop the crab cake. Drop the crab cake, dog,' I yelled. Didn't even knowd dogs liked crab cakes," Pepper continued while washing the sandwich down with his mom's freshly brewed ice tea. "But he juss up an' ate it, then licked his chops as if ta ask fer more. My mom was laughin' so hard she almost fell ta the floor. My two sisters were laughing and Ty and David were laughing. Everyone was a laughing 'cept me," he said.

"Looking back now, I s'pose 'twas funny but since I figured everyone would say it was my crab cake he ate, I saw nuttin' funny 'bout it at the time," Pepper explained. "When my dad came home that evening an' my mom told him what happened, he looked straight at me wit' one of those impish grins he gets on his face and said, 'Well, son, I s'pose now he has a name.'

"'Huh,' I answered him, dumbfounded. 'Whata ya talkin' 'bout? What name, Dad?'" Pepper continued with his story.

"'Crab Cake,' Dad said. An' the whole family juss laughed 'emselves silly once again, this time harder than before. I looked down and there was the dog juss a waggin' his tail a mile a minute, juss as if he liked the name. So I thought, since 'twas unanimous, why not? An' that's how he got his name." This time it was Thursy laughing for all it was worth. He loved hearing Pepper tell stories. To him it was entertaining. Then Pepper abruptly switched subjects.

"Ya ever think about what ya wanna do when ya grow up, Thursy?" asked Pepper as they leisurely enjoyed their lunch. Surprised at Pepper initiating a new conversation and caught off guard, Thursy mumbled something as he tried answering and chewing his food at the same time. Pepper suspected he said no and preferred not to discuss his future.

"What about you, Pepper?" asked Thursy after swallowing the mouth full of food he was chewing and now able to be heard somewhat clearly.

"Probably gonna go ta college," Pepper answered. "Least I'd like ta. Really ain't got no ideas what I'd take up," he continued. "Dad says I'm still too young to decide that. 'Plenty o' time,' he says. 'Sides, I'm liable to change my mind twenny times 'fore I get ta college," he said.

"But I do like writin', Thursy. And I offen think o' actin' or readin' the news fer radio. Might even like ta appear on that new picture radio they got out now. They say it's called television. Juss like you guys got. An' every now and then I think 'bout being a lawyer, an artist or better still, a photographer." Then he added as an afterthought, "One thing's for sure, Thursy, I don't wanna hafta end up in a fact'ry punchin' timecards. That'd bore me ta death."

"Man, sounds like you wanna be everythin', Pepper," Thursy commented in awe as he took the last bite of his sandwich. With his mouth full, Pepper indicated for him to help himself. There were still more sandwiches and Thursy accepted, adding, "I'm still hopin' I can pass fourth grade 'n' not be held back again."

The two boys lay back on a bed of leaves and dreamed of what the future might hold for them. One thing it did not hold was their immediate access to the best fishing spot on Rehmeyer's Run.

Soon the fullness of their stomachs and the warmth of the mid-day sun had them enjoying the peacefulness of napping. Their dog, still nearby gnawing his bone, moved closer to the two and finally joined them in their mid-day siesta. Upon wakening, they'd continue their quest for a good fishing spot.

Chapter 8

Pepper awoke with a tickle. A near weightless feather, soft as down and drifting lazily in the breeze off a high flying bird, had settled on his nose, causing it to itch. Sneezing, he suddenly realized they had fallen asleep. Walking to the top of the ridge and looking down, Pepper noticed the fishing spot was absent of any other anglers. He quickly woke Thursy. Crab Cake was already by Pepper's side.

"C'mon, Thursy," he spoke softly to his pal. "No one's down there. The spot's empty. Let's hurry down 'fore some one shows up an' grabs it."

Thursy was in the middle of a good dream. "Mmmm, ooooh, aaaah, mmmm," he groaned. And then rolling over in the leaves, he returned to his slumber.

"Okay, buddy," said Pepper. "That'sa way ya want it? I'll juss go on down myself an' have me the entire spot," he told his buddy, kicking him gently in the rump.

The lad shot up like a rocket. "Ya 'bout ready to finally do some serious trout fishin'?" Pepper asked his groggy fishing partner. And before Thursy could answer, Pepper continued. "If so, grab yer pole an' foller me an' Crab Cake."

Led by their dog, the two young lads walked as fast as their legs would carry them down the slope to the bank of the fishing hole. Gazing across the wide calm bend in the creek, they stopped and watched alertly as the afternoon's serenity was shattered by the arching back of a rainbow trout as it cleared the surface, snaring a snack of fresh live bug in mid-air, just above the water's line.

Excited, they swiftly baited their hooks and cast their lines. Finally, after all the troubles they've encountered, they were going to catch trout. Maybe even catch Ol' Uncle Louie, himself. Thinking they could surely use the $100 reward, all seemed well with their world once again.

Both boys sat on the grass of the slightly sloping bank by the stream waiting for the fish to strike. After thirty minutes of patience and no bites, Thursy suggested they may be using the wrong bait. "I saw some guys downstream usin' tiny feathers tied ta even tinier hooks," said Thursy. "Ya couldn't even see the hooks. Don't know how they got the worm on, Pepper."

"Them's artificial lures," Pepper informed him. "Them's called flies. Ya don't put worms on 'em. Ya don't even use live bait, Thursy. Those guys were fly fishin'." Thursy listened carefully as Pepper told him all he knew about fly fishing from reading old Boy's Life magazines he had found stored in a box on the floor of their attic. "Most fly fishermen tie the lures 'emselves," he continued. "Ya gotta have nimble fingers ta do it, Thursy. My Grandpa Chronister said 'ta do it right an' have it work, takes a real pro.' It ain't for everyone."

But Pepper really didn't think different bait which was used by others made much difference. He had always caught trout in Rehmeyer's Run and had always used freshly dug worms. That's because his grandfather and he had always caught trout in the Yellow Breeches creek and both had consistently used freshly dug worms. To be accurate, his grandfather was quite frugal and would never have agreed to spending good hard earned money on fishing bait when worms were available, free for the digging.

"What the problem seems ta be, Thursy," said Pepper, "is that the fish are full from eating too much food other fishermen threw to 'em. Here 'tis midday, an' by now they don't got no appetite. Remember," he told his buddy, "the best times for catching trout's in the early morning an' late evening hours. That's when they eat, Thursy, right after getting up and just 'fore goin' ta sleep. With the exception of having lunch, they ain't no different than you and me."

"You calling me a fish?" asked Thursy, standing up and raising his voice as the hair on the nap of his neck bristled. "If ya are, Pepper Whelan, ya'd better take it back, or I'll knock ya from here ta clear across the stream."

Pepper chuckled as he stood too. Noticing Thursy's hands rolled into fists, he said, "Nah, nah, good buddy." Then resting his one hand on Thursy's shoulder, he continued, "I'm juss saying, like all life, fish got reg'lar schedules, just like me an' you. You misunderstood, pal. I's only usin' that as an 'xample."

Upon hearing him raise his voice in a threatening tone, Crab Cake shot up like a light and quickly sprang towards them. Coming to a dead halt between the two boys, the dog sat and faced Thursy, warning him to reconsider his aggressive actions by simply looking up and staring. Thursy quickly got the message as he unrolled his fists.

Suddenly Pepper's line jerked. Within seconds Thursy's did, too. Both boys instantly forgot about their confrontation and raced to their poles. More important issues grabbed their attention. There were fish nibbling at the worms on the end of their hooks.

His grandfather once told Pepper that each time you cast your line, some one wins. Either you win by landing the fish, or the fish wins by not getting caught. It was time for Pepper to win this game of fishing.

The young lad waited. Once more a nibble and then the line went limp. They were down there, no doubt about it. Now a stronger nibble. "Not yet," Pepper told himself, knowing it wasn't a rainbow but a different specie of fish. "Patience boy, patience." What he waited for was the hard strike a rainbow makes and then its run. Only then would he set the hook.

Thursy was just as patient, taking his cues from Pepper. "Don't set the hook on bites, Thursy," he said. "They're not rainbows. Wait 'til it strikes an' runs, Thursy," Pepper whispered. "Then pull back hard ta set the hook. An' don't fergit to use the baseball cap ta land it. You don't wanna lose 'nother one."

Crab Cake watched as the two boys basked in their glory. The dog knew very well they were onto something. He had joined Pepper in too many fishing trips not to know. Crab Cake had a good recollection. He remembered the procedure. Between the two, he sat and cocking his head to one side and then to the other, he silently watched.

Now, another jerk of the line. This one the strongest of them all. "Not yet," Pepper uttered to himself. "Not yet," he repeated excitedly. "Juss wait. He wants that worm."

The fish didn't have it yet, but he was losing patience with this nibbling business. *Soon he'll strike*, thought Pepper. And with that thought completed, his line went under, his pole bent and Crab Cake barked loud and breathlessly.

Pepper jerked the pole, setting the hook. He couldn't see the fish, but knew he had him. Not having a reel on his pole, there was no line with which to feed. As a consequence, the fish had no where to go except up. And up he went. Jumping high out of the water thrilled the two boys and put them as close to angler's paradise as they've ever been. The moist sides of the rainbow glistened as it caught the rays of the mid-day sun.

Surprised it was a rainbow trout, Pepper held on with all his might. He knew the nibbles were from other fish. He also knew a rainbow strikes and runs. In this case, the rainbow must've seen the little fish nibbling, scared them off and then went for the bait itself.

"She's a beauty," hollered Thursy with a high level of exhilaration in his voice. "Biggest 'n' pertiest rainbow I ever did see, Pepper." Secretly Thursy wished the fish would have been on his line, but nevertheless, he was still happy for his pal. He had already forgotten about the ruckus he had caused only minutes earlier.

Back into the water the fish dove and tried in vain to take off. Once again he fought by jumping out of the water. Once again the sun did its job, painting the sides of the fish with the spectrum of the rainbow.

Suddenly, as Thursy watched the fight between Pepper and his fish, his line bent. Deep down it went. "Thursy," yelled Pepper, keeping his eyes on his own line but catching a glimpse of Thursy's bent pole from his peripheral vision. "Yer line. Set the hook, now!"

An unexpected sense of adventure gripped the boy as he reached down to pick up his pole. Crab Cake's eyes switched from Pepper to Thursy and back again. The dog barked loudly and with much enthusiasm. He seemed as thrilled as the boys.

Unlike Pepper's homemade pole, Thursy's equipment was a store-bought casting rod and reel. He set the drag and jerked hard on the rod, setting the hook. Now both rod and pole were bent in high arches, each with the weight of their own respective fish. When Pepper's fish jumped out of the water, Thursy's was deep under the surface and vice versa. In and out, in and out the two Rainbows jumped, glistening in the rays of the sun. Thursy started reeling in his catch, but Pepper quickly stopped him.

"Nah, nah, buddy," instructed his friend. "Feed it line. Let it run, an' then reel it in. Keep doing that an' it'll tire itself out an' be easier ta land." Thursy did what he was told. Slowly he fed more line to the fish. Downstream it went, fighting with all the energy it could muster.

In the process of the excitement, with all the noise and Crab Cake's barking, the actions of the two boys started drawing a crowd. Seeing both boys had hooked not just a trout but two beauties, other anglers had lined both sides of the banks and before the boys could land their catch, they started casting. *Oh no*, thought Pepper. *Give us a chance to land 'em.*

But that would only have been wishful thinking. Not everyone was as considerate of the other guy as Pepper was taught to be. In the process of lines being cast here and there, exactly what Pepper feared would happen, happened. First, Thursy's line became tangled with two other lines from the opposite side. Trying to reel in his catch, the line became snared and in the process the great rainbow spit the hook, freeing itself.

Thursy was furious. "Couldn't ya at least waited 'til we landed our fish?" barked the disappointed lad. "Ain't ya got no respect for other anglers? Ain't ya got no common sense?" It sounded more like a furious Pepper than it did an upset Thursy.

He opened his pocket knife and quickly cut his line, freeing the other lines in the process. As upset as he was, this time he just wanted to leave the area and the stupidity of those around him. But his pal, Pepper, still had one hooked and was struggling to land it before the same thing happened to him.

Across the stream sat three new guys, ready to throw in their lines in the direction of Pepper's. Crab Cake growled loudly as they moved their poles into casting position. Stopping in mid-cast they stared at the dog. "Drop those lines in the water 'fore I land this fish an' my dog'll be dropping all three of ya," promised Pepper. "An' if he misses, my buddy an' I's gonna do it."

It wasn't the sight of Pepper, Thursy and Crab Cake that scared the three inconsiderate anglers on the other side. They knew they were wrong. Pepper had hit the nail on the head. But more so, it was the tone in Pepper's voice and how he said it that bothered them. They thought more than twice about taking a chance.

Thursy was shocked. He had never heard Pepper speak so calmly and with such intimidating force. Thursy stared across the water at the three nitwits and gave a devilish grin. Of course he had never seen Pepper at the height of his passion before, either. Never had he ever witnessed him in a situation like this.

The three goofballs across the creek laid down their rods and watched the struggle between Pepper and the mighty trout. "Looks like a big un, Pepper," said Thursy. "Juss might be 16, maybe 18 inches long."

"We'll know soon's I land it, Thursy," answered Pepper. His heart was now racing and sweat was dripping from his brow. With every ounce of energy, he pulled on the pole, trying to bring the big fish close enough to net it. "Keep the hat ready," he told Thursy. "When I bring it in close, I'm gonna try liffin' it outta the water. That's when you slip the hat unner 'n' liff it up. Whatever ya do," he reminded him, "don't let go o' the hat."

By now, others across the stream were rooting Pepper on. Most had heard the threat Pepper made to the three nitwits sitting across from him and agreed Pepper was right. Out of respect, they pulled their lines. Crab Cake watched his master. Every now and then he'd let out a loud bark in the general direction of the others just to let them know he hadn't fallen asleep.

Now the glistening rainbow appeared to be tiring and Pepper started making headway in his efforts to land him. Looking at Thursy, he said, "Buddy, think I'm gonna need help. Here you hold the pole and gimme the hat." When another angler across the stream saw what they were using for a net, he offered the boys his. Pepper graciously accepted, thanking him humbly.

Thursy lifted the pole, moving the fish closer to shore. As he did, Pepper took hold of the slack line and drawing it in, wrapped it tightly around the pole's tip. The fish slowly made its way toward the bank. One more wrap around and he'd be able to lift it out of the water.

In the excitement of the moment, the boys never saw the sky darkening.

Deep in a valley between two high ridges surrounded by trees, it's difficult noticing an approaching storm until it's almost there. The first clue for them was seeing the crowd across the stream slowly disappear, all except for the man who offered them his fishing net. Even the three goofballs were gone.

Thursy lifted the pole again and Pepper grabbed the line, wrapping it around the pole tip like before. The rainbow trout was near the edge of the water. All that was needed was for Thursy to lift the pole and for Pepper to slip the net under the fish. Once that was completed, they'd both take hold of the net's handle and bring the big fish onto shore.

Lightning struck and the thunder cracked almost instantly, telling Pepper that a bolt struck nearby, possibly somewhere very close. Both boys knew the last place they needed to be during a thunderstorm was either under or near trees. Simultaneously the two looked skyward to see the flash of another bolt and hear its accompanying roar. The skies opened up and a downpour soaked their clothes tightly to their skin. Water ran down their heads and into their eyes, preventing them from seeing clearly. Crab Cake stayed right by their side.

Thursy lifted the pole too soon and too high in trying to clear the big fish from the water. Before Pepper could respond by placing the net under the fish, the line snapped, proving the fish weighed far too much for the eight pound test line the young lad had been using. That was the standard strength line with which most kids equipped their rods and reels. Pepper, with his homemade pole, was no exception. Sadly he handed the net across the stream to the fisherman who loaned it to him and again humbly thanked him for his generosity.

Now the rain was coming down in sheets and the boys were virtually soaked. "C'mon, Thursy," Pepper said. "I know a cave nearby." And up the side of the hill they ran, across the woods to a clearing and into another part of the woods. They ran more than a quarter of a mile with Crab Cake right with them before seeing the dark impression in the side of the hill, the entranceway covered with wet shrubbery.

Both boys and their dog made a beeline for the cave and, pushing back the shrubbery, entered as the rain pelted their bodies. "Wow," laughed Pepper, his clothes dripping wet. "Mom was right. She said it might rain. Even wanted me to carry along an umbrella," he continued laughing. "Whew! That was a nasty one."

"Came out of nowheres," added Thursy. "Guess that does it for fishing today. Man, I never saw it comin'."

"When yer in a valley 'tween two wooded hills, it's hard ta see an approaching storm 'til it's almost right there on top of ya," Pepper explained. "That's 'cause when we're there, we're sitting so low, the high hills hide the

68

horizon."

Sitting on a rock just inside the cave, the boys watched as the rain poured down on the hidden entranceway's shrubbery and felt the spray brush softly against their faces. Moving back deeper out of the line of spray, they heard a voice from deep inside the cave demand, "Don't even think o' staying here." Something in that voice rang familiar to the boys and immediately startled them as they heard it continue. "Just beat it, an' take that mangy mutt wit' yas."

Chapter 9

Pepper and Thursy looked at each other with surprise. That voice? "O' course," said Pepper to himself. It sounded just like the voice of one of the criminals, the ones who assaulted the Game Warden and left him for dead. It sounded like...Crazy Eyes.

But what in the name of good trout fishing were they doing hiding deep in a cave? Both boys and Officer Helfrich had thought they had escaped and were gone from the area. Neither the boys nor the wardens knew anything about loot that might have been hidden in the bottom of the fishing hole. And no one would have suspected they were hanging around only as long as it took them to recover that booty.

Neither boy could see the men. Nor could Crab Cake, but he knew they were there. Remembering how they had treated Pepper and Thursy earlier in the day, the dog growled fiercely when he first heard their voice.

"Nah, nah, Crab Cake, not now," commanded Pepper. "Shhhh. Be real quiet, boy."

Thursy, not realizing who they really were, turned toward the rear of the cave and blurted, "We just wanna stay here 'til the rain stops, Mister. We ain't gonna bodder ya. We'll stay in the front, honest!" he pleaded.

"Well I'll be dipped in a barrel o' fresh rainwater," Crazy Eyes said to Tattoo as he slowly walked to the front of the cave in full view of the boys. "Look who the storm juss blew in. Our good friend from the fishing hole, his mangy mutt and anudder jubenile delinquent. What a coincidence! Maybe, just maybe, we got some use fer these guys. If the heat gets too hot fer us, Tattoo, ya know what I'm sayin', don't ya buddy, we might o' bought us a ticket outta this jungle," he reasoned.

"Perhaps you juss guaranteed us our freedom, boys," he said, slyly lowering his voice, rising and then walking to the full light in the front. "I see no reason why we can't accomadate ya wit' the full hospitality of our humble abode." Then bellowing an evil laugh, while tying them securely with more of the rope that Tattoo had, he added, "and there's no reason for ya to leave after the rain stops, absolutely none whatsoever! Juss make yerselves at home here an' stay nice an' dry. But keep that mutt outta my way or else someone's gonna get hurt," he ordered fiercely. "Ya unnerstand?"

71

Thursy fully understood his mistake and looked at Pepper hopelessly. Pepper was already thinking three moves ahead. How could they escape the clutches of these criminals? Of course Crazy Eyes and Tattoo were not aware that the boys had been witnesses to their 'murder.' They also had no clue that the Game Warden was still alive, thanks to Crab Cake, Pepper and Thursy.

Peering out the corner of his eyes, Pepper saw an object shaped like a handgun lying on a natural shelf formed by a ledge of rock on the right side of the cave. Then he remembered the warden and how the two got the drop on him, stealing his sidearm. That was the warden's revolver. If he could just get it, their chances of escaping would be good.

Crab Cake lay close to the cave's opening, out of range from the two criminals. He sensed they had no love for him and decided to keep his distance. Nevertheless, the small Border Collie kept his eyes on the two seedy men but mostly on Pepper and Thursy. If any physical harm came their way, the dog would be on the perpetrators in a flash.

Crazy Eyes and Tattoo both sensed the same and decided to sit back and contemplate their next move. With the boys thinking how they can escape, the criminals thinking of their next move, and the dog thinking he'd like to protect the boys by attacking the two felons, a good deal of thought processing was going on inside that cave while outside a great thunderstorm raged on.

"Psst, Thursy," whispered Pepper. "Ya think ya can get their attention? If ya can, I think I can grab the revolver. May be our only way outta here."

"Let me think," mouthed Thursy, pointing first to himself and then to his brain. "I hafta come up wit' an idea that's good, udderwise 'twon't work," he whispered.

"Keep on a thinking, Thursy," said Pepper. "I'm gonna do the same."

Inside, the cave lit up instantly for a split second as bolts of lightning outside flashed nearby. With the rumbling of thunder and the down pouring of a driven rain in wide sheets, coupled with the abduction scene inside, it made for a scary scenario.

Then it dawned on Pepper that all was not lost. He remembered his father telling all the children that if they ever get into trouble, to stay where they were. Even though authorities don't consider a person missing unless they're missing 24 hours, they'd be found within those 24 hours. Surely their parents knew they'd be waiting out the storm in a cave. Pepper as much as told his mother that on Saturday afternoon when she badgered him about taking along an umbrella.

When evening came and the boys failed to appear at home, it's a guarantee their folks wouldn't wait 24 hours. They'd come searching now. They'd have half the neighborhood with them checking out what might have happened. With what the three did for the Game Warden, why Officer Helfrich would probably be leading the rescuers. Pepper felt much better.

However, little did the boys realize that Pepper's mother had no idea where the cave was located. It was uphill, more than a quarter of a mile from his secret fishing hole, a spot on Rehmeyer's Run of which Pepper told no one. The cave was an opening in a wooded hill covered by heavy vegetation and shrubbery and shrouded by the canopy of foliage from tall trees. So well hidden was its entrance, even standing next to it would have been difficult for anyone to spot. Pepper stumbled upon it accidentally late last fall when Crab Cake chased a rabbit through the brush and into the cave. How Crazy Eyes and Tattoo found it is anyone's guess. They would never say.

Crab Cake stayed close to the entrance eyeing the rain. The faithful companion kept his head close to the ground with his eyes focused on the two criminals. Their time would come, and when it did, Crab Cake would be ready.

Doris Whelan stared out the farmhouse kitchen window at the sudden storm. Wondering what was taking place with her son and how he was staying dry concerned her. She had a need to know what was happening, but her hands were tied.

Pepper's father was working. While the family did farm the land, Jack Whelan had a second job. A building he rented in Shrewsbury to refinish antique furniture for clients enabled him to add extra income to the family coffers. Most of his work was done in the evening hours and on days when there was little else he could do on the farm due to either seasonal or inclement weather. His work was considered outstanding. Jack Whelan was known for his professionalism, and word soon spread far and wide that he was as close to a perfectionist as any you could find.

Pepper's father was also devoted to his family. If Jack had been home when the thundercloud burst, he would have immediately driven the family car to find his son. Since they only had one car, Doris Whelan was powerless to help.

"Don't worry, Mommy," little Ty said, as he stood by his mother who was still staring out the kitchen window. "Pepper knows how ta take care of himself. Besides, he's got the dog wit' him an' Crab Cake'd never let any thing bad happen to Pepper."

Doris affectionately smoothed Ty's hair down with her hand as if to thank the young lad for such kind words of consideration. "Yes, maybe your right, Ty," she assured him. "We'll probably see him walking up the lane in time for supper and then all our worries will disappear."

The rain continued to fall. The repeated flashes of lightning accompanied by the crackling thunder startled Doris and Ty and caused them more worry than what the falling rain did. With each loud boom of thunder, the two held tightly onto each other. Then, after each released the other, they'd repeat the same whenever the next crash followed its flash of lightning.

When would it all end? They didn't know. Looking out the window toward the lane, they saw a river of water rapidly running down the slope toward the small brook that crosses the lane near Sawmill Road. "I sure hope the old wooden bridge doesn't get washed out," Doris said to no one in particular, "otherwise yer father won't be able ta get in, or if he is in, he won't be able ta get out," she reasoned.

"And if this continues," she said to Ty, "the brook'll swell wit' wooder, which flows inta the crick, which flows into the stream, which flows inta Rehmeyer's Run where Pepper is fishing, an' if it gits too high it could sweep him away." She was on a roll. Everything that could happen to poor Pepper, would. Her poor mind was now going faster than a race car, but she couldn't help herself. To her, one of her children was considered missing, and like the good and concerned mother that she is, she was at her wit's end. But there was nothing she could do but wait.

Ty took his mother by the hand and led her to the long family kitchen table. It was still four hours until the evening supper meal. "Sid down a while, Ma," he told her. "I'll fix ya a cuppa hot tea and make ya some toast."

"No, not now, Ty," his mother said. "I'm juss in no mood ta eat anything or drink any tea. Juss leave me be. I'm gonna be okay, in time. I juss wish Pepper woulda taken the umbrella like I asked him to. I told 'im it might rain."

"But Ma, that's what ya always do fer us! Ya fix us a cuppa hot tea an' some warm toast. An' it always makes us feel a liddle better. I'm sure it's gonna make ya feel a liddle better, too," little Ty told his mother.

Doris looked down lovingly at her son. So far Jack and she had succeeded in teaching their children that others in their lives were equally as important, and in some cases, more so, than themselves. "Thank you, son. You're absolutely right. I'll have a cuppa yer tea and summa yer toast." Then very softly she whispered to no one in particular, "I pray hard he found the cave."

Outside the cave the rain still fell in torrents. Long before they were tied up, the boys knew their fishing for the day was over. With the heavy rains, the creeks would be muddy and rising. And with the rising waters, the rapids would be too fast to hold a line and all fishermen know those aren't the best of conditions to try for trout.

"Pssst! Thursy," whispered Pepper. "I can't reach the gun. Did ya think o' anything ta get us outta here?" Crab Cake still watched the two as he lay by the cave's entrance.

"I'm still workin' on it, Pepper," answered Thursy. "Gimme some more time. My brain doesn't work fast as yours." By now the two were tired. Their hands had been tied together in front with a rope that connected down to their tied feet. Both boys knew they had very little time with which to make their move. If they were going to make one, they had better make it soon. When the rain stopped, they felt sure they would either be moved elsewhere or would meet their demise.

"Thursy," whispered Pepper again. "Where's your tackle box?"

"Same place as yer pole and bait can, Pepper," the lad answered. "Down by the fishin' hole where we both lost our rainbows. Why?"

"If we had yer tackle box, we might o' been able to open it 'n' get your fishing knife, the one ya used to cut your line," Pepper explained slowly, carefully and with a bit of sarcasm in his voice. "Wit' our hands tied in the front, we'd be able ta see what we'd be doing and togedder, we might o' been able to cut each udder's ropes and free ourselves. But never mind. We's never gonna git outta here now."

"That's a fillet knife I keep in my tackle box, Pepper," Thursy whispered even more sarcastically. "That's not a pocket knife."

"Okay then, Thursy," Pepper shot back. He really wanted to call him a 'Wise Guy' but held his tongue. "If ya gotta git so perticuler and technical, then do ya have a pocket knife?"

"O' course I got a pocket knife! All fishermen have pocket knives," he lectured. "They're used ta cut tangled line. Why wouldn't I have one?"

"Okay," Pepper shot back. By now he was starting to get peeved. "Where do you keep your pocket knife?" he asked slowly, emphasizing each word.

"Where I always keep it," answered Thursy more coldly than before. "Right here." He lowered his eyes towards his front pocket. Then little by little and very pointedly, each of the next words he spoke dripped with ridicule. "That's why it's called a pocket knife."

Having been one upped, Pepper realized the silliness of the situation. They were both in this predicament together and needed each other if they expected to escape. "Sorry, my friend," replied Pepper, apologizing for making the worst of an already bad situation. "I deserved that!" It was one of the few times he ever called Thursy 'friend.' "Do ya think ya could work it outta the pocket?"

"I can try, Pepper," answered his newly discovered friend, more civilized this time and in a tone that said he was accepting the apology. "Keep those two occupied by distracting 'em in some way. I'll see what I can do."

Thursy went to work moving this way and that, trying to work the pocket knife up to the top and out of his front pocket.

Suddenly Tattoo spotting his squirming and motioned to Crazy Eyes to look. "What's wrong wit' that one?" he asked.

Pepper just looked at him, shrugged his shoulders, and asked, "Whatta ya mean?"

"Hey?" yelled Crazy Eyes, standing up and starting toward the boys. "Don't play dumb wit' me. Why's he squirming like he got a bad case o' da worms?"

"Oh that," Pepper answered as if it was an every day common occurrence. He had to think of something good, and fast. "That's ah... ah... because ah... because he has... ahhh... worms," he said, lowering his head and pretending to be embarrassed.

A light went on in Pepper's head. "Oh yeah!" he confirmed his diagnosis reassuringly. "Sittin' in any one spot fer any length o' time makes 'im squirm like a slippy worm. Tsk, tsk, tsk. Poor guy!" Pepper continued, shaking his head. "He's had 'em fer long as I can 'member. Happens all the time." Pepper was on a roll. Nevertheless, he kept telling himself to just convince them. Don't overdo it.

"That's why the school teacher keeps moving 'im from desk to desk every day," he added. "If ya could move me a little fardder away from 'im, I'd be deeply obliged to ya," Pepper said in an innocent, naïve, begging voice. "When he gits ta squirming bad as that, summa the worms work 'emselves loose an' can jump on anyone sitting close by." The two seedy characters were becoming convinced. Pepper was now closing his case. "Once ya git 'em," he said with a straight face, "no telling what might happen. The itchin' drives ya bongos. Nuthin' ya can do about them. They's mighty hard getting rid of."

Thursy was doing everything in his power to keep from laughing. So to mask those suppressed laughs, the boy pretended to be in pain by contorting his face in the weirdest shapes imaginable, and at the same time, feigning a cry of pain while squirming with much gusto.

Had this been a scene from a comedy, without a doubt it would have had the audience filled with tears from laughing so hard. In their fear of "catching" whatever it was Thursy "had," the two evil men bought the story lock, stock and barrel. They even separated the two more by moving Thursy closer to the front entrance. Even Crab Cake moved away when he saw Thursy squirming. Then Crazy Eyes and Tattoo walked deeper into the cave, away from the two lads.

This was not the result which Pepper was expecting, but despite the gloomy weather outside, the situation inside the cave now looked a whole lot brighter than what it did moments ago. But the gun still lay near the side of the cave out of the reach of the boys.

Thursy continued to squirm. This time Crab Cake was watching him with more curiosity. The dog stood up and sniffed the boy, then lay down to watch him squirm some more. Looking at Thursy, the dog cocked his head to one side, and then to the other, as if to ask, "What in the world are you trying to do?"

Suddenly Thursy saw the round, shiny, metal tip of the black pocket knife stick its head out the top of his left front pocket. "Pepper," he whispered. "I think I got it. It's near the top. Juss a liddle more squirming ta go." Thursy continued going about his business of squirming like he really did have worms in his pants.

"Keep on a goin', Thursy," encouraged Pepper. "Keep on a goin', buddy. You're doing good. Juss don't lose it now." If Thursy could get the knife and cut his ropes, he might be able to sneak close to Pepper and cut his. And with the two creeps near the back of the cave, the two young boys and their dog might be able to make a running escape.

"Just a liddle more, Pepper," said Thursy. "I think I got most all o' it." When the pocket knife plopped out of Thursy's front pocket and fell between the lad and the dog, Crab Cake picked it up with his mouth. "C'mon, Crab Cake," commanded Thursy. "This is no time ta play games." But Crab Cake just wagged his tail and took off towards Pepper.

"Pepper," whispered Thursy. "Tell your hound ta stop playing games. He's got the knife in 'is mouth and won't drop it."

"Crab Cake, cool it," commanded Pepper in a stern voice. Upon reaching Pepper, the dog dropped the knife near his hands. "Good dog, Crab Cake," Pepper said. "Good dog. Now go lay down by the entrance. G'won." With that order, the dog returned to the spot where he lay before. It was as if he had never left.

Pepper tried to pick up the knife in his tied hands but could only get within inches. He tried rearranging his sitting position but that only put him in a more awkward position. In the process, his foot kicked the knife to the other side of the cave out of view and now the only way he could reach it was by himself scooting over a little at a time.

"Hey," yelled Crazy Eyes once more, spotting Pepper and coming to the front. "Whadda ya think yer doin'?"

"Muss be them worms," Pepper said, thinking fast. "Ya took too long ta move 'im an' some got in me. That's how fast they spread. Man it's driving me crazy. C'mere wunst," he said to Tattoo, standing in the background watching the scene with much nervousness. "Can ya gimme a hand an' scratch 'em fer me?"

Tattoo just looked at Pepper strangely, said nothing to him, turned around and walked back deep into the belly of the cave.

By now the rain was letting up and Crazy Eyes made a corporate decision. "C'mon" he ordered Tattoo. "Let's get outta here 'fore them worms get ta us. With their worms, we don't need these squirmy guys as a ticket ta freedom. 'Sides, the last thing I need is fer you ta start goin' nuts wit' worms."

"What about them guys?" the taller one of the two crooks the boys heard the Game Warden refer to as Tattoo, asked, pointing to Thursy and Pepper. "We just can't let 'em here!"

"Ya want their worms drivin' ya batty? Look how screwy they is," he said while both boys continued squirming. "Juss s'pose these here worms do sumpin ta ya brain causin' ya not ta think? Huh? Then what?" he asked, hoping it would make Tattoo think. "Ya wanna end up like these two characters?" The two boys continued squirming and scooting on their rumps as a show for Crazy Eyes and Tattoo. "'Sides," continued Crazy Eyes, sarcastically, "we gonna be nice to 'em. We's gonna leave 'em inside the cave outta all this cold, damp, nasty weather. Now c'mon."

And in an instant, the two seedy criminals were gone like a bat out of a cave at dusk.

Chapter 10

"Pepper," called Thursy. "Look! We gonna be okay, Pepper. They forgot the pistol." There, lying on a small natural shelf on the side of the cave, was the Game Warden's revolver which the two had stolen and was all but forgotten by the dangerous duo.

Then, in an instant, one of the two returned. "Sorry to disturb you gennelmen," the one the boys called Crazy Eyes said, facetiously, "but in our haste to depart from your fine company, we seemed to have forgotten one of our most valued possessions." He turned to where the gun lay on the shelf of the cave wall, and cackling with laughter, he picked it up, placed it into his inside jacket pocket and after gingerly sidestepping both lads, bid them farewell by saying, "Don't let the worms bite ya." With that he cackled some more while departing as quickly as he arrived.

"Well that takes care o' the pistol, Thursy," said Pepper. "All we got left now is the knife. Let's not do anything stupid to lose that, ol' buddy. Hurry an' git untied. Then untie me."

"Gee Pepper, I'd like ta," said Thursy. "I really would. But if you're so daggone close and can't reach it, how do ya 'spect me to get to it any faster if I'm sittin' much fardder away?"

In the surprise of seeing Crazy Eyes return, and then being hit with a blanket of fear that perhaps they may have changed their minds, Pepper had suddenly forgotten all about how he accidentally kicked the knife to the other side of the cave. "Sorry again, Thursy," said Pepper softly. This time he was embarrassed. "I'm gonna try ta work my way over 'n' git it."

Crab Cake acted as a lookout at the cave's entrance. Pepper's faithful companion was thrilled the two hombres were gone. If the boys hadn't been in direct danger, Crab Cake might have attacked the two. But doing so could have meant the end of the boys and of him, and somehow the little Border Collie knew he was more important to them alive than he was dead.

Besides, by staying by the door, he acted as insurance, keeping the boys safe. If harm came to the kids, Crab Cake was in a position to either attack the perpetrators or run for help. If the two creeps tried to corner the dog, he could still run out of the cave and go for help.

The last thing the abductors wanted was attention drawn to the cave during the violent thunderstorm. Crab Cake was the boys' ace in the hole. The two criminals knew it, the boys knew it and Crab Cake knew it.

"Thursy," yelled Pepper. "I'm juss 'bout there. The scooting worked. Now all I hafta do is to get the knife in my hands an' open it."

Pepper lay on his stomach and wiggled closer to the shiny pocket knife. It rested on the floor of the cave near a large rock. Raising his head, the lad noticed movement on a nearby rock. Then he saw his worst nightmare come true. There on the flat top of the rock where the gun had rested lay a poisonous snake, a copperhead, coiled and ready to strike.

Pepper feared snakes more than any other thing in his life. "Thursy," called Pepper. "I can't get the knife. There's a snake ona rock an' I think it's gonna strike."

"Don't move," cautioned Thursy. "Stay still. Snakes got poor eyesight, Pepper. They only notice motion. Stay perfectly still. I'm gonna work my way over to ya an' distract it while you go fer the knife." It was a plan that made sense, at least to Pepper.

Thursy wiggled his way toward the back of the cave where Pepper was near panicking. As he wormed his way closer, his words of encouragement helped calm Pepper. Slowly the copperhead uncoiled and with his tongue moving in every direction, finally determined there was nothing nearby that would put it in any kind of danger. The snake backed off. Then it saw Thursy's movement and started its slithery slide towards Pepper's friend.

"Now," called Thursy. "Get the knife now, Pepper." And as if he was taking a command from a Drill Sergeant, the ten-year-old lad reached over to the knife with his tied hands, picked it up with his nimble fingers and scooted away from danger. Then with his head bent down, he grabbed the edge of the blade with his teeth. Holding the body of the knife in his fingers, he pulled. The knife opened.

It didn't take long for Pepper to cut his ropes. Turning to Thursy, he realized his friend was now in as deep a trouble as he himself had been just moments ago. Thursy froze, but the snake had zeroed in on his movements. This time the serpent would not be fooled, as he once again coiled ready to strike. Moving back his head in a classic position, the copperhead opened his mouth wide, exposing the fangs which held its deadly venom.

From out of nowhere, sailing through the air as if on a special mission, flew Crab Cake. Instantly the dog positioned himself between the boy and snake. And just as quickly, the snake struck, burying its fangs deep into the right front leg of the dog. The dog yelped. The snake backed off. Pepper grabbed his dog and the snake slithered away under some rocks.

Holding Crab Cake in his arm, Pepper quickly cut the ropes on Thursy, freeing his friend. Lifting Crab Cake closer to his chest and snuggling his face close to his, he fought back tears as he saw his dog's eye lids slowly flutter. The dog was fighting valiantly between keeping them open and having them close. "Thursy, we gotta get Crab Cake to a vet... or a doctor. We gotta get 'im some help."

Thursy was still shaking. A venomous snake bite intended for him was taken by his friend's dog, possibly saving his life. He stood up, his legs wobbly from fright and his hands unsteady and trembling. Still he was determined to help Pepper save his dog. "C'mon, Pepper," he ordered. "Keep Crab Cake calm and follow me."

The two lit out of that cave faster than they entered in the mid-day downpour. Running down the slippery wooded hill, they fell on their hind end more than once, each time standing tall and continuing their journey to save Pepper's beloved Crab Cake.

The downpour sent Officer Helfrich on his way when all the fishermen left for the day. No one else was anywhere near Rehmeyer's Run or the dirt road that led there. Not even any local anglers living in the area who might have waited until the crowd dissipated.

At the road, the boys turned right, heading to the 'Y' and up past old Amos Springler's house. The retired house and barn painter was sitting on the front porch watching the storm clouds as they made their way from the western sky across to the eastern horizon. "Whasha big hurry?" he called to the boys, hiccupping as he slurred his words.

"We need help, Mr. Springler," Pepper answered, standing on the berm of the road. "We need help real bad." And with tears streaming down his cheeks, Pepper related how Crab Cake saved Thursy life by taking the bite from a poisonous copperhead snake.

"*Misher* Springler?" slurred Amos, his chest swelling with pride. Rarely has anyone ever referred to him as *Mister*. It felt good. "C'mon, kids," he extended an offer, "get ina truck. I'll take ya ta where youse goin'."

Pepper suspected Amos had been drinking but felt he had no choice but to accept his offer. He sat in the middle holding Crab Cake and Thursy sat on the end. Much too late, his suspicions were confirmed when he saw Amos wobbling toward the truck and into the driver's seat. As soon as he sat down next to Pepper, the smell of booze engulfed the cab of the truck. Amos Springler reeked of alcohol. He had been drinking since before noon.

Up the road they went, sometimes running near its right edge, sometimes near the left, but most of the time Amos drove straight down the middle. When they got to the road leading to Chet Cline's house, Pepper told Amos to turn right there, but Amos had a mind of his own and onward he went past the bridge, past the White Oak School House and onward toward Sawmill Road, the one that leads to Thursy's.

"Turn right here, Mr. Springler," Pepper said once again. But Amos kept driving, this time much faster than before. It was as if he didn't know the boys and their dog were in the truck. Climbing the hill past Hilderbrand's, Amos pulled a flask out of his hip pocket, unscrewed the top and lifting it to his mouth, took a swig. Then handing it to Pepper, he offered him a drink. Pepper took the flask and flung it out the opened right side window.

Seeing the flask go flying out the window, Amos jammed his brakes so fast the truck slid off the right side of the road and into a ditch. Quickly the boys got out, and with the dog in their arms, they ran up the road with every ounce of energy they could muster.

The closest vet was 25 miles north in the City of York. Crab Cake's eyes were beyond glassy. The dog was fighting hard to keep them open. Pepper started accepting the fact that his dog may never make it.

Tears slowly fell once again from Pepper's eyes. Putting his hand on his shoulder, Thursy encouraged his friend. "C'mon, Pepper, we can make it, my friend. We gotta make it. For Crab Cake's sake we gotta."

At the top of the hill they looked down to the right at Roy Haney's farm. On the porch sat his oldest son Larry whittling away on a stick. Running across the field to the house, Pepper reached the porch. He was now fighting back a full outcry. "Larry," he pleaded, "can ya help us?" And because Crab Cake was now slipping in and out of consciousness, Pepper gave Larry a condensed version of what had happened. "Drive us ta the vet's hospital on South Queen Street in York," he begged, "please, Larry. We can make it in 45 minutes, 30 if ya drive real fast," he said. "I'll pay whatever ya want. I'll even buy the gas." Pepper had very little money, but whatever he did have, he was willing to sacrifice to save Crab Cake.

Larry Haney's father, Roy, was known in the community as a penny pincher, but, nevertheless, all in the family were considered by everyone to be good people. Larry was more generous than the others, and Pepper knew if any of them could be counted on to lend a helping hand it would be him. Pepper was desperate. It showed!

Larry smiled a little, than broke into a small chuckle. He wasn't being mean.

This was just his nature. The Haneys were farmers with horses, cattle, swine, chickens and cats to keep the mice population down in the barn and around the other farm buildings. Larry hunted each fall and never allowed himself to get that close to animals where he would become attached. It was just the way he was raised.

When he saw the tears in Pepper's eyes and heard the plea in his voice, he couldn't quite understand what all the commotion was about. His philosophy was, animals are born, they live and they die. That was it. No need to get bent out of shape when something happens to them.

"So ya want me ta drive ya ta York?" he asked Pepper in his slow draw and with another light chuckle. As was his custom, a long piece of dried timothy he picked up from a hay bale, and on which he had been chewing, was hanging out from his mouth. "Probably no need ta," he said softly, looking down at the dog and petting it on the head. Crab Cake's eyes were closed. His breathing was shallow. "The Doc's in the barn now wit' the mare. She's 'bout ready to foal any time now."

What a stroke of luck! Pepper gave the biggest sigh of relief in his young life. He was positive Someone high above was watching over him. Upon hearing that, he rushed to the barn where the vet was working on the mare. Thursy and Larry followed.

"Looks like ya might have a 'mergency here, Doc," Larry told him. "If the mare's not ready yet, see what ya can do ta help my two friends."

Pepper gave the condensed version of what happened to the vet and the doctor went to work immediately. "Is Crab Cake gonna be okay, Doc?" asked Pepper anxiously after the vet spent twenty minutes working on Crab Cake.

"If you had a knife and would have cut his leg where the snake bit him, the flow of blood would have helped drain the poison. But you probably didn't have a knife on you. Right now it looks bad, my friend," the vet said as he put his hand on Pepper's shoulder, trying to calm him. "I cut Xs on the two fang marks and drew a lot of blood out with a suction pump. Whether I got enough of the venom out to save your furry friend, I can't tell yet," the doctor sighed. Then, to give some hope to the boys, he added, "If he stayed calm and his heart wasn't racing on the way here, well, that's in his favor."

The doctor gave Crab Cake a shot to calm him, one as an antidote and another for pain. He suggested the boys let him keep the dog overnight. "You've got quite a dog there, young man," the doc said. "He put his life in the line of danger to save the life of your friend. Your dog's a hero. But he's in some bad shape, fellows," the vet assured them. "And right now the next

83

twenty-four hours will be crucial."

"Doctor," asked Pepper, "if ya keep 'im overnight, I wanna stay wit' 'im. If he makes it, I wanna make sure I'm there to encourage him."

The doctor looked deep into the red teary eyes of the ten-year-old, remembering how it was when he was Pepper's age. He, too, had lost a faithful companion because there was no vet available. It had served as a catapult for him deciding on becoming a veterinarian. He also understood that no matter what he might say, it would be highly unlikely that he could talk Pepper out of going. And who knows, maybe the boy staying by his dog will become an encouragement to the little Border Collie.

"There is one promise you must make to me, Pepper," the vet told him. "The only way I'll allow you to stay with the dog is if your parents are aware of where you are."

"I'm gonna run home right now an' tell 'em myself, Doc," said Pepper. "We only live over the hill on the udder side o' the woods an' down the udder hill." Still, it was a good mile away. The mare had not yet had her foal. Pepper knew the vet would be there for at least another hour. "Be right back," he said to the vet.

Pepper Whelan called Thursy, and together the two took off across the fields faster than they have ever run in their lives. Instead of using the winding field road, straight up over the field they ran, taking the short cut into the woods.

The top of the wooded hill was the halfway point between Haney's and Whelan's. To the right, down over an incline was Patterson's house. Thursy left at that point, explaining he needed to be home and doubted if he could stay with Pepper overnight at the vets. Pepper bid Thursy goodbye and thanked his friend for his help.

The fishing tackle they left behind would have to wait for some other day to be collected from Rehmeyer's Run, lying on the bank of Pepper's secret fishing hole. As he continued, Thursy called after Pepper, returning the thanks, this time for Crab Cake saving his life.

Pepper thought about what the vet had said. If they had had a knife, they might have been able to help the dog by cutting Xs on the bites and draining the venom through bleeding. But Pepper was too embarrassed to admit they had one. Scared, badly shaken and fearing the loss of his dog, Crab Cake, consumed so much of Pepper's mind that he never thought of using the knife.

Pepper continued down the hill, out of the woods and into the newly plowed field that was waiting to be planted in corn. His shoes were becoming very heavy from gathering mud in the plowed fields after the recent cloudburst. Still he ran, although not as fast as when he first started. The weight of the shoes gathering mud was holding him back.

He made sure to remember to slip off his shoes before entering the house, otherwise his mother would have conniption fits. It was a term used frequently in the Pennsylvania Dutch area meaning, going crazy, and most folks have used it at one time or another in jest.

Pepper made it to the end of the grassy lane and slowed to a walk, stomping as much mud from his shoes as he could on the grassy turf. He passed the chicken coop, the outhouse and as he approached the big pear tree at the edge of the garden, he sensed something strange.

Normally, some family member would have seen him come out of the woods and down through the plowed field. One of the kids would have said he was coming and been out to greet him by now. His mother certainly would have been standing on the back porch masking the fear she went through that day during the thunderstorm by making sure no mud was tracked into her house.

His smaller brother Ty would have been on him like a fly is to honey, demanding of Pepper to tell him all about the fishing and then asking to see his catch.

Pepper slowed to a moderate walk. He moved toward the back porch and stopped dead in his tracks. There, coming from the cement sidewalk, were tracks. It looked like they were prints made from muddy shoes. There weren't just one, but two sets. The tracks led to the porch and right up to the back door. On the porch Pepper could clearly see there were no waiting pairs of shoes.

Pepper stood behind the 150-year-old Maple tree. Its trunk was so wide it easily hid the ten-year-old. Pepper had to think. He was on his own now. There was no Crab Cake to watch him. Thursy was home and he probably wouldn't see him until school the next morning. The tracks could not have belonged to his father. Jack Whelan knew better than to track mud into his wife's kitchen. He glanced at his watch. It was only 5:15, still too early for his father to be home. Besides, there was no car parked in the open end garage.

Pepper slipped out from behind the big maple tree and moved back against the side of the house that faces the garden. This was the same side that faced the newly plowed field he had just crossed, and if no one had seen him, then there was a good chance no one would see him checking out the house.

A wooden barrel stood against the spout catching rainwater. His mother and sisters used the soft water to wash clothes and to shampoo their hair. Pepper covered the rain barrel with three wide, thick, two by sixes and boosted himself onto the top. Standing up and leaning to the right against the window, he peeked into the living room from the edge. He could see the parlor. But the second room, beyond where the kitchen entrance could be seen and where the family's Heatrola stove stood, was blocked from his view. What little he could see in the kitchen was the view through the doorway which included a small section of the long family kitchen table.

Pepper climbed down and this time grabbed an old 5/8 bushel basket used for picking tomatoes. For strength, he picked up three more just inside the garden's fence and stuck each one inside the other. Turning them upside down and standing them against the other window, he climbed up. The baskets gave him just enough height to see above the windowsill and what he saw startled him. Quickly looking once more and making sure he wasn't just imagining things, the sight before his eyes sent shivers down his spine and all the way to his toes.

There standing in the kitchen with their backs against the window in which Pepper was peering into were Crazy Eyes and Tattoo.

Chapter 11

The two criminals were using the same gun they stole from the Game Warden after beating him, tying him up, throwing him in the creek and leaving him for dead. Now they were holding Pepper's mother, his two sisters and little brother David. But where was his brother Ty? Pepper peered into the window again. "If Ty's in there," he softly murmured to himself, "he muss be somewheres outta view."

These were two dangerous men and Pepper knew it. While he wanted so very much to stay with his dog, Crab Cake, his heart broke once more knowing it would be impossible. His allegiance now was to his family. They needed him more. Pepper looked into the living room through the window again and this time he spotted his mother.

Doris was standing in front of the Kalamazoo kitchen range, facing the living room window, looking directly at Pepper. She showed no signs of surprise, instead looking blank, as though she saw absolutely nothing. Pepper held his pointer finger to his lips signifying to his mother to stay quiet. Then he slipped down out of sight.

Pepper backed down the tomato baskets, and slipped back behind the back yard maple tree. From somewhere behind him he thought he heard a voice. Listening carefully, it spoke again, sounding something like, "Pssst!" as if someone was vying for his attention.

Pepper looked behind him. He saw no one. Again he heard the voice. "Pssst!" He looked to one side then to the other, all the while staying hidden behind the wide old maple tree and out of view from anyone who might have ventured out of the kitchen and onto the back porch. No one was in sight.

Pepper turned to look behind his left shoulder and once more heard the "Pssst!" Looking in the direction of the old stone smokehouse that stood across the lane near the potato field, he thought he saw some movement.

It was the same smokehouse with the sloped roof from which Crab Cake would jump into the waiting arms of Pepper whenever he'd whistle. Maybe just a cat, he surmised. "Pepper," the voice whispered. "Over here." This time Pepper zeroed in on the direction of the sound. Indeed it was coming from behind the smokehouse.

Pepper whispered back, "Is that you, Thursy?" He suspected Thursy figured out there was trouble at his house and came to help. But then Pepper remembered he saw a car driving up the road and away from his house. It was Thursy's parents with his new friend in the backseat.

"No, Pepper, it's me," replied a voice. "It's me, Pepper. Whatsa matter, don't ya know who yer own brother is?"

Now Pepper recognized Ty's voice. That explained why he didn't see him at the window. "Ty," he called. "Stay there. I'll work my way over." Pepper was the only one who ever called him 'Ty.' He was also the only one whom Ty allowed to call him 'Ty.' The rest of his siblings called the soon to be eight-year-old, Tyrone.

Pepper looked up, down, front and back to make sure the coast was clear. He quickly darted 50 feet back to the old pear tree and hid behind it for a moment until once again he found himself checking to make sure no one was watching. From there he moved up behind the peach tree and then got down on all fours to slowly crawl to the back of the smokehouse where Ty was waiting.

"Pepper, I'm scared," said Ty, rushing into his older brother's arms. "They got Mom, Paula, Sarah 'n' David 'n' they're holding 'em wit' a gun." Tears were streaming down the young lad's face. He was visibly shaken, sobbing from fear and looking for reassurance that his mother, sisters and smaller brother would be fine.

"Nuttin' bad's gonna happen to 'em, Ty," Pepper tried guaranteeing his younger sibling while he himself was searching for the strength to be brave. "Long as you an' me's out here, those guys ain't gonna harm Mom, the girls or David. They may look dumb, but they ain't," he said, wiping the tears from the face of his little brother and holding back his own. "They know if they bring any harm ta 'em, we might be able ta identify 'em. So until they catch us, no harm's gonna come ta Mom or the kids," he assured Ty.

"One way we can help 'em is ta keep 'em criminals from catching us and maybe figure out a way ta get some help. Vishtay?" he added, using a common colloquialism from the area meaning, "You understand?"

Ty felt better. He nodded his head, wiped his wet nose on his long shirt sleeve, dried his eyes and then sat closer to his bigger brother for protection. Pepper look around, surveying the lay of the land.

"Ty, do ya think ya could make it up that hill to the potato field an' hide b'hind the garage?" Pepper asked his younger brother while pointing to his left. "Soon's the coast is clear, I'm gonna follow ya. Stay low an' wait fer me there."

Without answering, Ty looked around and lit out for his new destination. Arriving at the designated spot, he laid low behind the garage, waiting for his older brother. Pepper started in the direction of the garage but quickly ducked back when he saw the back kitchen door open. Sticking his head out, one of the criminals looked about quickly. *Whew*, thought Pepper. *That one was too close fer comfort.*

It was Tattoo. He walked onto the back porch and looked down the lane. All was quiet. Then he looked up the hill in the direction of the corn field and toward the woods. No sign of anyone in that direction, either. Slowly he moseyed out across the lawn to the edge of the lane and stared directly at the old smokehouse. Taking the butt of a cigarette he had been smoking, he flicked it onto the grass next to where Pepper was hiding, not more than five feet away.

Knowing he was fast enough to win a race with the old man if Tattoo spotted and decided to go for him, Pepper would run. But doing so could endanger the lives of his captive family. Tattoo took one more look up and down the lane, saw no one and returned to the kitchen where the other four family members were being held at gun point.

Pepper breathed a heavy sigh of relief. He looked skyward and said a silent prayer of thanks. Then with the near speed of an impala, he made a bolt for the potato field and from there, the garage, where Ty was waiting. "Ya did well, Ty," his brother praised him. "When sumpin' like that happens, stay quiet an' very still. R'member, if they can't see or hear ya, they ain't got no idea where yer at."

"Who are they, Pepper, and whadda they want?" queried his little brother. "What can we do ta help Mom, the girls and David? Do ya think we can reach Dad? I know he can help." The little boy's questions came fast and furious, one right after the other without waiting for answers. He simply needed reassurances that everything would turn out for the best.

"Ty, do ya think ya can do one more thing ta help? Can ya make it ta b'hind the barn an' wait for me there, juss like ya made it here?" Pepper asked his little brother. "Don't forget, Ty," he reminded him, "when ya get there, ya gotta stay quiet, lay low an' wait fer me."

This time Pepper checked the coast more carefully to make sure all was clear. "Okay, Ty, get ready," he ordered. "Now go." And off Tyrone Whelan went, running as fast as his weak little legs would carry him, up the grassy slope to behind the barn where he laid low, remained quiet and waited patiently for his bigger brother to arrive.

Ty didn't have to wait long. Pepper was close behind. Perhaps a minute separated the two. "C'mon, Ty, in the barn," ordered Pepper. "With cattle down below, you an' me's gonna be warm in here. 'Sides, it's gonna keep us outta sight an' allow us some time ta figure outta plan," he said.

"First thing we gotta do is git word ta Dad for some help or try signaling him when we see his car a comin' down the road," he explained to Ty. "Then we gotta git Mom, the girls an' David safely away from those two characters." It was a mighty tall order for two small boys, especially two without their dog, but Pepper realized they had no other choice.

"Pepper." Ty's eyes got big. He suddenly realized he had not seen the dog. "Where's Crab Cake? What happened ta Crab Cake, Pepper? He was wit' ya this mornin' when ya left for fishin'. I was lookin' out my window. I saw 'im. Where's he at now?"

Sitting high in the barn loft on stacked bales of straw, Pepper explained to Ty from the beginning what happened. Ty gave looks of deep concern when he heard about the warden being hurt, their kidnaping experience by Crazy Eyes and Tattoo and the snake bite Crab Cake took for Thursy. He laughed with delight when Pepper told him how Crab Cake tangled all the fishing lines chasing a rainbow trout upstream and how they foiled the crooks by pretending they had worms.

"Is he gonna be okay, Pepper?" asked Ty. "I love that little doggie as much as you do, Pepper. I don't wanna see him die." Tears were starting to form in the little boy's eyes.

"The vet said the next twenty-four hours is gonna be crucial, Ty," Pepper answered his brother, laying his hand on his shoulder for more reassurance. "All we can do now's pray."

The naïveté of a child became apparent as little Ty knelt down on the straw of the upper barn floor, held both hands together pointing upward, bowed his head and prayed.

Pepper also bowed his head, leaving Ty take the lead in his prayer with the Almighty.

"Dear God. I know ya got more 'portant things on Yer Mind than helpin' little doggies, but I learnt in Sunday School how Youse so merciful an' I juss wanna r'mind Ya that Crab Cake's been like 'nudder brudder ta us," he prayed.

"Wit' Yer help, he did save the life o' Thursy who sometimes gits hisself inta more trubble'n he oughtta, but he's still a friend an' a perty good guy, so that muss count for sumpin'. If Yer keepin' count, dear God, it's gotta count fer least one good point in Crab Cake's favor."

By this time Pepper's eyes were so misty he couldn't see clearly without first wiping them. Ty continued in his conversation with God. "And he walks us ta school every day an' meets us when we get offa the bus ta walk us home. He really does a perty good job o' protecting us, but Ya already know that," he prayed.

"If Ya add up all 'em points, God, I'm sure Youse gonna find that li'l doggie's well worth savin'. So if Ya'd guide Crab Cake safely through these next twenty-four hours, we'd be mighty obliged ta Ya for all Yer Special Blessings.

"Oh yeah, one more thing, God," he continued. "Ya knowd I do a lotta fightin' wit' my sisters but that don't mean I wanna see any harm comin' to 'em tonight. Sometimes I juss can't help myself," he confessed. "And my mother, too. Ya knowd I don't always do what she wants me ta, but she's still a real good mother, an' me an' Pepper don't ever wanna lose her. So if Ya can see Yer way clear ta help 'em outta this mess they's in, we'd be mighty thankful to Ya for that, too. Amen."

"Amen," repeated Pepper, wiping his eyes on his sleeve. He looked at his little brother. "Ty Whelan," he said, "that had ta be one of the best prayers I ever did hear. That was straight from the heart, Ty, an' that's the way ya always gotta pray. Where'd ya ever learn ta pray that perty?"

"Sunday School," Ty humbly answered. He felt good that his older brother was so pleased. It was the least the little fellow could do to help make things go easier for the two. Besides, it seemed to calm him and help him with his anxiety.

The two sat there for the longest time, ten-year-old Pepper with his arm around his seven-year-old brother, staring out the barn through the narrow openings between the vertical slats of siding. They could see all the way up the narrow dirt road past Lucas Barnes and Elwood Gampee's farm and into the short stretch of woods before Sawmill Road turns right and dead ends at the Potosi Road. It was from this direction that his father would come.

The late afternoon sun of early spring slowly settled in the west and dusk was fast approaching. Still lost as to what to do, the boys waited patiently for their father's car. Pepper's mind drifted back to his dog and how he wanted to be at his side, but he reminded himself that he was needed to help his family. He lay down on the straw, closed his eyes and silently said his own small prayer that God, in His infinite mercy, would save the life of his canine friend.

Like a bolt from out of the blue, Pepper sat upright on the straw. Ty shot up too. "Little brother," Pepper said, looking down at him and feeling like a fool.

He suddenly realized the mistake he was about to make. "It's impossible! We can't juss sit up here'n *wait* fer Dad. If we do, it's curtains fer Mom, the girls an' David. We hafta go an' *find* Dad. An' we gotta be quick 'bout it!"

Chapter 12

The two boys crawled to the hay side of the barn and cautiously looked out between the slats at the farm house. The wide part of the kitchen faced their side. A window to the right of the sink and one at the end of the table gave anyone a clear view of the barn yard area. With the setting sun and darkness closing fast, it would've been difficult for anyone to spot eyes peering out between the barn slats.

Pepper could see his mother with her back toward the barn. His sisters were out of his field of view. While Pepper was conjuring a plan in his mind, he wasn't sure whether to leave his little brother there or take him along. "Ty," he finally said. "You're gonna hafta come along. How's your legs?"

Tyrone Whelan had had polio four years earlier, leaving him partially paralyzed from the waist down. But with the leg braces and the encouragement of so many, mostly from his big brother, Pepper, whom he worshiped, he was able to make it back to where he could hold his own in walking and some running. Baseball with the family each Sunday afternoon afforded him the chance to run the distance between bases. His siblings allowed him to run in their stead whenever they got a hit. It was this practice, which, instead of atrophying, helped strengthen the peripheral muscles of his lower leg.

"I can run, Pepper," he said convincingly to his brother. "You saw me run the bases," he added hopefully. "I'm a real good runner, Pepper!"

"You may not hafta run that far, Ty," Pepper told him. "All I'm asking ya, is that ya keep up wit' me. If ya don't think ya can do that, tell me now."

Ty insisted he could run from the barn to the Potosi Church, a distance of a mile away, and back again. Pepper knew it was wishful thinking for the little boy. But he also knew they wouldn't need to run that far. All they had to do was to get clear of the farm house view, a distance of perhaps 350 yards.

"Ty, downstairs in the lower part o' the barn on a middle beam by the first cow is a flashlight," Pepper said. "I use it in the darkness o' mornin' so's I can see ta clean off the cows 'fore I start milking 'em. Be careful goin' down, but get it fer me if ya can, would ya please?"

With the flashlight in hand, he asked Ty to take a pitch fork with him. Pepper also picked up a pitchfork and a full roll of binder twine. Peering out the back

93

barn door, all seemed clear. Swiftly they made their way across the lower pasture running toward the Lucas Barnes farm.

Lucas had an older brother, Leonard, who taught night school at the York Business College. He was probably the only male in the area with a college degree. If Lucas or Leonard had been home, Pepper would've asked for help, but lady luck abandoned the two boys for the moment, and they continued on their way up the dirt road toward Floyd Brouse's farm.

Brouse had been in constant competition with Roy Haney over hiring the local kids whenever crops were ripe. If Haney was paying them three cents a basket for strawberries, Brouse would pay them three and a half. Haney paid ten cents a basket for tomatoes but when Brouse found out, he upped his pay to twelve. Even green beans weren't safe from the wage wars. After hearing that Haney was paying three and a half cents a pound for the slender, stringy legumes, Brouse upped his to five, an unheard of price at the time.

Naturally, word spread like wildfire among the neighborhood kids. It was nothing to see them working Haney's fields in the mornings, hearing about a price hike from Brouse and then bolting for his fields that same afternoon.

These two made the nation's fierce labor negotiations, constantly deadlocked between management and union officials, look like a friendly game of Old Maid. To the kids, this was neither a difficult, nor a highly complicated labor problem with which to comprehend, let alone solve. Whoever paid the most, that's for whom they worked. To them, it was just that simple.

"Ty, if we'da stayed there in the barn," Pepper finally explained to his brother who was just about to ask him why they were looking for their father, "Dad would'a driven right up the lane inta a trap. He'da exposed hisself to the two hoodlums 'fore we'da gotten to him. If we'da ran down to tell Dad an' they'da seen us, then all would've been lost. Hard ta tell what they'da done ta Mom an' the rest," he emphasized. "Now we hafta stop Dad *before* he gits in view o' the house. Long as Dad's somewhere out there," he said pointing towards the Hamlet of Potosi, "an' we're out here, the ladies an' David's gonna stay safe. Udderwise everybody's life's gonna end up in real danger."

Onward they walked toward the crossroads that made up Potosi. Upon reaching the hamlet, they sat on the front steps of its white church and waited. When their dad passed, he'd have to pass by that very spot. With the flashlight, they'd wave him to a stop. And when he saw his boys out this far, this late in the evening, he most certainly would stop.

The two young lads laid their pitchforks and roll of binder twine down on the grass by the steps of the church. Pepper watched up the hard Potosi Road

94

that eventually dead ended into the Susquehanna Trail South. Watching for the headlight beams of his father's 1934 black Ford he knew would be coming his way helped wile away the time. Ty watched the other way. Both boys wished Crab Cake was with them.

A dark green car came rumbling down the road from the trail, its headlights glaring ahead, going much too fast for Jack Whelan's '34 Ford. Before the boys had a chance to flag it down for help, having no stop sign at the crossroads, it continued at full speed straight ahead until the road changed from macadam to gravel. Then it slowed down just enough to prevent damage to its underside, stirring a great cloud of dust in its wake.

"He'll be by, Ty," said Pepper. "Don't lose faith." To keep Ty's mind off their troubles, Pepper tried changing the subject. "Ty, wit' all that's happened I ain't had a chance ta ask ya what ya was doing outside hidin' b'hind the smokehouse wit' Mom an' the girls inside?"

"I was hidin', Pepper," the little boy confessed, embarrassingly. "I didn't wanna go inside wit' those two bad guys."

"It's okay, Ty, it's okay. Ya got no reason ta be 'shamed," his big brother told him. "As a matter be the fact, ya did the right thing."

Pepper, in his attempt to comfort Ty, hoped he had just put him at ease. He had noticed as they were walking up the road to the church that Ty appeared to be tired. He knew Ty would never have admitted it, and for Ty's sake was glad they had the church steps on which to rest. "But how'd ya manage ta get outta the house an' hide?" Pepper continued his query.

"I's never in the house, Pepper," replied his little brother. "I's outside in the garden diggin' worms fer ya, hopin' when ya go fishin' next time, ya'da take me along wit' ya."

Pepper's heart sank. He knew how his little brother looked up to him. He knew how much Ty loved to hear Pepper tell stories of Crab Cake and him fishing. But Ty would have struggled walking that distance to Rehmeyer's Run in White Oak Valley and Pepper knew it.

"That's when Mom called me. I said, 'I'll be right there, Mother.' But time musta passed fast 'cause by the time I finished an' walked in t'ward the house, I saw the screen door was open an' when I peeped in, I saw those two guys. One of 'em, the big ugly one wit' the funny eyes, was holding a gun on David, Paula, Sarah an' Mom." Only amongst themselves did the children ever referred to their parents as *Mom* and *Dad*. With the exception of Pepper, and out of respect, they always called them Mother or Father to their faces.

"So ya went ta hide b'hind the smokehouse 'til help arrived?" asked

Pepper. "That's perty smart thinkin', Ty. Them guys musta heard Mom callin' ya an' decided ta wait 'til ya came in, an' then, bingo, they'da got alla ya, juss where they want'd ya. That muss be why the one wit' the tattoo came outside. He wasn't juss out there ta have a smoke. He was lookin' 'round fer ya, Ty."

"I didn't go hide b'hind the smokehouse right away, Pepper," Ty finally revealed after listening intently to his brother. Ty remained quiet for an unusual amount of time, and then said, "I went fer help."

Pepper was stunned. A seven-year-old child brave enough to go for help? If Ty wasn't kidding his brother, and there was no reason why he would be, he immediately sensed a feeling of deep pride for his younger sibling. "Ya not ferhoodling me, are ya, Ty?" asked Pepper.

Ty looked up at his older brother and slowly shook his head no. "Well that's great, Ty," Pepper said, putting an arm of comfort and reassurance around him. "That's great. Where, Ty? Where'd ya go?"

Ty told him the whole story from when the bad guys arrived until Pepper heard Ty issue his first "Pssst!" from behind the thick stone walls of the smokehouse.

The young lad snuck into the cellar through the back basement door, and after drinking some water from the underground spring, listened at the bottom of the steps that led to the kitchen. "Those two weirdoes tole Mom if she didn't tell 'em what time Dad got home, she'd be very sorry. I heard Mom tell 'em, 'anytime now, anytime, if he doesn't stop off at a bar,'" Ty told his brother. "So I took off 'long the banks o' the brook that runs inta the meadow from unnerneath the spring in the cellar," he said.

"Ya know, juss like you, I ain't too crazy 'bout snakes, Pepper, so I stayed 'long the edge in the high grassy part o' the pasture, outta sight, 'til I reached the dirt road right 'bout where the three cedar trees are at," he said. "Then I run inta the woods an' on t'ward Thursy's house. I figure you'd be there or on yer way there from fishin' an' you'd know what ta do."

"Well, what happened when ya told Thursy an' his parents?" asked Pepper. "I saw all three of 'em drive up the road long 'fore I heard you gimme that first 'pssst!'"

"I never got to 'em, Pepper," the little boy confessed, now almost in tears. "If I'da gone right up ta the house 'stead o' over ta git me 'nudder drink o' wooder from that spring pipe that comes outta the side o' their hill, I'da never missed 'em," he said, apologetically. "An' Mom an' the girls'd probably be okay by now," he added.

"But I's scared, Pepper," he continued, "an' all that runnin' musta made me thirsty again, 'cause I started losin' my voice. I thought I'd git a drink 'fore trying to tell Mr. Patterson what happened. Least he cudda used the phone ta call for help." By now, big tears were falling from the eyes of this innocent child. The safety of his mother, sisters and smaller brother weighed heavily on his conscience.

"Ya can't blame yourself, Ty," Pepper reassured him. "Ya didn't know they was leavin'. Ya did the right thing, li'l brother. I'm proud o' ya."

"Then, when I seen 'em leave wit'out havin' a chance to ask 'em fer help, I juss sat right down on the road 'n' cried 'fore startin' back ta the house. This time, juss 'fore enterin' the clearance, I cut through the woods on the left an' hiked ta the top. Then I crossed over the fence row an' follered it down ta the potato field. When I seen ya standin' b'hind the big ol' maple tree, I slipped down behind the stone smokehouse. And, well," Ty concluded, "ya know the rest, Pepper."

Pepper spotted the headlight of another car coming up the side dirt road toward the hamlet's only intersection. As soon as it reached the macadam part of the road, the blue and black new Plymouth picked up speed and through the intersection it raced, the driver gunning it as it climbed the hill toward Carmen's dairy farm and onward to the Susquehanna Trail.

"Don't no one slow down when they drive through Potosi?" asked Pepper to no one in particular. "Guess they need a big ol' stop light here, if fer no udder reason than ta control the dust these cowboys always make."

Turning on the flashlight, Pepper glanced quickly at his watch, and then turned it off. The batteries were low and he needed to save them to flash down his father. The time was now close to eight o'clock. The boys were getting hungry. Pepper reached into his pocket. He still had an apple left from the lunch his mother had packed. "Here, Ty, eat this," he ordered his little brother. "I ate so much for lunch I's almost too full to do any fishin'. This was left over." Ty looked at him smiling. He knew Pepper was lying, but he wasn't about to tell his big brother he knew. Instead he accepted the juicy red apple and bit into it heartily.

"It's gettin' late, Pepper," Ty said between bites. "Do ya s'pose Dad stopped offa some bar ta do a li'l drinking?"

"You know Dad don't drink at no bars," Pepper said, shocked to hear what Ty asked. "As a matter be the fact, he hardly ever drinks. Oh, he might have a bottle o' beer or two durin' the family corn roast every year, or maybe a toast at Thanksgiving, Christmas or Easter, but that's 'bout all. What makes ya ask me a question like that?" As much as Ty worshiped his older brother, that's how much Pepper worshiped his father. To hear his little brother question his father's drinking habits, or rather the lack thereof, hurt Pepper deeply.

"Then why'd Mom say what she did ta those two creeps? Ya know, when she tole 'em he'd be home 'anytime, if he doesn't stop off at a bar.' Mom muss think Dad drinks every night at bars!"

Pepper laughed a good laugh. With all that had happened to him today, it was a laugh he definitely needed. "Tyrone Whelan," he started slowly and carefully. "If Mom'd said Dad'd be home anytime soon now, an' he didn't show up, these guys'd been all over her. They'd figured she's been ferhoodling 'em an' no telling what they mighta done," Pepper explained. "By sayin' he stops at a bar ev'ry now an' then an' drinks, she juss borrowed some time an' invented an excuse when Dad doesn't show up on time. That, they could probably unnerstand," he said.

"Mom knowd he wouldn't be home from work 'til late. But if she'da said that, it coulda been a green light for those two creeps ta have their own way, an' who knows what they mighta done ta little David? By thinking Dad might walk in on 'em any minute, an' not knowing what Dad looked like, they minded their Ps and Qs. Mom was smart," Pepper went on, "she knows Dad don't drink in no bars. Mom juss used that story to her 'vantage. After all, she still got two daughters an' a son ta pertect, as well as herself."

Ty thought about this for quite a while. Then he put his arms around his brother's neck and said, "Pepper, I'm lucky ta have ya fer a big brudder. I juss hope I'm gonna be as smart as you when I'm yer age."

"Yer already as smart as me, Tyrone," Pepper assured him as he hugged his brother tightly. "Yer already as smart. As a matter be the fact, I think yer smarter'n I ever was at yer age."

Ty looked up the Potosi Road to the top of the hill and noticed a car's head light shining from beyond the hill. For the longest time its brightness did not increase. Pepper noticed it too. "It musta stopped by the road and parked, leaving its light on," he casually mentioned to Ty. But then it slowly became brighter, and as it reached the crest and started down the hill, the large globes of a mid-thirties vintage automobile became evident. Of course it could have been Phil Whelan's Ford or anyone's car from the community. Most farmers kept their cars longer than the average American, repairing them constantly until they could no longer be driven. Slowly it chugged toward the intersection.

Pepper reached for his flashlight, and after walking into the middle of the intersection, waved it back and forth. Ty started to join him, but instinctively, in order to keep the youngster away from any possible danger, Pepper told him to gather the pitch forks and wait by the side of the church.

As the car reached the intersection, and with Pepper standing in the middle of the road waving his flashlight, it slowed to a stop. Now Pepper could see clearly. It was an old black Ford sedan, and shining the light into the driver's side, the young boy saw his father behind the wheel.

With tears of deep gratitude in their eyes, both boys gave a yell of sheer joy.

Chapter 13

"And just what are you two boys doing up and out at this hour of the night, young fellas?" Their father demanded to know. Jack Whelan's English and grammar was probably the best of the entire family. Nevertheless, he queried them in a tone he rarely used with his children.

Discovering very early in parenthood they could control their children better with love and understanding than they could with anger and violence, his wife and he adopted the former as a basis for parental discipline.

"Dad, turn left an' park b'hind the church in the parking lot," Pepper asked him politely. "There's trubble at the house ya oughta know 'bout 'fore driving up the lane." Jack Whelan made a quick left turn into the lot, parked the car and the two boys jumped in.

Their father listened intently as Pepper and Ty told him the entire story, from the time Pepper left the house in the morning to go fishing until now.

"What in the name of good common sense were you planning on doing with the pitchforks?" asked their father, somewhat amused, but nevertheless befuddled.

"I tole Ty ta bring 'em along," said Pepper, "juss in case we needed 'em ta defend ourselves or if ya needed 'em ta rescue the rest o' the family."

"Well, you certainly have prepared yourselves well for the worst," Jack Whelan told his two sons, while shaking his head in almost disbelief at what the boys have endured. "The two of you are to be commended for your actions. You've had quite a day so far," he added in what appeared to be an understatement.

"You've both helped contain a possible explosive situation. That's good, because that's thinking. Remember," he said, "you can get a lot further ahead and much faster by first thinking than you can by just reacting. And, as you grow into an adult, you'll come to find out you'll win more of life's battle by thinking first than what you will by not thinking." Jack Whelan was always looking for a lesson in life to teach his sons.

"Now before we go forward without a plan," he said calmly while including his two sons in on the grand scheme, "we must think about what's the best way to rescue the rest of our family."

Stabler's Cabin's was located on the Susquehanna Trail, about a mile out the Potosi Road and about 300 feet north of where it dead ends. Jack Whelan and the boy's started in that direction. Their destination: Stabler's. When they arrived, Charlie Stabler was on duty, standing behind the counter in the dining area serving hamburgers, hot dogs, snacks and watered down coffee.

Jack first met Charlie about two years earlier when he stopped to ask for directions to the old forty acre Townsend Farm that was advertised for sale in White Oak Valley. At the time the Whelans were living in the east side of York on Wellington Street and, with a growing family, decided life in the country was a better environment for raising children than the city was.

They sold their home on Wellington Street, house number 933, and agreed on a price for the Townsend farm. When the children's school in York let out for the summer, they packed up their furnishings and headed for White Oak Valley, and they have never been sorry for having made that move.

"Gotta use the phone, Charlie," Jack said. "What's the number of the State Police? We've got troubles at the house."

"No need to call anyone, Jack," answered Charlie. "For the life of me, I'll never be able to figure out the incredible luck you Irish have always had." He shook his head, laughing and nodding towards the front door. Jack turned and with a sigh of relief saw two Pennsylvania State Policemen enter the restaurant. They were distributing flyers to all businesses describing two escaped criminals who quite possibly were last seen by two local boys.

"These two outlaws are suspects in the attempted murders of a State Game Warden earlier in the day and of an older couple up in York Springs earlier last month," the officer said, handing a flyer to a patron sitting at the counter drinking coffee and eating a sandwich. "All three survived their injuries and are under police protection for identifying purposes. However, we also believe the two to be extremely dangerous," he added, "because we believe the outlaws think they killed all three."

Approaching the patrolman, Jack Whelan introduced himself and his two sons. Then he had the boys tell the officers all they knew about the events of the day. Immediately, the older of the two cops returned to his car to radio for backup. Within minutes, five more State Police cars pulled up, four of them carrying two more officers each. The fifth car was occupied only by the driver, a Captain Gangloff who immediately took charge. Stabler's Cabins would be used as a base camp to lay out plans for the ex-con's capture. Charlie offered them as much room as they needed.

"Lives are at stake," Captain Gangloff made sure everyone understood. "The wife of this gentleman and mother of these two boys, including three more children at the house," and pointing to the boys, "their siblings, are in great and immediate danger. Do not fire unless it's cleared with me. That is a strict non-negotiable order. Any violation of that order will call for swift and immediate dismissal. There are absolutely no exceptions," he emphasized.

"Mr. Whelan," the captain continued, "we might have to use your assistance. You'll be under the protection of armed security at all times. Would you agree?"

"If it means saving my family, even if I'm wounded or lose my life, that's why I'm here," Jack Whelan clearly stated. The boys saw in their father a determination and dimension they had not seen before.

Earlier in their young lives, they had heard stories from their mother about their father's heroism in the Second World War; about how he was awarded the Purple Heart for bravery; about how he fought valiantly in the Battle of the Bulge and the Normandy Invasion. But since their father never talked much about his experience in the service, the information came to them second handed from a person who was not there, but who deeply admired and loved Jack Whelan, their mother.

When the captain was sure he fully understood the layout of the Whelan farm and its surrounding public and private roads, with the help of Pepper and Ty's father, he laid out his plans.

"We'll start with two sets of two cars each, one following the other. The lead cars will use lights. The cars following will not," said the captain. Having the advantage of taillights and a full moon on a partial cloudy night to guide the cars that follow, it was hoping would help to some degree.

"Cars number one and two will proceed toward the Whelan Homestead from the direction of the Pattersons," the captain directed. "They'll reach that starting point by turning left onto the Hametown Road opposite the church south of here. From there they'll proceed east to the White Oak Valley Road, turning left there, and when they reach Sawmill Road, they'll turn left again," the captain said. "Upon reaching Patterson's, car number two will park in their driveway with the officers exiting and traveling on foot to the edge of the woods."

Captain Gangloff continued, "Both officers will then turn left, walk up the wooded hill and approach the house from behind the fence row adjacent to the plowed corn field. Once they reach the old stone smokehouse, they'll wait there for further instructions."

These movements were successfully completed with no adverse activity occurring and after one, a rookie, lit a cigarette to relax his nerves, the other, a veteran of the force, reported to the captain they were in position and all was clear.

In the meantime, to cover their movements, the captain, in an effort to attract attention from inside the farmhouse, had car number one continue up Sawmill Road, past Whelan's lane, past the Barnes home and straight on into the woods toward the Floyd Brouse farm. There it parked and waited for further instructions from Captain Gangloff.

The captain had two more cars approach from the direction of the Brouse farm. Again, similar to the plan of the first two cars, car number four followed car number three, driving without lights and using the taillights of car number three along with a full moon for guidance.

Like car number one, car number three's mission was also to attract attention from inside the farm house by slowly driving past Whelan's lane to the Patterson home. There it would turn around and proceed back toward the edge of the woods with its lights off. At that point it would stop and wait for further instructions.

In the meantime, under the cover of car number three, car number four stayed 50 yards behind its pace car and with its lights off, pulled into the Barnes driveway and parked behind their house. Both officers exited their patrol car and proceeded across the road to Gampee's meadow. From there they crossed to behind the Whelan barn on foot and waited for further instructions.

Upon carrying out their clandestine movements, over a crackling, noisy, two way radio, the two officers immediately reported their successfully completed mission.

From across the fields west of Potosi, the captain had car number five, with its lights on, drive south along a field road toward the west side of the house. On the hill behind the potato field's fence row, high above the barn, the two patrolmen would wait for further instructions with their lights extinguished.

The captain would be controlling the rescue from the portable command post in car number six while parked on the side of the road that stretches from Brouse's to a hill behind the Barnes homestead, on the east side of the farm. Jack Whelan and the boys would be with the captain; Jack in the front seat, the boys in the rear. The Whelan home would be surrounded.

With hills on the north, east, southwest and west, lined with tall white oak trees, it was easy to understand where the area got its name and, with the exception of a small stretch of wooded hills and treacherous outcroppings of rocks to the southeast of the Whelan homestead, the law enforcement officers felt they had all exits covered. Besides, no police car would ever be able to negotiate that rocky incline nor was it likely that two old men could manage to conquer it. All sides, the police determined, were well covered.

Now was the time to implement the plan. Now was the time to see if it would work, at least enough to save the lives of a wife and mother and three of her children. Now was the time for action. The next hour could possibly hold the fate of four innocent hostages.

Two State Policemen patiently passed the time behind the old stone smokehouse waiting for further orders. Two more waited for instructions from behind the barn. And on top of the western hill, behind the fence row next to the potato field, another two officers sat waiting in their unlit car number five. In the woods near the Brouse farm, two officers in car number one lingered. And at the bottom of the hill, hidden in Patterson's woods, sat two more in car number three.

Suddenly the back kitchen door opened and out came Tattoo with a cup of coffee in one hand and a cigarette in the other. Down the sidewalk, all the way to its end, he walked. Facing the barn, he looked around and halfway back, then looked up the hill to his right. Then he returned to the back porch.

Before re-entering the farmhouse kitchen, he turned back toward the smokehouse and walked south down the lane toward the outhouse. Looking around he saw nothing of interest and again returned to the back porch. From inside the opened door, the two smokehouse officers could hear another voice asking if it was all clear. "Yeah," answered Tattoo. "Musta been a raccoon or one o' them nasty groundhogs they got all over this state," he said. "There's no one out here."

Jack Whelan heard the veteran cop's voice from behind the smokehouse radio Capt. Gangloff about Tattoo's movements and the conversation the two cops heard. "Remember," the captain reminded them, "no one moves until I say so. And no one fires unless either their lives are in immediate danger or I give the word. There are lives at stake and I want all four of them saved."

For 25 minutes they sat and waited patiently. Finally Jack and his two sons saw seven more patrol cars approaching, each car carrying four armed officers. Counting the captain, that made a total of 39 armed Pennsylvania State patrolmen on the scene. "Were these guys considered to be that dangerous to warrant a whole army?" asked Jack. The captain assured him he was doing everything necessary to save lives.

"You men are the secondary line of defense," the captain explained to the new arrivals, laying out the plans to the sergeant and ordering him to have his men surround the house at a distance of 300 yards. "If these two criminals should somehow give the slip to the primary defense of officers, it will be your duty as the secondary defense to stop them by any means necessary," he instructed.

"That means, once they're away from the captives and the farm house," he continued, "if need be, fire a warning shot in the air. And if they continue their flight, fire again to halt them."

Through the captain's radio static, he directed the two cops waiting behind the barn to cautiously approach the front and to remain out of site near the corn cribs. The two policemen parked in the woods were ordered to exit their patrol car and approach the house by way of the private lane, then slowly proceed through the ball field meadow and hide behind the summer house while waiting for further orders. The two behind the smokehouse were ordered to vacate their spot and proceed to the south side of the house next to the garden. And the two who were in the car parked on the hill were to move on foot to the spot vacated from behind the smokehouse.

Car number one, with the two cops waiting at the edge of the woods near the Brouse farm, was ordered to proceed through the woods, lights off, and back into the Gambee driveway across from the Barnes farm, parking behind the house out of sight. There they'd wait to head off an escape if one should occur.

"Is everyone in position?" the captain asked, all radio receivers crackling his question.

The ten-four replies came rapidly across the airwaves, each answer stepping on another's or coming a second or two later.

"Standby and wait for my instructions." And with that order, the captain engaged the car's gear into first, slowly drove back the road toward the Brouse farm, turned left at the dirt crossroads and started down the slight incline of Sawmill Road. After coming out of the woods, he extinguished his headlights, passing car number one in Gambee's driveway and proceeding to the Whelan private lane. The captain turned right into the lane and around to the back of the farm house.

After ordering Jack and the boys to stay behind the stone smokehouse, the captain first turned on his car's flashing red bubble gum style domed light. With a gun in one hand and a bullhorn in the other, he ordered the criminals to give up, while using his patrol car as a shield.

"We've got the house surrounded," yelled the captain. "There are 39 armed Pennsylvania State Policemen out here. You can not escape. It's virtually impossible! Release the ladies and little boy. Come out with your hands high in the air and no one will get hurt."

Silence! Not a peep of noise was coming from the farmhouse. From behind the smokehouse, Jack slipped down to the captain's car. "Captain," he said, "perhaps they're not in there."

"They're in there, all right, Mr. Whelan," the captain answered. "You heard the report from my officers behind the smokehouse, didn't you?"

"Release the woman and children and we'll talk," the captain bellowed to the seedy suspects over the bullhorn.

Still nothing. Not even a moo from the cows in the barn. There was nothing but dead silence. Only the trickle of water in the spring brook that runs out from beneath the basement could be heard in the still of the late evening.

"You're absolutely sure they're in there?" insisted Jack Whelan.

"Where could they have gone, Mr. Whelan? Where on God's green earth could they have gone? The valley is completely surrounded. And unless I'm mistaken, I don't recall seeing an airplane flying out of that house."

"But, Captain," Jack insisted, "what your men reported to you was witnessed more than a half hour ago. Maybe they escaped."

"Escaped to where, Mr. Whelan?" the captain argued. He was becoming increasingly frustrated at Jack's insistence that they might not be inside the house. He was even beginning to consider it as personal criticism. "The house is surrounded. The valley's surrounded. Even the great Houdini would never have been able to escape this dragnet," he insisted. "To where did they escape, Mr. Whelan? By some quirk of fate, mysteriously into the thin air?

"You have two minutes in there to make up you minds, and then we're coming in," the captain's voice boomed over the bull horn.

Still nothing. Absolute quiet! It was becoming increasingly eerie. Uneasiness engulfed Jack. Perhaps his wife, daughters and son have been murdered. Perhaps the two criminals took their own lives. It's abnormal not to get a response, at least some kind of response, even if it is a negative one.

"Captain," said Jack, "I'm going in. If they're still alive, perhaps I can be of some help serving as your eyes. At least we'll know where they are in the house. If they're not there, then there's no need to scare the ladies, if they're still alive."

"Sorry, Mr. Whelan," the captain insisted, "I can not allow you to do that. This area is now under my jurisdiction, and as such, I am responsible for all lives, including yours."

"Captain, perhaps there's something you should know." Jack Whelan was not about to give up. Diplomatic measures were needed. "With all due respect," he started, "I was with Special Forces behind enemy lines in the early part of the war. Uncle Sam trained me in clandestine espionage and then used my communication skills to negotiate with the enemy, thus saving lives of captured POWs when the situation called for it. This is no different, Captain. Over the years I have maintained and, from special governmental programs, updated those skills."

The captain saw that Jack Whelan was determined and his story about the Special Forces did seem quite credible. "Okay, Mr. Whelan, if you insist. But you must go in unarmed.

"Attention, please. If you can hear me, wave a towel out the crack of the door," ordered the captain. Still there was no response. "Okay, you two in there. I'm sending in Mr. Whelan under a blanket of peace. He is unarmed. He will be there simply to negotiate with you for the release of his wife and children in exchange for your freedom. If any harm should come to him, all hope of us ever agreeing to your freedom will end forever."

Jack Whelan walked slowly toward the back porch. He climbed the one step then the second. Standing on the porch, he looked back toward the old stone smokehouse. In recognition of their father's bravery, Pepper and Ty stood up and, as a sign of support, gave the thumbs up sign. Slowly Jack walked across the porch toward the back kitchen door. Cautiously, he opened it and looked in. Four chairs were missing from around the table. "Hello," he said. "Is anyone here?"

The only response he could hear from his question was a low mumble coming from inside the parlor. Little by little Jack worked his way into the kitchen with much care until he reached its center. Standing next to the Kalamazoo kitchen range he asked again, "Is anyone here?"

Once more a low moan was the only response he got, this time somewhat louder. Then he heard what sounded like a stomp of a foot and shuffling of furniture. Jack turned toward the parlor, looked in and saw no one. Entering the room, he turned to his left. The room was empty. Turning around with the intention of returning to the kitchen, he suddenly became startled, staring at the scene in front of him. There in the second parlor room, tied to the four kitchen chairs and blindfolded, their mouths stuffed with towels, were his wife, two daughters and little son.

He raced to the back door and hollered, "All clear," then tore back into the second parlor room and started untying his wife, daughters and finally his son. Shaking, Doris hugged him so tightly, he swore he'd never be able to breathe again. Next came embraces of deep love and gratitude from his daughters,

Sarah and Paula, and son David.

Within seconds the house was flooded with state policemen. "Where are they?" the captain asked. "Where did they go?"

"They went down into the cellar just after the one with the tattoo came in from walking outside to check on things," Doris Whelan answered the captain. "He told the one with the strange eyes that he heard a two-way radio crackling behind the barn, saw a car in the moonlight behind the fence row above the potato field and noticed cigarette smoke coming from behind the smokehouse. Then they tied us up and went to the basement. That's been at least 45 minutes ago."

Jack Whelan looked at Captain Gangloff as if to ask why he seemed so surprised. "Did they hurt you or the kids? Did they demand money? What was it they wanted?" Jack asked his wife.

"I never did get a clear demand from them, Honey," she answered, still shaking. "They were rambling on 'bout some hidden loot. I couldn't make heads or tails what it was they were saying. Then they started on 'bout a dog and two boys. I tole 'em I only had one boy who was away from home at the moment. An' then tryin' ta pertect Pepper, I did a terrible thing in front of the kids, Jack. I lied. I said I didn't know anything 'bout a dog."

"You didn't lie, Sweetheart," her husband told her in an effort to comfort his wife. "You merely did what any good and loving mother and wife would have done to protect her children."

Suddenly Pepper and Ty came rushing in, hugging their mother, sisters, little brother and father. If they felt their whole world was falling apart earlier in the day, it now felt as if some one with a greater power than they had ever known, power beyond anything mankind had ever devised, suddenly, as if it had never happened, glued their world securely back together again.

Now all they needed to become a complete family once more was to have Crab Cake with them.

Chapter 14

Captain Gangloff opened the door to the cellar and peered down. Switching the light on, he slowly descended the steps, looking to his left and then to his right until he reached the bottom. Immediately behind him was Jack Whelan.

"That back door," asked the captain, pointing to an oversized door against the east wall of the basement. "To where does it lead?"

"Out the back, across from the entrance to the summer house," answered Jack, while the captain opened the door. Jack, noticing the captain was fooling with the door, probably checking to see if it was unlocked, volunteered, "We always keep it tightly secured, especially when just the wife and children are home. No one from the outside can enter, but from the inside, they can leave."

Out the back they walked. The small brook, originating from the underground spring in the basement, trickled down toward the rear of the meadow which the family uses for a baseball field. It runs southeast, joining a larger stream which originates to the north. From there the stream runs south through brush and high weeds, crossing the road just inside the woods and paralleling Patterson's property.

Looking in the direction of the woods the captain said, embarrassingly, "They got about a 45 minute head start. The one area we couldn't cover, that southeastern wooded hill with the outcroppings of rock, they used to their advantage, but we'll catch them. Where's your telephone?"

"There is no phone here," said Jack. "The closest one is at Patterson's home, and they live down the road on the left after entering the woods."

Captain Gangloff knew where they lived. After all, he was the one who laid out the failed plans to capture the outlaws. He stared at Jack as if to ask how they could live in such modern times as the 1950s without a phone, but discretion commanded him to think the better of insulting this man after all the cooperation he gave the police, and he held his tongue.

Walking up the back yard slope toward his car, he radioed for more assistance, this time asking for bloodhounds. Jack interrupted the captain to remind him that if the two crooks followed the streams, by walking in the water, they would have left no scent. In such a case, the dogs would be useless. The captain ignored him.

Doris put a huge pot of coffee on the stove, made chicken salad sandwiches

111

and in the oven warmed homemade cinnamon rolls. Both girls immediately pitched in to help.

As if somehow knowing help was needed, Mrs. Brouse, Barnes, Gambee and Haney arrived uninvited with trays of pastries and pots of hot coffee for the officers. Mrs. Haney told Doris how word got to them from Stabler's Cabins. They knew help would be needed and so she even brought along ten dozen eggs and six loaves of bread. After the long stakeout, the patrolmen would be hungry.

In this special community, when one family becomes threatened, all feel threatened. Believing strongly in the principle of safety in numbers, they've never faltered in helping their own during times of need. All the neighbors pitch in and help, always pulling for each other. It's just the way things are done in White Oak Valley.

Under cover of the full moon's declining illumination, hampered by the rush of an overcast sky, Crazy Eyes and Tattoo made their way southeast. Past the outcroppings of rock the cops could not cover and over the top of the treacherous wooded hill behind the Patterson home, they continued their escape.

Upon reaching the road to Cline's, they stayed low, quickly crossing and moving into the woods on the opposite side. From there the terrain became more isolated from civilization, if that was possible in this sparsely populated, hilly, forested section of Southern York County. The cloud cover increased, dimming the glow from the moon until it was gone. Hurrying along, with no specific destination in mind, the two hoped to fully escape the long strong arm of the law by morning.

Once they reached the creek, they continued walking upstream in the water to throw off any traces of tracks. Covering their trail, they proceeded until reaching the point where the creek's wide deep bend makes it unfeasible to continue that route. So crossing to the other side, they started uphill, once again traveling along the top of the ridge. By morning, they hoped to be out of the area and on their way to everlasting freedom. They continued running as stars dimmed behind the cloudy skies.

A paddy wagon carrying seven bloodhounds soon arrived at the Whelan home. As they were being unloaded, the skies opened up. Thunder and lightning caused another downpour equal to the one earlier in the day. With the sudden cloudburst and rain water washing debris here, there and everywhere, little hope was left of bloodhounds picking up any scent of the two and quickly capturing them. "These guys are running with luck, good luck," Captain Gangloff said to his sergeant. "But it won't always be like this. There will come a time when that luck will end and that time is soon approaching."

Loading the hounds back into the wagon, the captain explained to Jack how the rain washed away the scent needed for the dogs to track them, as if he didn't know. From being in the service, it was one of the first lessons Jack learned in his special training. Still, he listened to the captain patiently and diplomatically. Together, the two entered the farmhouse for a cup of hot coffee and some warm pastry.

Before long, all who were involved in the rescue were dry and warm, their stomachs free of hunger pangs and their mission to preserve the lives of the innocent, successful. But somewhere out there in the torrential downpour of the moment, not all might have been as cozy, especially with the two perpetrators who brought this mess onto innocent lives.

For those inside, at the moment, there was some consolation in knowing the two renegades were suffering in the cold rain, soaked and miserable, while they were comfortably eating good home cooked food in the dry, warm and safe kitchen of the Whelan farmhouse.

With rain water dripping off their heads and into their eyes, the two wanted hombres continued their journey eastward. "Maybe we oughta turn and head in 'nother direction," suggested Tattoo, "juss ta throw 'em off in case they send in the hounds."

"What? Ya think 'em hounds don't know when ya turn one way or 'nother? Huh? They track by smell, Tattoo, not by sight," Crazy Eyes yelled. "No wonder yer never gonna be any smarter'n ya at right now. Ya gotta head fulla warm, week old rice puddin' fer brains."

Then realizing he desperately needed his comrade if there was any hope of escaping, Crazy Eyes did an about face and softened his comments. "Listen, Tattoo," he said, "if we turn, we gonna lose our sense o' direction in these here woods. Right now, looks like you and me's headin' southeast towards the river. Once we git there, we can foller the western bank south 'til we cross over the border inta Maryland," he said.

"Piece o' cake, Tattoo, juss a piece o' cake. From there, all we hafta do is foller the river ta the Chesapeake Bay and over ta the eastern seaboard where they got three states that make up the whole peninsula. When one state starts searchin', we just move to 'nother. And when we do git ta that three state peninsula they call Dalemarble, we gonna be free once an' fer all from the state fuzz in this blasted Commonwealf."

By now the rain had soaked their clothes to the skin and with nightfall arriving, temperatures were falling. The two hoodlums experienced a wet cold that sent chills down their spine. Following Rehmeyer's Run, Crazy Eyes and Tattoo traveled upstream near Pepper's secret fishing hole, over the wooded hill, across a field and into the woods where they re-discovered the cave in which they had hidden earlier.

Out of the driving rain, they lit a fire with dry wood left behind. Hungry and cold, they removed their clothes and placed them near the fire to dry. Oddly enough, the soaking rain was a welcome relief to both as they had not bathed in weeks, while at the same time, the rainwater did much to dilute the smell from their dirty, filthy clothes.

From out of the pouring rain, two rabbits suddenly entered the cave. Noticing them immediately, Crazy Eyes went wild eyed with hope. Tattoo did the same. "The gun," said Tattoo, holding out his hand to his partner, "gimme the gun, Crazy Eyes. That's our supper."

Taking the warden's pistol from Crazy Eyes, Tattoo aimed it squarely at the one, but dropped them both, when, at the last minute, the second rabbit ran directly behind the first. Tattoo lifted the barrel of the gun to his lips and blew away the smoke. "Two rabbits with one shot. Not bad, eh, Crazy Eyes?" he bragged. Rabbit on a spit was a welcomed meal for the two. To them it tasted just like chicken.

"We gonna make this our base 'til things open up," Crazy Eyes told Tattoo while feasting on rabbit. "It's warm an' quiet, that's fer shore. It's abandoned and seems perty safe. 'Sides, there's that crick down there," he said, referring to Rehmeyer's Run. "And it'll never be as crowded as it was today. After the first day of fishing season, it always seems ta quiet down some durin' the week, pickin' up mostly on weekends and holidays."

"We can always fish fer food," Tattoo suggested. "I saw a coupla poles and some tackle when we passed by down there earlier after we left those two kids and their hound tied up here in the cave."

"I know you ain't agreeing wit' me, Tattoo, but I still say them poles and that tackle box belonged to them two kids who had the dog." Crazy Eyes insisted. "I suspect they was laying up on that hill all along, just a waiting for us ta leave sos they could fish there an' they saw us kill dead that there game warden. That's why we gotta find 'em, Tattoo. If we don't, being witnesses, they could spell trouble for us an' land us back in the slammer fer good."

"But ya got no proof, Crazy Eyes," Tattoo countered. "You heard their momma. She said she only had one older boy and that they didn't have no scroungy mutt."

"Don't need no proof, partner. This ain't no jury trial. The strong feeling I got's good enough fer me. I'd rather be safe than to ignore that strong feeling and end up being sorry," Crazy Eyes continued. "If them kids did see us, and I believe they did, and they squeal, it's curtains for me an' you. That's why we gotta find 'em. An' their dog, too."

"What if anudder game warden comes back an' finds us here? Or worse yet, the cops?" asked Tattoo, changing the subject because he was not quite convinced the cave was the place to make a base camp.

"Tattoo, that's the whole beauty 'bout stayin' here fer a while," Crazy Eyes said in an effort to convince his comrade in crime. "No cop worth his weight in buckshot's ever gonna figure we come back ta the very same spot we started at. After escaping their dragnet back at that isolated farm, thanks ta you an' yer keenness, they gotta figure we's smart 'nough ta head in a whole new dye-rection," he said. "An' in the meantime, whilst they try ta track us down in that whole new dye-rection, we just stay low 'til the heat's off. Then we make our move. Simple as that.

"But first we gotta git that box full o' loot from the bottom o' that there crick out there," he reminded Tattoo. "Udderwise, why even bodder ta hang 'round?"

"It's got too much in it juss ta let it sit there," Tattoo said. "My brudder said it was his share o' the robbery. Split only ten ways, that's a cool $25,000. 'At's a hunnert an' twenny-five C-notes a piece fer you an' fer me, Crazy Eyes. That shore's gonna keep us livin' nice an' easy down there on that Dalemarble peninsula," he said.

"B'sides, it ain't doing much good waitin' down there in the bottom o' that there crick fer my brudder. He ain't got much of a chance fer parole 'til after he serves 50 years. He's already 57 years old. So might as well use it ourselfs. No sense lettin' it go ta waste, is there?" he asked.

But Crazy Eyes just ignored his question and went on with what was on his mind. "If they'da lissened ta me, they'da waited 'til that bank had its payroll supply. Instead, they gotta git antsy pantsy and knock it off a day 'fore it gits there. 'Stead o' hunnert an' twenty-five C-Notes a piece, we be rollin' in so much dough, we'da flew outta here lass week 'stead o' hangin' 'round tryin' ta latch onto a metal box under the pretense of catchin' some stupid fish worth a hunnert dollars," he said.

From over the noisy, static, crackling police radio came a call for Captain Gangloff. Taking the message, he listened attentively. Returning that message with a ten-four, over and out, he placed the receiver on its stationary arm and walked into the house where he spoke quietly to Jack and Doris Whelan. Both nodded in agreement to whatever it was that the captain suggested.

Jack and Doris called Pepper over to the table. "Sit down, son," his father said. "That was Larry Haney on the police radio. He's still at the vet's hospital in York. When he heard over the police scanner what happened down here, he offered to drive down here and pick you up, then drive you in to be with Crab Cake. He's your dog, son. Your mother and I agree that you should be permitted to go in, that is if that's what you want to do."

"How is he, Dad? Is he any better?" the ten-year-old asked, strongly hoping his father's answer would bring him some good news for a change.

"Not good, son," his father answered, looking down at Pepper and rubbing him softly along the nape of his neck. "The doctor seems to think that your presence might help the situation. At least he thinks it's worth a try."

There was no reason for Jack and Doris to wait for an answer. Pepper's actions gave them all the answer they needed as he reached for his jacket and Brooklyn Dodger baseball cap. "I'll send along a written note, excusing you from school," Doris explained. Reaching into her purse, she handed Pepper a five dollar bill for food and whatever other necessities he may need. "Larry should be here within the hour."

The forty-five minute trip to York by way of the Susquehanna Trail went past Stabler's Cabins, Krout School House, through Loganville, Shantytown, Jacobus and on past Leader's Heights. Pepper couldn't wait until he saw Crab Cake once more. Riding with Larry Haney in the front seat of his gray Dodge pickup truck, it seemed to him as if the trip was taking forever.

"He ain't too good, Pepper," Larry told the boy. "May not make it. That's why the Doc thought you might wanna be by his side if he does go. But," Larry continued, "the Doc did say that his young age was on his side. The fact that the dog is only 'bout three or so's in his favor."

Pepper's eyes filled with tears, but turning his head and looking out the right window, he was able to hide his silent weeping from Larry's attention. He thought back over the past two years when he first got Crab Cake and all the good times he had with him. Again, Pepper lowered his head, saying a silent prayer of thanks for the safe recovery of his mother, brother and two sisters, then asked Divine Providence for His continued help in saving the life of his dog.

Reaching the hospital, Pepper rushed in, gave the nurse a no nonsense look straight in her eyes and said, "I'm Pepper Whelan. My dog Crab Cake was bit by a copperhead snake. He's here in your hospital. I'm here to see him."

Without any hesitation, the nurse led Pepper down a long corridor of steel cages used to keep the animals separate. Some animals were drugged so heavily it was all they could do to lift their heads. Others were recovering from drug laced operations designed to improve their quality of life. Crab Cake was resting quietly on a mattress in a large cage after receiving another antidote for the poisonous venom of the copperhead snake.

Still in critical condition, his shallow breathing continued. The next twenty-four hours would tell the difference.

Chapter 15

Pepper slipped off his jacket. A table was pulled into the cage. The nurse lifted Crab Cake off of the floor mattress which was then set on the table and the dog was placed back onto the bedding. This put Crab Cake eye level with Pepper. If he pulled through, it would be the first image he'd see upon awakening.

Pepper rested his arm on the dog and slowly rubbing his head behind his ears, he spoke softly. As he did so, he recalled the many good times the two have had in the two years they've been together. He thought of how Crab Cake loved chasing groundhogs. The dog would lie in high weeds, almost stalking their holes. Upon seeing them poke out their heads, he'd wait until they thought all was clear. Then as they left the safety of their underground bunker, Crab Cake would spring. With a panicked look of surprise on their faces, his fun was forcing the rodents into unwanted chases. Rarely did he ever catch any and at times, when he thought he had them cornered, they'd break away by quickly turning on the dog. Eventually, Crab Cake learned how to prevent such dangerous actions, although sometimes, not fast enough.

All through the White Oak Valley, his stints fishing with Pepper soon became legendary. When it came to fishing, Crab Cake had a special talent. He instinctively knew where and when the fish were biting. He'd stand near by the creek at a specific spot until Pepper would throw in his line. Invariably, the boy caught more fish when he listened to his dog than if he hadn't.

Pepper loved hunting, just not the killing part. Unless there was a distinct need for food to be placed on the table, he saw no need to kill. For reasons he thought long and hard about, but which he could never explain, this feeling never crossed over the line into his fishing activities. But then he always brought his catch home with him to eat.

Pepper and Crab Cake spent hours in the fields during the fall hunting season. The young lad would track and Crab Cake would flush. Many a time the dog taught Pepper where to look for ring necked pheasants. Slowly he'd work the fence rows, stirring up cockbirds as well as hens. When the dog chased one out from beneath the brush, Pepper would consider that a strike and mentally mark it among his "catch," leaving the bird as free as the wind, just as it had been before, and perhaps returning again someday to give the boy

119

and his dog the thrill of a new hunt.

To Pepper, one of the most beautiful sights in all of nature is the image of a couple of hen pheasants in flight against the background of a harvested corn field, followed by a ringneck leaving the underbrush of a fencerow against a field of oaks and maples changing their leaves to the myriad colorful hues of autumn.

"How did it go for you two today?" his father would ask as he sat down at the supper table, ready to satisfy an appetite worked up by hunting.

"Juss fine, Dad," Pepper would answer. "Crab Cake flushed out seven ringed necks. I managed ta get five of 'em. Course since I never shot any, there's still seven flying aroun' that wouldn't be there if I had packed a 12 gauge." Pepper had no problem with others killing game. It just wasn't his cup of tea. Other than fish, he had always had a certain regard and deep natural respect for the dignity of life.

Looking lovingly at his dog, the boy bowed his head again, silently concentrating on prayer. Asking Divine Providence to intercede on Crab Cake's behalf, healing him and helping him to a full and speedy recovery, Pepper finished and lifted his head. The dog was still motionless. With so much time on his hands, Pepper dwelt long and often on the condition of his dog. The more he thought about it, the more he fought back tears. When it came to Pepper's emotions, Crab Cake could stir them like nothing or no one else. That dog had his master twirled around his front paw.

It was pushing midnight, two hours past his normal bedtime but Pepper was on his second and, possibly, third wind. He couldn't sleep if he tried. Looking around, the boy noticed other animals, possibly in worse shape than Crab Cake, although for the life of him, he couldn't understand how. Across the walkway lay a dog with his leg in a cast. In the cage next to it, another was sleeping soundly, possibly assisted by medication. On the other side of the aisle a full collie, golden brown with splotches of white, whined in pain, its medication obviously wearing off. It was enough to tear at the heart strings of any dog lover. For Pepper it was even worse.

At one time Pepper thought he'd like to work with sick animals, maybe become a veterinarian. It certainly seemed to him as if it was an interesting field and was rewarding work helping animals back on their feet. But that was years ago and still, perhaps years away. Before the young lad would finish college he'd change his mind a hundred times. The important business of the day was to get Crab Cake well enough to go home. Pepper's eyes were heavy, but like before, he fought determinedly to stay awake. Again Pepper bowed his head in prayer. Crab Cake needed all the help he could get. This time, while still in prayer, his head stayed down. Slowly Pepper Whelan fell asleep from exhaustion.

"Jack, Honey," asked Doris in a tired voice. She had just gone through an ordeal of a lifetime and wasn't sure she could hold her own in conversation, but questions needed answered. "Who are those two guys, and what are they wanted for?"

"Sweetheart," her husband said, gently taking her hand in his and answering slowly, "they're known as Crazy Eyes and Tattoo. I don't know their real names," he told her, "but I suppose the police do. Earlier in the day, they were involved in an attempted murder of a game warden, but a certain dog and two boys we know saved his life. Authorities believe the two outlaws don't know that. They believe the two think they killed the warden. And I heard talk about a hidden box of loot, but I'm not sure what that's all about," he added.

"They're also wanted for the attempted murder of an elderly couple last month after robbing them at gunpoint, but the old man and woman survived. Authorities also have reason to believe the two criminals think they died," Jack said. "It was at a mom-and-pop grocery store located along state route 94 up near York Springs in Adams County."

She looked at her husband blankly, as if she had no idea who he was or what he was talking about. It was as if the trauma of the evening somehow suddenly hit and now was depriving her of the ability to follow simple everyday conversations. It was as if she suddenly realized what had happened and temporarily went into a case of mild shock.

"Just north of C & W Performance," Jack reminded her tenderly while holding her close, "the garage where we got such a good deal on our Ford."

Doris Whelan looked at him puzzled, as if she still had no idea what he was talking about.

"Honey," Jack continued, trying to bring her out of a trance, "it's where those two mechanics, Chet and Whitey Chronister, inspect our car every six months. Being a Chronister yourself, you joked about how they may be related to you. Don't you remember? You were with me. C & W? Chet and Whitey?"

The simplest connections seemed to be way over her head.

"Chet's got a son about Pepper's age. Just a little squirt of a kid named Ken. But still a nice lad. Remember how polite he was and how you once said it'd be nice if we ever found out he was related to us. It'd give Pepper someone else his age to do things with, like learn about cars."

Nothing! She continued staring blanks.

"You do remember the place where that one guy up there named Bossy, who claimed he was a mechanic, jokingly offered us a good price to change the air in all four of our tires, don't ya?" Jack was trying a little humor, hoping that would bring his wife around. "You had one of the best laughs of your life when he said he'd do the spare for free."

Still nothing. She stared blankly past her husband.

"The garage where that black Blue-Tic Hound they call Mitzi hangs around all the time," he emphasized, struggling to bring her around with some tidbit of familiar information. "That dog that Pepper and Ken always played with. They said the dog was named after that movie star. The store's on the opposite side of the road, just beyond and north of his garage and used car lot."

Jack took a deep breath before continuing. "Those old folks at the store never had a chance, Honey. I heard that after they already gave 'em all their money, the one criminal hit them upside the head with a two by four. The old man and woman's in a nursing home now. Probably never'll be the same again. Not at their age."

Coming out of her temporary shock, she instantly realized the real danger her children had been in. Nodding her head as an indication she understood, chills suddenly built up inside. Running down her spine she shivered and held on to her husband with all the strength she had.

"The cops knew what they were capable of," Jack said to his wife. "And even if they haven't, once people believe they've committed murder, to them additional murders mean nothing. As a matter be the fact, it becomes easier for them to commit the second, third and fourth killing than it did the original. Once they have the first one under their belt, or at least think they do, their danger level increases a hundred fold. That's why this situation had to be handled with kid gloves," he explained.

"We were lucky tonight, Honey," Jack said softly, "real lucky. Someone up there was closely watching over this family." Then as an afterthought, he added, "I think I'll purchase a firearm for you. I think I'll train you on how to load it and how to use it."

Doris looked at her husband with that same look she always gave him whenever she'd suddenly become stubborn. Both of her eyes opened wide, but only for a split second. The left eyelid would arch high near the brow while the right one nearly closed. Her mouth became set to argue every point as to why she would not be forced to have loaded weapons in her home. In Jack's mind, there was no doubt now his wife was completely free from her trance.

Jack knew her dislike for firearms in the house. "Just for protection whenever I'm not here," he added more as a suggestion than being insistent. Then Jack softened his request. "I'd feel a lot more comfortable if you'd agree."

"That's a tall order, Mr. Whelan," she told him. Whenever she called her husband 'Mister,' Jack Whelan knew his wife well enough to stop his conversation and listened carefully. "That's a mighty fast decision you're making without consulting me first," she insisted. "These are my children, too. I've got to think about that, Mr. Whelan. I'm going to have to give that quite a lot of deep thought." The conversation was usually as close to arguing as they'd ever come.

It was close to one a.m. when Jack and Doris finished their coffee. The other children had been put to bed and all doors securely locked. Periodically Doris would notice the headlights of a car coming down the road in the pitch black rainy night and would shudder with fear. If they were to continue to live on the farm, she'd have to overcome this fear. She knew it. Jack knew it too but refused to push her. Now was not the time. She needed to pace herself in getting her confidence back once again. And Jack was determined to do everything in his power to help her.

Standing, the two held each other as tightly as they've ever had before. For both it seemed for the longest time. And for both, it felt good. "I was so scared of you never seeing the kids and me again," she whispered softly to her husband. "When you walked through that door, it was like an answered prayer." By now her shaking had subsided.

Gently he cradled her face in his calloused hands and kissed her softly on the lips. "As long as I'm alive I'll protect you and my family with every ounce of energy I have," he vowed in a low whispered voice. "You need never fear of losing me, Doris Chronister Whelan. I'm still as much in love with you today as I was that magical moment eighteen years ago when I fell head over heels for you. And I don't think I'll ever fall out. With you, that would be an impossible feat."

Hand in hand, the two walked across the kitchen floor, turned out the lights and climbed the steps to their bedroom on the second floor. Lying down across the bed on top of the covers, they continued holding each other tightly. Finally Doris released her hold, turned and cuddled up into her husband's strong arms. As they fell into a deep sleep, partially from physical and as well as mental exhaustion, the same thought crossed their minds. What might have happened, had cooler heads not prevailed.

Crazy Eyes and Tattoo sat staring out the cave entrance at the pouring rain. "Could be worse," muttered Tattoo. "At least we's in the dry an' outta the rain." By now the clothes on their backs had been dried by the fire and their supper of roast rabbit satisfied them for the evening.

"Tomorrow we try again fer the loot, an' depending on how we do, survey the area an' maybe advance a little at a time," Crazy Eyes said to his partner. "An', Tattoo, the more I think 'bout it, the more I like yer idea of backtracking. The cops'd never suspect it, that is as long as we don't run into 'em."

"No more killings, buddy," Tattoo insisted. "The robberies I can take. The killings I'm having lot o' trouble with."

"Hey, hey," Crazy Eyes warned Tattoo, slapping him across the cheeks to bring him to his senses. "What's happenin' here? Ya going a bit soft on me? Yer in this mess deep as I am, ol' buddy," he reminded his younger comrade in crime. "Now's not the time ta let a little thing like a conscience git the better of ya. Ya fink out on me now an' run ta the cops," Crazy Eyes emphasized, jabbing his partner in the chest with his pointer finger, "I'll hunt ya down like the double crossing, stinkin', smelly polecat my other professional acquaintances always said ya was."

"Hey," Tattoo shot back, returning the jab to Crazy Eyes, "I said I didn't mind the stealin'. I juss don't think it was necessary ta kill that old couple in cold blood. They gived us their money, didn't they? If we's ever caught, they already got us fer armed robbery. Why we gotta have a murder rap hanging on our heads, too? Huh?" It was one of the few times the silent one of the two ever spoke up to the bigger guy.

Crazy Eyes was taken aback at the assertiveness of his partner. Seeing he was determined to stay his ground, he decided for now he'd drop the subject and try getting some sleep. There was no need to antagonize Tattoo any more than he already had, especially right before bedtime. It was hard enough sleeping on the cold, hard, ground of the cave, let alone doing it with one eye open while watching your back with the other.

Crazy Eyes had always believed that the hitting of those two old folks with a two by four was a moot issue. To him, the old couple was dead. While it was an unfortunate happenstance and he was remorseful, he couldn't do a thing about it now. Besides, it had happened last month. Crazy Eyes had always believed that life was meant for living in the present, for looking toward the future and certainly not dwelling on the past.

From deep in the back of the cave, near a rock formation, Crazy Eyes thought he saw something move in the iridescent shadows of the dying campfire. He stood up, gun in one hand and long heavy piece of wood in the other to investigate. When he was satisfied nothing was there, he passed it off as tricks the light from the flickering campfire was playing on his eyes and picked up more wood for the fire.

Within minutes the campfire was ablaze again, producing sufficient heat for the two criminals, and anything else that might be wandering throughout the cave. Crazy Eyes looked at Tattoo and saw him sleeping, his snores becoming louder with each breath. Then he laid his head down on the ground, and with the revolver in his right hand, the large club of wood in his other, he closed his eyes. It was past midnight. He had better get some sleep.

Tomorrow was already here.

Chapter 16

A chilly mist hung over the valley early that morning as if the area was in the clutches of a low hanging cloud. Jack walked to the bedroom window looking north toward the Barnes' farm. By his nightstand he turned on the black Arvin table radio very softly so as not to awaken his wife. The weatherman was calling for clearer skies and sunshine toward noon. He wasn't sure whether to believe it or not. After all, rarely was the weatherman ever right in the spring of 1951.

Jack dressed and started the chores Pepper normally did. When he finished, he loaded the wood bin with an ample supply, putting fresh wood in the stove in preparation for cooking breakfast. He climbed the stairs once more, waking his wife and finally the three school children. Little David remained in bed until after the rest had left for school.

Since Crab Cake was not available to tend to his daily responsibilities, that of escorting the children to and from the school bus stop, Jack decided he would drive them to the old White Oak School house and pick them up in the afternoon, at least until better arrangements could be made. It even crossed his mind to keep the children home a day or two, but the better of the two minds prevailed. "Let's not let them think it was any worse than it was, Honey," whispered Doris after getting up. "The best thing for them is to keep their minds occupied. There's no better way to do that than with schoolwork."

At breakfast, Doris wrote a note to Pepper's teacher, explaining his absence. No excuses were used. Only the truth, that he was spending time with his critically ill dog at the animal hospital in York. Sealing it in a white envelope, she handed it to Tyrone, with instructions to deliver it personally to Mr. Rohrbaugh. Among the boys and girls in the family, there had always existed a certain sibling rivalry. So naturally Ty's chest swelled with pride when he was handed the note. Instead of his sisters, his mother had finally trusted him with a document of great importance.

Tattoo opened his eyes first. The fire had just about gone out. Looking first at Crazy Eyes, who was still snoring, he turned around, in search for dry wood. Noticing a pile toward the back of the cave, near an accumulation of rock, he walked back. With his bare hands Tattoo reached down and grabbed five chunks of dry oak. A sneaky serpent, not seen before by the quiet criminal, slithered out from behind the clump of rocks and continued through the arch of his legs, resting abruptly on a piece of wood. Tattoo froze.

The snake turned toward the bad guy and hissed, sticking out his tongue and waving it every which way. Tattoo, remembering that snakes have poor eyesight, knew enough to stay still. Snakes do not see clearly. They sense the direction of their prey from its motion. Carefully he glanced at his unwanted visitor. It wasn't a copperhead. He knew what they looked like. Then he heard the rattle. An eastern rattler! *More venomous than a copperhead*, he thought. *Just remain calm and don't move.*

The snake moved about between Tattoo's legs, turning one way and then the other, searching for motion which would indicate its enemy. Suddenly a loud bang caused Tattoo to jump. There was Crazy Eyes standing behind Tattoo with a large piece of wood in his right hand. Tattoo looked down. The snake was gone. "Snakes! Hate 'em," Crazy Eyes yelled, drawing back the weapon. "I think I glanced it off the head," he said. "Shoulda hit it head on."

"Let's not wait 'round ta find out," Tattoo insisted. "I came back ta get some wood fer the dying fire an' end up confronting a rattler. I'd sooner face an army of state policemen. I s'pose I owe ya one, ol' buddy. But fer now, let's make tracks an' leave this den o' snakes."

The two crooks walked to the front, put new wood on the fire and sat between the fire and the entrance. Looking out at the cold, misty morning before them, they thought about which way they'd head when the sun warms up the air and after they've tried once again to retrieve the loot. Crazy Eyes wanted to backtrack. Tattoo did too, yesterday. But now, after having to have dealt with Mr. Slithers, he wanted desperately to just continue onward toward the river.

The only thing they seemed to agree on was that they did not want any more confrontations with snakes, poisonous or otherwise.

A gentle hand shook Pepper. The nurse stopped by, checking up on the patient. "He ain't moved since I been here," Pepper whispered, as if he didn't want to wake Crab Cake from a much needed sleep. "Ya sure he's still alive?" he asked, holding back sobs.

The nurse held a stethoscope to the dog's chest, listening for a heart beat. "He's still hanging in there, Pepper," she said. "He's quite a trooper. As long as he doesn't give up," she assured him, "neither can we. If he does come around, he's going to need us here, especially you."

"I read where a copperhead's poisonous but not 'nough to kill a person," Pepper said. "Their bite s'posedly juss makes you sick. Why'd it affect Crab Cake so hard?"

"You need to understand, Pepper," the doctor answered before his nurse had a chance. He had just entered the area, and neither had heard him come in. "What they're talking about is an adult. A person under 75 pounds can easily die from a copperhead bite. A large adult usually gets very sick," the doctor explained. "Crab Cake only weighs about 40 pounds. So the venom had a worse affect on him than it would have had on a St. Bernard dog," the doctor said gently to the young lad.

"Also, when a human is bitten, nine out of ten times an X is cut over the fang marks and much of the venom is sucked out," the vet continued. "This helps prevent serious reactions and also aids in the adult recovering faster. That wasn't done for Crab Cake, so his reaction was much more severe than it would have been if it had been done."

"How long ya think he'll be here, Doctor?" asked Pepper. "I ain't gotta lot o' money saved, but I'll give ya what I have, and if you let me, I'll pay ya off soon's I get it. I juss don't wanna lose Crab Cake," he pleaded. The sobs were coming faster. Pepper tried to hold them back but lost out to his emotions.

"Let's not worry about that," the doctor reassured him. "First things, first, son. Right now it's more important for Crab Cake to get well." The words rang in Pepper's ears like beautiful soft symphony music. "When your dog recovers and goes home, then you and I will sit down and come to an agreement like refined, civilized gentlemen. I'd even be receptive to having you work here to pay the bill. But we'll discuss that later," he said as he left the immediate area.

Pepper bowed his head to say another prayer, that of thanks that Crab Cake was still alive. A second prayer asked once again for Crab Cake's quick recovery. And a third one asked Him to bless the good doctor. Besides, if he works off the bill, maybe he'll give him a part time summer job. Pepper would love that.

Pepper felt a slight bit of pressure against his right arm. He opened his eyes and noticed Crab Cake's forepaw was resting against it. Did the dog move? Is he responding to the anti-venom serum? Is this a sign of good things to come? Did the Almighty give Pepper a sign that Crab Cake would come around? Would the dog be able to come home with him within a week or so?

A plethora of questions ran rapidly through the young lad's mind. His level of hope was higher now than it had been since the dog was bitten. Then realizing his optimism, he softly muttered, "Maybe it was juss *my* arm that moved against *his* paw."

He looked at his faithful friend lying on the table motionless, his breathing shallow, fighting with every ounce of the life force within him in order to survive. Pepper laid his head down on his arms and closed his eyes once more. Soon he was off again to dreamland where he relived the many good times he and Crab Cake had had together.

The sun broke from out amongst a bank of dark clouds, giving Crazy Eyes and Tattoo a window of opportunity, one that would enable them to continue their getaway. After searching in vain for the "buried" loot box one more time, the two men gave up, realizing they could no longer hang around for fear of being recognized.

Surely by now their mugs were on the front page of all the local papers. They needed to escape the area and then when things settled down, return during one of the warmer summer months to retrieve the treasure.

Leaving the cave, they climbed to the top of the wooded hill. Staying high along the ridge and hidden by the trees, the two wanted hoodlums made their way back from where they came. As they approached old Amos Springler's home, the retired barn painter was sitting on a dilapidated stuffed chair that was reeking from the mildew of spilt beer and resting near the edge of his front porch. Amos was in about the same state of inebriation you could usually find him in this time of the day. After all, he had been drinking since he woke up early in the morning.

Crazy Eyes and Tattoo spotted him taking a nip from his flask from high along the ridge in the woods. Descending the hill toward the Springler homestead, they noticed Old Shep. As they approached, the nearly blind dog slowly made his way back to Amos, growling at the two criminals in a low tone.

"Whatsha matta, ol' boy?" Amos slurred. He looked toward the direction the dog was pointed, but was too far sloshed to focus on any one thing. "We gonna (hic) have com (hic) pany for su… su… supper (hic)?" He struggled in asking his faithful old friend. Old Shep gave one loud bark, then lay down on the porch along side his master's feet.

The two would be murderers slowly approached the porch, eyeing the dog ever so carefully. Finally they came into Amos Springler's focus. "Gennelmen," Amos muttered with much carefulness, nodding his head and tipping his dirty old feed mill cap while acknowledging their presence. "If dere's anyting (hic) dat Ol' Shep an' me can do fer ya (hic), chust let us know, ain't dat right, (hic) old buddy?" he asked the dog, patting it on the head.

Crazy Eyes and Tattoo could not believe their luck. Here they were, not knowing which way to go, and stumbling across this drunken stumble bum with a blind dog. They would be remiss in their professional duties of self preservation if they didn't take him up on his offer. After all, the last thing the two crooks wanted to do was to insult the good nature of the local populace.

"Ya shore could, ol' timer," said Tattoo, taking in the sight of the drunken septuagenarian. "Our car broke down an' we's on our way to a garage fer help. Ya think ya could give us a lift?"

"I guess yer in luck, (hic) gennelmen. My neighbor just pulled the (hic) truck outtuva ditch after trying ta help two boys and a dog yesterday. She's a runnin' (hic) mighty fine now. So shtep right this (hic) way, fellers," he slurred. "Ol' Zelda'll be mighty happy ta (hic) 'commodate you where ever it is yer goin'." He pointed to the same truck that hauled Pepper, Thursy and Crab Cake less than 24 hours earlier, the very one in which he thought of so highly.

In no time flat, the four were motoring down the road in Ol' Zelda. Crazy Eyes sitting on the outside, Tattoo on the middle, Old Shep in the back cargo bed and Amos Springler behind the wheel, driving down the narrow dirt roads like a drunken maniac, which, of course, he was.

For a brief moment, the two crooks wished they were back in the company of the poisonous eastern rattler.

Chapter 17

Jack Whelan drove his three children to the school bus stop at the old White Oak School House. With Ty's help, his father had finished the chores Pepper did every day. Before they left for school that morning, Doris Whelan hugged each child tightly, whispering softly in their ears that she loved them. "Listen to your father an' make sure all three of ya behave yourselves," she reminded them.

"And stay together," Doris added. "Each of you always watch out for the others," she said. "There's gonna be a lot of questions your schoolmates are gonna be asking ya. If you're not sure of the answers, juss say, 'I don't know.' There's nothing wrong with not knowing," she reminded them. "That's why we're always learning."

While the previous evening's incident had happened too fast to make the morning papers, it was sure to appear in the evening York Dispatch. Already it was on the morning radio news. With few television sets in homes, save for the Pattersons and Haneys, it was unlikely anyone in the area would have seen it on TV. Besides newspapers, the biggest form of communication in the community was word of mouth. That, of course, and with anyone having a telephone.

Jack dropped the kids off at the old White Oak School house and waited until the bus arrived. As soon as other students spotted the Whelan children, they wanted to know first hand what all happened. "Were you in great danger?" asked one. "What did they look like?" asked another. "Is Pepper and Crab Cake okay?" asked the third. "I heard Pepper, Crab Cake and Thursy were shot and won't make it and that they're all three in the same hospital now. Is that why they're not here today?" The questions from the imaginations of their young schoolmates were endless.

Suddenly Thursy showed up. He had gotten a much later start than usual but still he had gotten close enough to hear the ongoing conversation. "Do I look like I's shot?" he asked. "Do I look like I'm in the hospital wit' Pepper an' Crab Cake? Huh? Do I look like I ain't here today?"

Instantly, a crowd of country school students gathered around the young lad, wanting to know all about the adventures he had gone through yesterday. Thursy was elated. Never in his wildest dreams did he ever think he'd be this popular. The young lad, who was considered by many of his classmates to be an outcast and even a dullard only last week, was now basking in his glory.

"One question at a time, please," he insisted. "One at a time." To whether they were shot, he answered, "Almost. Had I not gotten my pocket knife out and cut the ropes to escape, we'd probably have been shot to smithereens by now." As to what they looked like, Thursy answered, "Meanest lookin' hombres I ever did see in my life. Meaner lookin' than that notorious pirate, Blackbeard. The one we learnt about in school? Both of those criminals yesterday looked like the devil himself."

As to whether they were in great danger, he answered without skipping a beat, "Danger was so great, both our lives passed swiftly in front o' each others eyes." With every question, Thursy was embellishing each answer, and loving it.

Of course the girls were taking all this in. The older boys suspected correctly that Thursy was milking his adventure for all it was worth and the younger kids just stood there agape, staring at their newly found hero. Jack Whelan just chuckled. *The lad went through more than anyone would ever expect a young boy to go through*, he thought. *Might as well let him enjoy it.*

Then another question was posed to Thursy. "Where's Crab Cake?" asked a smaller boy. "I heard he went along fishing with you guys and was killed by a giant rainbow trout."

Very unexpectedly, Thursy became serious. "Had it not been for that dog," he spoke in a somber voice, "Pepper and I would probably not be alive today."

From inside the old Ford sedan, Jack rolled down his side window and listened as Thursy stopped joking long enough to tell the story of how Crab Cake saved Pepper and him, mostly him, from the deadly fangs of the poisonous copperhead snake. "Right now, he's at the York Animal Hospital on South Queen Street. He's in critical condition, and," he sighed, "he may not make it. Pepper's with him now. Please say a big prayer that he pulls through."

As the bus pulled up to the stop, and the kids boarded, Thursy turned from his captive audience so they wouldn't see him wipe the moisture from his eyes on his long sleeved, plaid, cotton flannel shirt.

Along the way, as the bus traveled the narrow and winding dirt road, it was halted by an accident. All the students went to the right side of the bus, peering out the window, and saw a very old beat up pickup truck lying upside down deep in a ravine. It had turned over and landed on its top sometime during the middle of the night. The police were there now, directing traffic and securing the area for an investigation.

They had checked out the registration and already knew the vintage truck belonged to old Amos Springler. Earlier in the morning a neighborhood motorist reported seeing an incredibly old collie dog whimpering and walking slowly with a heavy limp down the road toward the Springler residence. Amos Springler was no where to be found. Ol' Shep, deaf, blind and with arthritis, now seemed to be all alone.

"Ya can't 'spect me to keep up wit ya wit a wounded leg," the drunken, retired barn painter told Crazy Eyes and Tattoo. By now the booze was wearing off and in its place a massive headache was forming.

"The only reason yer still alive," Crazy Eyes shot back, "is 'cause my partner's taken a shinin' to ya. He's also taken a leave o' his good, criminal common senses. He's turnin' soft is what he's doin'. Been listenin' to his heart 'stead o' his head. An' that bleedin' heart o' his has issued you a reprieve," he said. Then using his finger to emphasize each word, he continued, "But soon's I straighten him out, you's history. If ya had kept all o' the truck on all o' the road, 'stead o' juss half the truck on half the road, we wouldn't be in the predicament we's in now. So don't gimme none of yer drunken' lip, ya 'nebriated bum."

"Let him go," Tattoo asked of Crazy Eyes. "Let him go. He's more trouble'n he's worth an' he's holding up our progress. 'Sides, he's nuttin' but a town drunk. Regardless o' what he says, who's gonna believe him?"

"I listened to ya when ya insisted not ta kill him," Crazy Eyes shouted at Tattoo. His eyes were getting wild. Now he was demanding, "Ya hear me good, Tattoo. He's gonna serve us good as a hostage if it's needed. This soused up stumble bum'll go free only when I says he goes free, no sooner an' no later."

"But my dog, Ol' Shep," pleaded Amos, "who's gonna feed an' water 'im? He needs me." Amos was almost on his knees begging. Like an apologetic, repentant alcoholic the morning after, the thought of losing his faithful companion left him remorseful for having imbibed so many alcoholic drinks over such a short period of time.

The three were now at the top of the hill, near the back woods that separate Haney's farm from Whelan's. Staying inside the tree line, they kept low and moved eastward toward Patterson's. The plan was to cross the dirt road and head up the hill, the very same hill they used the night before that was covered with outcroppings of rock. They figured the cops were elsewhere looking for them, and even if they weren't, they knew the police couldn't track them there. They were successful the night before because of that very reason and the odds of a repeated success were in their favor.

Once they were back deep into the woods, they'd release Amos. With his injured leg, it'd take him forever to seek help and by that time the two would be out of the area.

Slowly the three continued, crossing the road, climbing the wooded hill and staying hidden in amongst the trees along the top of the ridge, giving them the advantage of seeing below. Upon reaching Chet Cline's house, they noticed two horses standing in the fields.

"Pssst! Tattoo," whispered Crazy Eyes. "Ya ever ride a horse?"

"Not for 'bout ten years," answered the younger of the two, "but I used to ride them alla time."

"Well, yer 'bout to ride 'em again, ol' buddy," said Crazy Eyes. "Ya think ya could check the barn for coupla saddles and whatever else it takes to ride 'em?"

"Why only a couple saddles, Crazy Eyes?" Tattoo queried, looking confused as if he didn't hear him right. "There's three o' us."

"Because there's only two horses down there in the field, you numbskull." Crazy Eyes was beginning to wonder if they'd ever make it out of the valley with what he considered to be idiots.

"Well, what about him?" he asked, pointing directly to Amos, who by now was resting on the ground waiting for the two criminals to finalize their latest plans.

"Just get the two saddles and whatever else is needed. I'll handle him," the goofy eyed one said. "Now go, an' for Pete's sake, be careful. Stay low."

"If he ain't here when I get back, Crazy Eyes," insisted Tattoo, "you's on yer own. Ya can go yer own way an' I'll go my separate way. Like I said last night, Crazy Eyes, I'm through wit' the killings."

It was the second time in as many days Tattoo stood up for what he believed. Crazy Eyes knew he needed him not only for companionship, but more importantly to get out of the woods and on the road to freedom. After all, regardless of his shortcomings, Tattoo did have a pretty good sense of direction. The goofy eyed one of the two decided to play his partner's hand, at least for a while. The time was not quite right to make a scene. There'd be plenty opportunities for that. Right now, they needed transportation, any kind of transportation. They needed it pronto and they needed to rid themselves of the drunk.

It was late on the Tuesday afternoon after Monday's opening day of trout season when the bus pulled up to the old White Oak School House. Dropping the kids off from the first day back at school, the adventures of the past twenty-four hours were on the tip of everyone's tongue. It was the only topic heavily discussed among the students. Simply stated, they spoke of nothing else. Consequently, Mr. Rohrbaugh had turned the subject into an open forum and had allowed all seven grades to talk openly about the previous day's exciting events.

Jack Whelan stopped across the road from the bus stop, waiting for his children. He had taken time off from his job to make sure they would be safe returning home. Thursy also rode with the Whelans as far as his home.

"How's Crab Cake, Dad?" were the first words out of young Ty's mouth. "Is he gonna make it?"

"I haven't been in to check his progress yet, son. Pepper's still with him," his dad answered. "As soon as supper's over, I'll be driving in to get a first hand report."

"He's a tough hombre, isn't he, Dad?" Ty was using a word to describe Crab Cake which he had heard over the past two days and was looking for any sign of hope that the family pet would survive. But in his wisdom, his father refused to give the young lad false hope.

"He's a medium size dog, Ty," Jack Whelan told his son. Knowing it would be harder on the children if the dog passed away after telling them he was doing fine when he wasn't, his father would not sugarcoat reality. Jack also recognized that the death of any living being is as much a part of life as it is to actually live, and without crushing their hopes, just like adults, children need to accept it.

"Crab Cake took a pretty big shot of poison, Ty," he told his son while driving home along the dirt road. "No cuts were made in his paw to drain that poison. And since he's only a medium size dog, his system took quite a jolt. Even if he does survive, he could end up disabled for life. If that's the case, the best we could possibly do for Crab Cake is to put him to sleep."

The little boy could no longer hold back the tears. While Crab Cake followed Pepper everywhere, the Border Collie was just as friendly to Ty as well as the other children.

The vintage Whelan Ford pulled into Patterson's driveway, leaving out Thursy. "See you guys tomorrow," Thursy said as he exited the car and ran for the back door of his home.

Before backing out and heading down the road toward home, Jack paused for a moment to wrap his arms around his young son, who by now had large tears sliding down his cheeks. This was just too much trauma for the little seven-year-old tyke to take. He had never known death before, and the thought of losing Crab Cake sounded traumatic.

"If Crab Cake doesn't make it, son," Jack assured him, "it won't be the end of the world. We'll all just have to stick together and help each other over this terrible bump in the road. But, I promise, we *will* make it, son. We have to. We're Whelans."

"If Crab Cake dies, Dad," Ty asked, "will he go to heaven?"

This one caught Jack Whelan completely off guard. What does he say to an almost eight-year-old who asks him a question like that. He doesn't want to tell him animals have no soul. That would be cruel to such a small and innocent young boy. Jack knew he had to think fast and he had to answer with confidence. Otherwise, if he stumbles, Ty may not believe him.

"Son," Jack began, "God made you and me, and everyone else in this world in his image and likeness. You learned that in Sunday School. And He made almost all things good, including animals. Well, I've never heard anything bad about dogs, have you? For the most part, they do a pretty good job helping us, don't you agree?" he asked, trying to draw Ty into the conversation with him.

Ty nodded his head yes, while sniffing a drippy nose, probably caused by his emotions getting the better of him, and lifting his sleeve to his eye, wiped it from the excess tears. He was starting to feel somewhat better. Conversations with his father had a way of doing that, even if it was only one way.

"Well, son, if we like animals, and we're made in God's image and likeness, stands to reason He must like animals too, you see?" Jack said softly to little Ty. "So, if that's the case, why would anyone be surprised if Crab Cake, who has always been a good dog for us, ends up in Heaven if he dies? I don't know about you, but I think it's pretty hard to imagine a heaven with all those people and no dogs or horses."

Ty agreed, and sniffing once more, he wiped his nose and eyes with his sleeve, looked up at his father and said, "Thanks, Dad. I feel better."

With his left foot, Ty's Father depressed the clutch of the old Ford, shifted the gear into reverse and started backing out of Patterson's driveway. An unseen voice called out, "Mr. Whelan, Mr. Whelan."

Out of the back door and down the steps ran Thursy as fast as his legs could carry him. Almost out of breath and trying to stop the car before it drove off out of sight, he called again for Ty's dad. "Mr. Whelan, stop. Please stop," he called, waving his hands in a panicky manner. "There's a phone call. It's for you, sir. It's the animal hospital."

Jack Whelan stopped abruptly, engaged the car in reverse gear, backed up to the driveway and pulled in. After drawing the emergency brake and turning off the engine, he exited the automobile and slowly climbed the side steps to the Patterson's back door. Upon entering the kitchen Thursy directed him to the phone in the dining room. "This is Jack Whelan," he said answering the call. "Yes... uh huh... yes. Well that's too bad. May I speak with him? Thank you." He lifted the receiver away from his mouth, rested it against him chest and took a long sigh.

"Pepper," he started. "I'm terribly sorry about the bad news." Jack himself was beginning to choke. What an awful burden, he thought, to have to tell the children what's happening. "Just hang in there, son," Jack said. "Everything's gonna be okay. I'll be in right after supper."

After Jack Whelan hung up the receiver, he thanked Thursy for stopping him. The neighborhood boy surmised what was happening. "Thursy," said Jack Whelan, "if you write a note and leave it for your parents so they know where you are, you may join us for supper and then ride along in to the hospital afterward. It might be better for Pepper to have a friend with him at a time like this."

"Is Crab Cake gone, Mr. Whelan?" asked the young lad. "I certainly hope not."

"So do I, Thursy. So do I," answered Pepper's dad. "But according to the doctor, all hope is gone."

It was now just a matter of time.

Chapter 18

As the sun made its way across the sky toward the western horizon, Crazy Eyes and Amos waited just inside the tree line of the woods for the return of Tattoo. "What could be takin' him so long?" Crazy Eyes asked Amos. But the old man was snoring away, catching a late afternoon siesta on the dead leaves of last fall.

"Wake up, you drunken stumblebum," demanded Crazy Eyes, kicking him in the side. "What makes ya think ya can catch shut eye while I gotta stay awake an' hafta worry so much, huh?"

Amos woke up with a jolt. He tried to stand but his leg was much too swollen. He hadn't eaten for the past twenty-four hours and was noticing hunger pangs. His truck was destroyed, his dog was missing and on top of that, he smelled strongly from poor hygiene habits. Belatedly, he decided it was the last time he would ever give anyone a lift in his truck.

Tattoo appeared over the horizon, crossing the field near the fence row. Across one shoulder was a saddle. Across the other was another. Slung over the saddles was other equipment necessary in the riding of a horse. He had first made his way to the woods by way of the fence row and then, under cover of the trees, moved south toward the other two.

"What in the name of a good, home, pan fried chicken dinner took ya so long?" demanded Crazy Eyes. It was evident he was suffering from hunger pangs. "Ya been gone mos' o' the afternoon," he reminded his partner. "If I didn't know ya any better I'da thought ya grabbed yerself a bite ta eat 'fore takin' off an' leavin' us behind an' all alone ta fend fer ourselves."

"You blind, Crazy Eyes?" Tattoo shot back. "Ya see these two saddles an' all this other equipment you wanted? Huh? Well, these ain't made o' bird fedders, ya know. They's heavy. 'Sides," he continued, "I had ta wait pret near the whole morning 'til alls clear 'fore I could make my move," he explained.

"An' then I had ta move uphill carrying this load a little at a time. Couldn't carry it all at once. Ya knowd I ain't no spring rooster no more," he reminded his partner. "An' you ain't neither. It might do well if we just take our time every now an' then. I'ma lookin' ta git outta here, not hangin' 'round permanent from droppin' over wit a heart attack."

"Never mind," said Crazy Eyes. "We gotta lot o' work ta do. Walk down

141

'long that fence row again an' slip these bits over 'em two nags. Make sure yer not seen. Stay low, and then lead 'em up here inta the woods."

Reluctantly, Tattoo followed his orders. When he had the two horses in the woods, Crazy Eyes told him to saddle them up. "I'll do mine," said Tattoo. "You do yers."

"You'll do both yers an' mine," ordered Crazy Eyes sternly. "An' you'll be quick 'bout it. We's wastin' too much time now as it is, justa sittin' here in this spot an' waitin' on you."

"I'll do my own," insisted Tattoo. "I'm tired o' bein' bossed 'round by you every time sumpin' gots ta be done. We s'posed ta be partners, but all ya ever do is yell, yell, yell an' order me 'round like I's one o' 'em nags. Man, Crazy Eyes," Tattoo admonished, "ya show more 'spect fer 'em 'ere nags than ya do fer yer own partner. Here, saddle yer own horse," he said, tossing the other saddle toward Crazy Eyes.

Crazy Eyes just stood there staring at Tattoo. The saddle lay at his feet. "Well, git busy," said Tattoo. "Whatsa matta? Don't ya even know how ta saddle a horse?"

Crazy Eyes continued staring at Tattoo. He actually looked as though he were embarrassed. "N-n-n-not really, ol' b-b-b-buddy," he stammered. Then very politely he asked, "Do y-y-y-ya think you c-c-c-could help me?"

Tattoo immediately stopped what he was doing to absorb his partner's answer. Then he started chuckling slowly until the more he thought about it, the funnier it became. He did everything in his power to keep from laughing heartily and embarrassing Crazy Eyes, but to no avail. Finally he let loose. Tattoo was cackling so hard the tears were rolling off his cheeks.

"Ya sent me alla way down 'ere fer saddles an' horses," he said, pointing to the meadow in the distance, "juss sos we can exscape an' ya don't even know how ta saddle them?" he questioned between laughs. "Next ya gonna be tellin' me ya never ridden a horse," he continued, still laughing at the irony of it.

"Not really, ol' b-b-b-buddy," he stammered again. "I rode one of 'em horses in a carnival once when I's a kid," he said, rather upbeat.

This time Tattoo really tried not to, but just couldn't control himself. He was laughing so hard he dropped to the ground and rolled. Even Amos joined in the laughter but due to the after affects of his hangover, really had no idea why he was laughing. He just decided he'd join the party.

"Crazy Eyes," asked Tattoo, wiping the tears he was shedding from his eyes, "juss how ya pr'pose ta ride that horse if ya only ever been on one fifty years ago, an' that'n, a tied up carnival pony 'at walks 'round in circles?"

"Ya can teach me, Tattoo," he answered. "Here, help me in the saddle an' take that rope," he said, referring to the rein while walking over to the horse, "then lead the way. As we move 'long, an' I git more comfortable wit' it, I'll work the ropes myself," he added. "After all, it can't be that hard ta ride a horse."

"Reins, not ropes, buddy," he said as he helped Crazy Eyes onto the horse and put both his feet into the stirrups, "it's reins." Tattoo gave Crazy Eyes one rein while he took the other after boosting Amos on behind him. He mounted his own nag and led the way. Setting out for the deep woods, the three remained inside the fence row for quite a distance. In time they were high on the hill overlooking Amos Springler's homestead.

"We's leavin' ya off here, ol' man," said Crazy Eyes. "Consider yerself lucky. Go on home an' if ya mention ta juss one soul that ya was wit' us, or even that ya saw us, we'll hunt you an' that blind mutt of yers down an' kill ya both. An' that, ya lucky drunk's a promise. Now git."

Crazy Eyes pushed Amos off the saddle and onto the ground. Standing up, he could barely walk but as the two moved away, they saw his blind, deaf dog gradually ascend the hill as Amos slowly hobbled down toward his house. The dog, being downwind, had picked up its owner's scent. Turning around, Amos saw the two take off at a swift pace for deep into the woods. He hoped he'd never see them again.

Upon meeting up with his dog, he sat down and put his arms around Ol' Shep, hugging him gently. The aged Collie licked Amos Springler's face and wagged his tail enthusiastically. The dog reacted as if it was the first display of compassion he had received in quite a long time.

When Amos finally made it to his house, he poured a fresh dish of spring water and a full plate of food for Ol' Shep. For himself he opened one of many beers he would enjoy that night. After all he had gone through, Amos Springler felt he had earned them.

The door to the special room where Crab Cake lay swung open. Pepper ran to his father and hugged him. "I prayed, Dad. I really did. I prayed real hard. Why didn't God answer my prayers?"

"Perhaps He's not finished yet, son," his father answered. "But even if He is, and the result is somewhat different than what we request, ... well, believe me, Pepper, because what we ask for doesn't always materialize, that doesn't mean He doesn't hear us or that He's not answering our prayers."

"We've done just about everything we could for Crab Cake, Mr. Whelan," the doctor told Jack. "He's just not responding. It's been more than twenty-four hours since this dog was bitten and usually if a canine this size doesn't respond within that period of time, there's not much more we can do. Rarely do they ever make it."

"Well, you tried, Doctor," said Jack, feeling somewhat guilty himself because he was starting to give up. "You gave it everything you had, and we appreciate your efforts. What do you suggest the next step would be?"

"That's entirely up to you, Mr. Whelan," the doctor replied. "But because the dog hasn't even moved since he got here, I think you might want to consider putting Crab Cake to sleep. It would certainly be the most humane thing to do."

"Is the dog in pain, Doctor?" asked Jack. "Is he writhing in pain from the poison?"

"Oh no," answered the vet. "I didn't mean to imply that. It's just that …well… economically… your bill could start adding up. I know you have a family and having had one myself, I understand they do take top priority. If you'd like, you may step into my office to sign papers authorizing me as your veterinarian to perform euthanasia on Crab Cake," he suggested. "You might want to consider this, Mr. Whelan. In the final analysis, it could end up being easier on everyone. Certainly much easier all around," he said, discreetly giving a nod of his head toward Pepper.

Jack looked compassionately at his son. He couldn't understand why the lad had to endure so much emotional pain in so short a time as he has had to do this week. A full stream of tears was now descending both of Pepper's cheeks. He knew his father was obligated to do what he didn't want to do. Pepper looked at his dad and nodded his head as if he understood. He bent down and hugged his dog, knowing it was near to the very last time he'd ever see him again. Then he stood up and rushed to his father's waiting arms.

Jack finally slipped quietly out of the room to join the doctor in his office. Thursy followed him, leaving Pepper all alone in the room with Crab Cake, a dying Border Collie and his best friend.

The dog was lying on his side, facing his master. Again, Pepper moved closer to the bedding, this time laying his head down next to the dog's and gently resting his arm across Crab Cake's body. "We've had so many good times together," he whispered to him, tears still streaming down his cheeks. He knew the end was very near.

"How am I ever gonna forget ya, Crab Cake? Huh? Remember flushing out all them ring-necked pheasants, rabbits an' other game whenever we'd go hunting?" he asked, knowing full well the dog, in the condition he was in, had no chance of ever hearing him. "Shore didn't take ya long ta learn ya don't corner skunks," he softly whispered, this time chuckling lightly as he remembered Crab Cake once being sprayed by a skunk he was chasing. "Crab Cake," he added, "you stunk for a week.

"I'm never gonna forget the time ya thought you'd caught that big ol' fat groundhog. The way he turned on ya, brought tears to my eyes, I was laughing so hard. I can still see ya hightailing it outta that field, yelping to beat the band with yer tail jus a flopping 'tween yer legs," Pepper continued, trying to implant within his mind an indelible memory of all the good times he had with his dog.

"I'll remember every one of 'em, ol' buddy, 'specially you chasing that big ol' beautiful, gorgeous rainbow trout downstream yesterday and tangling every fishing line on both sides of the creek. Sure I yelled at ya, Crab Cake," he sobbed, "but you know I really didn't mean nuttin' by it, don't you?"

His face was now buried deep into the fur of his dog. A very slight thump on the bedding was felt. Pepper just lay there, holding onto Crab Cake with all the love he could muster.

"I'm gonna miss ya whenever I dig worms again, Crab Cake," he whispered again. "Who's gonna help me? An' fishing ain't never gonna be the same again."

Once more a slight thump was felt.

Pepper looked up and stared at his dog. He surveyed Crab Cake's motionless body laying there before him. He saw nothing out of the ordinary that might have changed over the past twenty-four hours. Now standing and looking down at him, and resting his hand on Crab Cake's head, he said, "An' it ain't never gonna be the same walkin' ta meet the school bus or comin' home without ya there protecting us."

This time the thump was stronger than before. This time the young lad knew it was not his imagination. This time Pepper saw Crab Cake's tail lift up and drop back onto the bedding, a signal that told him there was still hope for his dog.

"Dad," Pepper screamed. "Doctor! Thursy! Come quick! Hurry!" He raced from the room where his faithful friend lay, to the doctor's office where his father was having a conference with the vet. "Dad, don't sign those papers ta put Crab Cake ta sleep yet," he pled. "He moved, Dad. He moved. C'mon. Take a look. There's still hope, Dad," he continued, pleading with tears of joy streaming down both cheeks. "There's still hope! Crab Cake moved!"

Rushing into the room where the dog lay, with Pepper leading the way and

Thursy following closely behind, the four stood looking at the dog, his eyes still closed and breathing as shallow as before. To them there was no change in the condition of Crab Cake. Surely what Pepper had seen was nothing more than an involuntary muscle reaction. That, or wishful thinking, his father suspected. Shaking his head, Jack Whelan put his hand on his son's shoulder before turning to leave the room for the doctor's office with the others.

"Crab Cake," Pepper whispered softly, as the young lad bent down and snuggled his face against his dog's. "Crab Cake? It's me, Pepper, your ol' buddy."

Whomp! The dog's tail lifted once again then dropped back down onto the metal table.

This time all four heard the sound. Turning back the three stood agape, staring in disbelief as Crab Cake opened his eyes ever so slightly and with his cold tongue, planted a wet one smack dab on Pepper's lips.

In time the young lad would change his mind, but until then, it was by far the best kiss he had ever received.

Chapter 19

For the third time in two days, Crazy Eyes and Tattoo approached the entrance to the cave. It seemed as if they just couldn't shake that habitat. Dismounting their steeds, they led the horses inside, tying them up near the entrance.

After gathering dry firewood, Tattoo lit a fire and the two sat, pondering their next move. Supper would have been nice but tonight, no rabbits were nearby. Not all was lost, however. Tattoo stood up, walked over to the saddlebags on his horse, reached in and produced a handful of jerky. "They put this stuff in there'n case they git hongry. They call 'em rayshuns," Tattoo said to Crazy Eyes, mispronouncing the word 'rations' as so many still do in that area. He offered some to his partner. "Don't know why. Looks juss like dried beef ta me."

"Why keep 'em inside them saddlebags?" Crazy Eyes asked, biting off a piece of the salty jerky and chewing it enthusiastically. "Hmmm! Stuff's not bad."

"For 'mergencies," Tattoo answered. "Juss in case they's out somewheres an' can't get ta the farm kitchen. All they gots ta do is juss take a bite o' this an' bingo! The hongries is all gone. Heard someone once say if ya keep it next ta the horse in the saddlebag, it adds ta the flavor."

After dining on the jerky, they both took their respective saddles and using them for pillows, bedded down for the night. "We ain't gonna hafta sleep on that hard barren cave floor tonight," Crazy Eyes reminded Tattoo. "This is gonna be like sleepin' in the Hotel Yorktowne," he said, knowing the hotel was one of the city's finest. "We gonna be real comfortable tonight. We gonna sleep good."

April has always been traditionally a wet, chilly, month in that section of the country. This year was no different. Outside the rain started again. Inside the two criminals would rest, plan their next move and get an early start in the morning. Thankful to be next to a campfire, they were warm and dry.

From deep in the cave a small rock moved from above, falling to the floor below. Crazy Eyes and Tattoo both shot up from their slumber. The horses moved uneasily. While his partner remained near the entrance, Tattoo grabbed a burning stick of wood and walked toward the back. Swishing it about, he saw nothing out of the ordinary. All seemed calm. Perhaps it was just their imagination, he thought. Returning to the front, he loaded the campfire with wood and settled down once more on his saddle bedding. Crazy Eyes was already asleep.

The state police cruiser pulled up next to Amos Springler's cabin. As usual, old Amos was sitting on the dilapidated chair near the edge of his front porch with Ol' Shep lying on the floor beside him. The two officers approached.

"Mr. Springler, do you own a 1932 black Ford pickup truck registered with the license plate number Pennsylvania 72854?" the older of the two officers asked.

"Well, that I chust can't shay, occifer," Amos slurred. He had been drinking heavily since Crazy Eyes dumped him off of their steed, and the combination of alcohol coupled with his Pennsylvania Dutch accent made it difficult for the Policeman to understand. "It'sh a '32 an' it'sh black," he added, running his words together, "but I chust don't rightly 'member what the number is."

"We're you driving it lately when it went off the bank into a ditch near the Haney farm?" the younger of the two state policemen asked.

"Hey, ya can't blame me fer that," Amos shot back defensively. "Them there two screwballs held a gun to ma head an' kept grabbing at the wheel. Took all I had in me, occifer, to keep it ona road," he insisted. "Then they stole them there two horses an' dumped me off here 'fore takin' off in that direction," he said, pointing toward the high wooded ridge that parallels his homestead.

"Had me ubducted fer dang near twelve hours. At'sh terrible. Man'd die o' thirst goin' that long without a cold one. Poor Ol' Shep," he continued, patting him on the head and feeling sorry for his dog, "they made me let 'im all alone wit' no one ta help. Now 'at chust ain't right, occifer" he muttered, "chust ain't right. Be a lass time I ever open up ma heart ta strangers an' offer ta help out anudder fellow human bean in need, I tell ya that!"

The beer was doing its thing, helping to make the old man emotional. "Affer all I done do for 'em an' the way they treat'd me. Why they threaten ta kill me! Who'da take care o' poor Ol' Shep? Huh?" he repeated his question. "Would you guys watch him? O' course ya wouldn't," he said, answering his own question. "Ya like a cold one, occifers?" he asked, offering the two policeman each a brown bottle of beer.

"No thanks, Mr. Springler," the one answered, holding up his hands in a stopping pattern. "And I think you ought to go inside and sleep it off. You've had quite a bit."

"I'm okay, occifer," Amos slurred once more. "Chust catch 'em crooks fer me an' lemme know. I wanna give 'em both the ol' one two right smack square ina choppers."

The two policemen just shook their heads in disbelief, almost chuckling to themselves that a person could drink as much as Amos Springler and still be able to stand up and speak coherently enough to be understood. Driving away slowly they watched in the glow of their headlights for any signs of the two.

In time they radioed headquarters the information they managed to retrieve from the old man before turning left at the 'Y' and starting down the road toward Rehmeyer's Run. Knowing about the cave high in the wooded hill above Pepper's secret fishing hole, they knew they had little chance of finding it in the darkness of night. What they didn't know was, inside that cave the two wanted vagabonds were fast asleep, waiting to finally make their escape in the morning.

Jack Whelan's old Ford sedan pulled into the driveway. He had just dropped off Thursy and explained to his parents where their son had been. All the way home Pepper rode with an air of relief. Crab Cake would make it. He was quite a feisty little dog. And Pepper was quite the happy young lad.

Running into the kitchen he hugged his mother, telling her all about the events the four of them witnessed that evening at the York Animal Hospital. "Crab Cake'll hafta stay for a while, yet, Mom," Pepper told her. "But it looks like he's really gonna make it."

"I'm so happy for ya, son," his mother told him, holding him close and kissing him on the forehead. "That dog means a lot to ya, and I would notta wanted to see its life end so tragically." Pulling out a chair at the table, she said, "Sit down and eat of bowl of hot chicken rice soup and a grilled cheese sandwich." Doris Whelan was known far and wide for her excellent homemade chicken rice soup. "There's some fresh cherry pie I just made for ya, and I'll heat ya up a cuppa hot chocolate. Ya must be starved." It would become the first meal Pepper had all day.

"When you've finished, son," his father told him, "I think you ought to get ready for bed. Morning comes fast enough and there are still early morning chores to do."

Pepper ate heartily, washing his meal down with ice cold spring water and hot chocolate made from fresh, rich cow's milk. Upon finishing, he thanked his parents for standing by Crab Cake, hugged and kissed them goodnight and headed up the steps to the bedroom he shared with Ty. His little brother was fast asleep, deep in the land of dreams.

Before lying down under the covers, Pepper said a special prayer of thanks for saving the life of his dog. Then he asked the Almighty to continue bestowing His special grace on Crab Cake, speeding his return home where Pepper felt the dog could regain his strength much faster than what he could lying in an animal hospital.

"Pssst. Pepper," whispered Ty, opening one eye and staring at his older brother. "Is he okay? Is he gonna make it? He didn't die, did he?"

"He's gonna make it, Ty," Pepper cheerfully answered, patting his brother affectionately on the head. "Crab Cake's gonna make it." Then in a very low voice, he proceeded to tell his little brother everything that happened since Crab Cake arrived at the hospital the evening before. It was like a bedtime story. Before he could finish, Ty drifted off once more into the land of dreams.

Downstairs, Pepper heard his father tell his mother, "When he gets home, Doris, there'll be medicines we'll probably have to administer, I'm sure."

"That's going to expensive, Jack. Where will we get the money, Honey?" she asked. "We're just scraping by now as it is."

"We're not doing so bad, sweetheart," Jack answered. "We'll make it. I'll take on some extra work. But whatever, I'm not gonna have my son go through any more trauma. Crab Cake is one of the family, and we'll do for the dog what we would do for any other member of this family," he assured her. "There's just no other alternative, dear. And when this is all over and behind us, someday we'll be able to look back and laugh… and thank each other for taking the right road."

As Pepper finished his chores that Wednesday morning and was heading into the kitchen for breakfast, the enormity of what transpired over the past two days suddenly struck him. He was overwhelmed by the danger he had encountered, especially the lives which were at risk. And he wondered if he would have been able to perform as he did if he had thought about it first.

"We don't do things out of the ordinary because we want to, son," his father told him at the breakfast table, "we do them because we have to. And even though there may be careful planning in the process, it's more of a reaction than a planned activity," he said.

Then Jack gave Pepper this example, "You're up to bat. When you choose to swing the bat at the pitched ball, you may have planned to hit it, but it's you seeing the ball in the right spot and instantly reacting to it that produces results," he said. "And that's sort of what happened Monday. You understood what had to be done to save your mother, sisters, brothers and dog, and you did it. Both you and Thursy are heroes."

That morning, after arriving at school, Mr. Rohrbaugh invited Pepper and Thursy to share their adventures with the rest of the class. The story broke in the front page of the *Gazette and Daily*. Now the entire world knew. And to a certain degree, Pepper became very self-conscious.

When the bus arrived, news reporters were already at the school waiting to interview the two. Mr. Rohrbaugh allowed them that opportunity, giving them 15 minutes before class started. If they could not finish in that allocated time, they'd have to wait until after school.

Questions flew about rapidly, pencils jotting down their every word and flash bulbs were popping as if President Harry Truman himself was speaking. Local radio stations were on hand recording their every word. Even the television station had a crew there to cover it for the lead story in their short evening news program.

When the fifteen minutes were up, Pepper was relieved. These guys seemed like they were trying to put words in his mouth, trying to embellish a story in order to make it sound juicier. Pepper wished they would write and tell the truth, just as it happened.

After school was over for the day, it was the same thing. Mr. Rohrbaugh took the boys aside and told them if they didn't want to talk to the press anymore, he'd protect them. But Pepper spoke up first, thanking his teacher and telling him he'd just as soon get it over with as have them follow him all the way home.

Knowing there would be no Crab Cake waiting to greet the four, the school bus ride home that day seemed strange. Pepper never realized he'd missed the dog as much as he did until he discovered he was no longer with him. Of course this was only temporarily. Crab Cake would be back. And when that happened, Pepper would make up for all the good times his dog and he had missed.

Lying low in the tall brown grass, high above the school bus stop, Crazy Eyes and Tattoo noticed the time and watched cautiously as the bus made its last stop of the day, dropping off, among others, the Whelan children. Like the day before, Jack Whelan left his job early to pick up his children. As long as the two criminals were still on the loose, he made it clear to his customers it was necessary that he does this. They agreed, thus providing him the freedom he needed to protect his family.

"We wouldn't be in this mess if you'da tied those horses better, you numbskull," Crazy Eyes said, glaring angrily at Tattoo. "If I didn't have ya tagging along, I'd be far gone from here by now."

"Yeah! Sure you'd be," answered Tattoo sarcastically. "That is if I didn't spot all them cops at that farmhouse... an' if I didn't lead us the way outta the woods... an' if I didn't catch us them two horses an' lead the way. Sure ya'd be, big man," he said mockingly. "Sure ya'd be."

"Juss once, why can't ya think like an average human thinks instead o' like an idiot?" Crazy Eyes continued, relentlessly. "Why don't ya juss use that good, criminal common sense all us natural criminals is born with? It'd be so much easier."

"How was I ta know there was still a snake in that cave? If ya knew, why didn't ya tell me?" Tattoo said in defense of himself. "And how was I ta know it'd spook the horses? I can't read horses' minds. I was sleeping. I didn't know they'd break loose from their fear of snakes until after they'd up an' skedaddled."

"Tattoo," whispered Crazy Eyes, gently poking him in the arm trying to get him to drop the subject, but more to get his attention. "See that old building across the schoolhouse yard? The one covered with gray shingles sitting on that hill juss off ta the left? I think we could stay there tonight 'til we re-plan our new escape.

"Ya crazy? Someone lives there. Everyone ina valley's looking for us," Tattoo said. "If we's seen by anyone, that only means we gotta take 'em wit' us, otherwise they gonna report what they seen."

"Shhh!" Crazy Eyes admonished. "Not so loud. Someone might hear ya. No one lives in there, Tattoo. They used ta live there," Crazy Eyes corrected his partner. "But now they live in the schoolhouse over there," he said, pointing at the weathered one room White Oak School House one hundred yards to the right.

"Looks like they might use it to keep chickens in now. Ya know what that means, don't ya, Tattoo? Eggs, food, maybe even a plump juicy chicken," he said, "and a shelter ta keep us outta this damp cold weather. With all them trees 'round, no one's gonna see us, partner. C'mon, Tattoo, let's head on down."

Waiting until all the kids had left and the Whelan children were picked up by their father, they slowly scooted down the hill on their stomachs when they found the coast clear, staying low so as not to be seen. By moving around toward the back of the building, they were protected by a wooded hill. There they slowly opened the door and peering in, had found lodging for the night.

It certainly wasn't the Hotel Yorktowne, but then they didn't expect it to be. On the other hand, they were finally away from that cave, away from the smoke of the evening campfire, and most importantly, free from that den of snakes.

Chapter 20

Thursday went by fast and after school on Friday, Larry Haney stopped by the house. Their mare had finally had its foal and the vet had mentioned the possibility of Crab Cake coming home. "I gotta go inta York," Haney said in his slow drawl to Doris Whelan. "If Pepper wants ta ride 'long inta git the dog, I'm goin' in anyways. I know he ain't been hisself lately, least not since the dog was snake bitten," he said, "but who has, Mrs. Whelan? Who has? Doc thought the dog was doin' good 'nough ta come home an' that it might also be perty good fer Pepper."

"Stop by after supper, Larry," Doris Haney told his neighbor. "I think Jack may wanna ride along, too. After all, I'm sure there's the matter of a bill to take care of."

For Pepper, the ride to the hospital seemed much longer this time than what it did Tuesday when he rode with Haney in to see his dog. Upon arriving he raced through the doors into the waiting area and onward through the double doors to the infirmary. Spotting Pepper, Crab Cake barked joyously, his tail moving at an incredible rate of speed for so sick a dog. All that was needed was a smile on Crab Cake's face to be absolutely sure he was one happy camper.

Before the nurse could fully open the gate to the dog area, Pepper was in like a light. Crab Cake immediately jumped into his outstretched arms and licked his face.

"He is a miracle," the vet told Jack and Larry, within earshot of Pepper. "You saw him Wednesday. Barely a breath left in him. It seemed his very life force itself had been drained. Everything in the book says that dog should not have survived. But then, like some humans," he continued, "sometimes there are animals that just refuse to go by the book."

"Well, Doc, I can't tell you how much we are so deeply grateful for what you did," Jack said, struggling to find the right words to convey his gratitude. "Had it not been for you, my boy would be suffering badly," he added, shaking the vet's hand and graciously thanking him.

"Mr. Whelan," the Doctor informed Jack, "I think you already know this, but I'm going to say it anyways. You see that young lad in there holding that Border Collie?" he asked, referring to Pepper and Crab Cake. "That's the one who deserves the thanks for saving the dog, not me. If you remember, we were about to give up on Crab Cake and put him to sleep. You have quite a remarkable son, Mr. Whelan... quite a remarkable son!"

"How much do I owe, Doctor?" Jack asked, reaching for his wallet and expecting the worst. They had experiences with veterinarians before, but never this particular one.

"Let's step out into my office, Mr. Whelan," the doctor suggested. "First, you know the dog is not out of the woods, by no stretch of the imagination. He'll need to take medicine for at least the good part of a year. I'd like to see him back here in two weeks. I'm giving you some pills to get him started and a prescription to be filled for more. Keep him on this until we're sure there is no more poison in his blood stream," the doctor ordered.

"As far as a bill goes, let's just wait and see how Crab Cake responds before we start worrying about bills. You've got enough on your mind. No need to take on any more right now than what's necessary," the doctor said.

Jack pulled a twenty dollar bill out of his wallet and handed it to the doctor. "Your generosity and compassion is well noted and quite appreciated, Doctor," Jack said. "But even you have bills to pay. Take this and credit my account. I'll send more as I get it."

"Mr. Whelan, I'm sure I need not tell you how impressed I am with your son," the doctor said. "Perhaps, with your approval, of course, Pepper might like to work in here a few days a week during the summer. It would not be very glamorous work, Mr. Whelan. He'd be cleaning stalls, feeding, watering and walking the patients and generally helping out wherever needed," the doctor said.

"The part-time position pays regular scale wages and, most importantly, calls for some one with compassion for animals. It's obvious your son has that, that and much more. He said, "I mentioned something to him this week when he too became concerned about the bill. Much to his credit, Mr. Whelan, I think your son, Pepper, would like to work off that bill."

"Give me some time to think about that, Doctor," Jack answered. "In the meantime, take this money and apply it to what we owe. Use it to pay some of the bills our dog created."

The ride home was one the young boy would never forget. Larry Haney drove, Jack Whelan rode shotgun and squeezed in the middle of the two was Pepper, tightly holding on to his dog as if Crab Cake were going to jump out the window and run away.

"It's been two days an' two nights livin' an' sleepin' in this here chicken coop wit' all these chickens," Tattoo complained to Crazy Eyes. "I ain't spending another night in here."

"Relax, my friend, relax," Crazy Eyes said in an attempt to keep his partner calm. "We juss need ta lay low a little while longer an' then we can make our exscape."

"How many more eggs can I eat?" asked Tattoo. "In the last two days, that's all we had. I'm having pains in my chest, arms an' shoulders right now. I'm telling ya, Crazy Eyes, it's all those darn eggs we been eatin'. I need some real food," he pleaded.

"No problem, Tattoo," said Crazy Eyes, sarcastically. "I'll just run over to Saubels Grocery in Hametown and stock up fer ya. That way ya can live more in the style ya been used ta in your long, 'lustrious an' privileged life!"

Tattoo knew he was annoying Crazy Eyes. Whenever his partner started talking sarcastically, experience had taught him to always be on guard. For some unexplained reason, Crazy Eyes had a nasty habit of just losing it. "All right. I ain't gonna complain no more," he agreed. "But at least let's talk 'bout where we gonna go from here. Being cooped up here wit' all these chickens juss a cluckin' an' a squawkin' the way they always do is driving me crazy."

"I don't like it either, Tattoo," Crazy Eyes admitted, "'specially since we gotta quietly leave each day until the eggs is gathered and the flock's fed. But look at it this way," he continued, "at least we got wooder ta drink an' food ta eat, even if it is eggs."

"Why can't we juss use the gun to kill another rabbit or squirrel or even a pheasant?" asked Tattoo. "That'd taste a great deal better'n eggs."

"We had six bullets in this gun," answered Crazy Eyes, slowly and emphatically. "We already used one ta kill them two rabbits the udder night. 'Spose we need the udder five ta d'fend ourselves. What good's a gun without bullets? Huh? 'Sides," he continued, "firin' the gun this close to where people live'll only draw attention. That's the last thing we wanna do," he said.

"Tonight, affer that Mr. and Mrs. Wertz and all those li'l Wertz's leave their humble schoolhouse abode fer town, we just gonna mosey on down there an' go through an' see what exter food they keep 'round fer unexpected guests," he exclaimed laughing evilly. "Tattoo, I think we's both gonna be mighty surprised."

The two hid quietly as they noticed a gray pickup truck moving down the road. Slowing to a crawl, the truck pulled up and parked at the Wertz's. Through a hole in the wall, Crazy Eyes and Tattoo saw Larry Haney get out of the cab and hold a conversation with Mr. Wertz. No voices were audible that far away, but their guilty minds roamed far and wide as to what was being said.

Perhaps they may not be able to raid the house later on. Perhaps they may not even be able to stay in the chicken house that night. Perhaps they are about this far from being captured. The two watched inquisitively, and when Haney drove away and Wertz went back into the house, they decided one would stand guard for four hours while the other slept, then switch places. It was the only way they could guarantee their security.

By now the Pennsylvania State Police had combed the woods in and around Rehmeyer's Run, White Oak Valley and the wooded hill with the outcroppings of rock behind Thursy Patterson's home. The only traces of the two were the horses stolen from Chet Cline's pastures. On Friday afternoon, the police discovered the two horses loose and grazing in a pasture near Delano Hyney's farm a few miles north of the cave. Missing were the saddles, blankets and saddlebags. That and all the beef jerky Chet Cline had kept in those saddlebags.

Figuring they made their escape on horseback, and then ditching the horses for a stolen automobile, the police widened their search to include an area south to the Maryland line, east to the Susquehanna River, north to the Dauphin County line and west to Gettysburg. All local law enforcement officers abandoned their immediate home region and concentrated on the focused area believed to be holding the criminals. Slowly they would be drawn into their dragnet, entrapping the two hoodlums once and for all. It was just a matter of time.

Like an old time sentry announcing the time and that all was well each hour, a police cruiser would periodically drive down the back dirt roads, checking this farm and that homestead and radioing into headquarters that at any given hour, all was well.

Amos Springler even slowed down on his drinking after realizing how close he came to losing his life and his dog... but mostly his dog. The last few days found him sober, at least until five in the afternoon. After that hour he'd only drink twelve bottles of beer between then and midnight instead of the usual twenty-four.

White Oak Valley was being lulled into a false sense of security, but no one knew it. Everyone thought Crazy Eyes and Tattoo had escaped, leaving the valley for good. As a matter of fact, talk had shifted to fishing again that weekend and having another opportunity of catching Ol' Uncle Louie. If anyone had told a stranger about the troubles that occurred there the beginning of the week, they would not have believed them. That's how laid back the area quickly became.

Not all believed the trouble was over. Among others, most notably was the opinion of the Game Warden, Officer Helfrich. Experience had taught him that once trouble starts and hasn't been corrected, odds are good it'll continue. And because of that, there was only one logical reason. It's because it's still out there lurking, waiting for just the right opportunity to strike again.

Jack Whelan believed that, too. Not surprisingly, so did his son, Pepper.

Chapter 21

A crowd was waiting as Larry Haney pulled his gray Dodge pickup truck into Jack Whelan's lane. Jack got out of the truck first, and carrying Crab Cake, Pepper followed. The first to greet them was Ty. Hugging the dog, he whispered how good it was to have him back. Next was little David. He also gave the dog a hug. Crab Cake's tail was operating in overdrive. He was definitely enjoying the attention.

Pepper's two sisters, Paula and Sarah, graciously stayed in the background, allowing the three boys and dog to bask in the joy of the moment. They knew this was Pepper's and Crab Cake's time. After all they had gone through, they deserved it. There would be plenty of time later for them to make a fuss privately over the dog's miracle recovery and to congratulate their younger brother, Pepper. Now was not that time.

Doris Whelan stood by her husband, watching all the fuss being made over Crab Cake. From out of the woods, racing across the pasture came Thursy. He was running as fast as his legs would move him. Wanting to be there on time when they arrived home, a telephone call from his mother had delayed his departure. As he approached, Pepper and he locked eyes. After all, it was Thursy whose life the dog saved by taking the bite from the copperhead.

Thursy walked up to Pepper and hugged him mightily, thanking him for being a friend. Then the neighbor boy picked up Crab Cake from the arms of Pepper and hugged him gently. No one could hear what he was saying as he whispered softly some words in the dog's ear, but as he handed Crab Cake back to Pepper, his eyes were glazed and misty. It was the first time Pepper ever saw Thursy get emotional.

Doris invited everyone in for homemade pie, cake, ice cream and store bought soda. Even Crab Cake had a dish of vanilla ice cream. The long farm kitchen table was surrounded with happy folks, delighted that one of theirs was back.

Thursy, enjoying a large piece of yellow cake with milk chocolate icing topped by a big scoop of chocolate ice cream, mentioned loudly for all to hear, "Crab Cake is a hero. Maybe he'd rather have some chocolate ice cream instead of vanilla." Lowering his spoon filled with the light brown colored ice cream, cake and chocolate icing, he moved it in the direction of Crab Cake.

159

But before the dog could enjoy the offering, Pepper intercepted, taking the spoon out of his friend's hand and putting it back into his dish. "Never give any dog chocolate, Thursy," he scolded. Then seeing that everyone was watching and Thursy was slowly becoming embarrassed, he softened his words. "You see, my friend, dogs ain't like you and me," he said, putting his arm on his shoulder. "Chocolate acts like a poison to them. Even a small amount can kill them."

"Pepper," said his dad, "I'm sure there was no intent on Thursy's part to harm the dog. He could not have known about that. After all, he's never had a dog. This Sunday I think would be a good time to see how Crab Cake reacts to our ball game. Maybe Thursy would like to join us after Sunday dinner."

Thursy quickly apologized for endangering Crab Cake and accepted the invitation to Sunday's game. "If you're not doing anything tomorrow, Pepper, maybe you'd like to join me in fishing," he asked his friend.

This time Jack spoke up. "I'm sure he'd like to, Thursy, but being in with the dog for two days this week put him behind in his chores. I'm sorry but Pepper will be busy tomorrow. However, if you'd like to come over and help him with anything, feel free to do so."

Thursy looked at Pepper. Pepper looked at Thursy, and Crab Cake looked at both boys. Even the dog must have thought he'd rather be with them chasing squirrels or rabbits or even trout than to watch them work.

But Pepper's dad had an ulterior motive. Certainly he wasn't being mean to Pepper as it had seemed so on the surface to Thursy. His reasoning was to keep the dog near the house, thus giving him a chance to regain his strength. There would be plenty of time for other outside activities.

Looking up from the table, Pepper caught Larry Haney walking outside from the corner of his eye. Taking a bite of ice cream, he noticed Haney motioning for Jack to follow. On the back porch the two spoke in whispered tones. It was the second time in two days that Haney would quietly and clandestinely discuss a subject with another man, the first being Mr. Wertz.

When they were finished, Haney and Jack returned to the kitchen as if nothing important had been discussed. But Pepper knew better. For the time being, he decided to keep Crab Cake in his sight at all times. He just wasn't going to take any more chances losing his dog. Crab Cake yawned as Pepper patted him. Then the dog laid down his head and closed his eyes. He had had a long and tiring day. A good night's rest would help to restore his strength.

Two indistinguishable figures made their way across the hill top just inside the woods. With the setting sun, it was easy for them to stay in the shadows.

The two floor chicken coop where they had spent the past two nights seemed minuscule way below. Left behind were the shells of eggs they had eaten the past couple of days. That and some old newspapers they had found along the way which they used to cover up at night.

During the day they'd gather the egg shells and papers, hiding them until the owners had made their egg collection. Before leaving they wrapped the shells in papers and stuffed them inside their jackets. On the way to their next unknown destination, they dropped them off at some abandoned dump deep in the woods, far away from any houses.

Along with them they took their personal belongings, the clothes they had on their back and a stolen Game Warden's gun loaded with five bullets. With a fervent desire to escape the White Oak Valley once and for all this weekend, they finally agreed to flee it at all costs, even if they couldn't find two certain boys and their dog. Looking back, it was nothing but trouble for the two. That and bad luck. It was as though destiny itself dealt it. Regardless, they had had enough of the inhospitable valley, its interfering people and its surly animals. Crazy Eyes and Tattoo were back on the move. This time, they felt, for good.

Moving west, they made their way along the ridge down to the junction of a second dirt road. Double checking to make sure no one was nearby, the two hurriedly crossed the muddy road and moved along the top of the western ridge. From there they laid low until the sun went down, then they slowly moved up the hill on their stomachs to the edge of the woods. Once in the woods and out from the eyesight of civilization, they stood up and walked.

A squirrel suddenly shot out from behind an oak tree and instinctively Crazy Eyes raised his gun and fired. He missed and fired again, this time hitting the bushy animal. From behind another tree a second squirrel ran across their paths and again Crazy eyes fired, dropping this animal on the first shot. "Ya outta yer mind?" whispered Tattoo. "Someone's liable ta hear us."

"Probably will, partner," answered Crazy Eyes, "probably will. But this time o' year they's gonna be figurin' someone's shootin' groundhogs or skunks. It's common 'round here, Tattoo. 'Sides, 'less ya want sumpin' different fer yer supper 'sides eggs, don't go startin' none o' yer complainin'."

Deep in the woods, the two built a lean-to and lit a fire. Making a spit out of green sassafras branches, they cleaned the squirrels, put them on the spit and placed them over the hot coals. Within half an hour they were eating bar-b-qued squirrel.

"What's it taste like?" asked Tattoo.

"Juss like chicken," answered Crazy Eyes, "juss like chicken." To Tattoo, it seemed like everything taste 'just like chicken' to his partner.

"That's the best we can do fer tonight," Crazy Eyes told Tattoo, pointing to the lean-to. "If that local yokel drivin' the gray pickup truck hadn't stopped ta talk ta the owner all that time, we'd still be asleepin' in a chicken coop 'stead o' out here."

"Ya think he suspects anything?" Tattoo asked his comrade in crime.

"Shore he does," Crazy Eyes answered, absolutely positive of himself. "Soon's the pickup truck up an' leaves, what happens? That owner comes right out ta the chicken coop lookin' about. Juss lucky we got ta sleep in it last night. Pushin' it anudder night might be the same as pushin' our luck too far. 'Twas time ta go, partner," he said. "Neighborhood suspicions, bein' the way they is, 'twas time ta go! In the mornin' we gonna break free from this valley an' make our way ta the Eastern Shore. Better getta good night's sleep, Tattoo."

Larry Haney was just leaving the celebration at the Whelan's. Pepper walked out the back door and stood alone with him. Haney was 21, out of school three years and worked his father's, Roy Haney's, farm. Not married, he dated many girls his age in the valley. Always one to give a helping hand to a fellow human in need, he was respected by just about everyone who crossed his path. Pepper looked up at the tall neighbor. "I want to thank ya for everything ya done fer us, 'specially fer Crab Cake," he said. "Had it not been for you, he might notta made it."

"Well," Larry started out in his slow, drawn out way of talking. "Youse woulda done the same thing fer me if I was in yer shoes. Ya see, Pepper, it's like the ol' mountain man always says, 'Birds of a flock, gotta feather together.'" Haney knew what he meant but still maintained such a unique way of always turning clichés upside down from their original wordings.

Pepper just smiled, shook his hand and thanked him again. Then he remained on the back porch, watching his friend start his truck and take off up the hill, using the field roads through the woods instead of the main dirt roads. Alongside the fencerow he drove. Inside the woods, the field road turns right and leads far back from where any houses can be seen.

One half mile into the woods the road takes a ninety degree turn to the left and crosses through a narrow opening between two trees and across some heavy rock. Without slowing down a driver could tear everything out from under the framework of a vehicle. Haney slowed to a crawl, downshifting into low and negotiated each rock. Squeezing the pickup between the two trees, he finally saw the last of the heavy rock in the glow of his headlights. Also in that glow, unfortunately, were the two jail birds holding a loaded gun on the Good Samaritan.

"Outen the lights," he was ordered. They were using a term mostly familiar to the farming community of the Pennsylvania Dutch area, meaning to turn off the lights. Immediately, Haney did as he was told.

"Well, well, well," Crazy Eyes declared, walking around to the left, looking at the gray Dodge truck and then at Haney. "What have we here?"

"Looks like our friend that whispers sweet nuthin's in the ears o' neighbors. Like the chicken coop owner yesterday," answered Tattoo. While Crazy Eyes held Haney's attention on the left, Tattoo had moved along the right side of the truck. Casually opening the door, he slipped onto the seat and reaching across the front, grabbed the keys. "Ya think them sweet nuttin's was him tellin' the owner we was camping out in his chicken house? How'd ya knowd we was there?" asked Tattoo.

"Next time ya use a buildin'," Haney said in his slow draw, "might be better fer ya if ya shut the door. Chickens got more brains than youse two. They juss don't open doors wit'out shuttin' 'em," he said sarcastically. "Ya see, they's still smart 'nough ta know an open door juss might let in the foxes."

"Oh! Looks like we gots us a real live comedian on our hands, here, Crazy Eyes," Tattoo said, looking at his partner. "Maybe with all dis talent in front of us here, we be able ta be entertained tonight," he quipped. "Okay, wise guy, outta the truck. Lean against that there hood an' spread yer legs, C'mon, move it! I ain't got all night."

Haney slowly did as he was told. Crazy Eyes tied his hands behind his back with binder twine he had found in the bed of the pickup. He stuffed more in his deep pockets for later use. Tattoo drove the truck through the thick brush of the woods next to their campsite with Crazy Eyes walking ahead holding the gun on Larry Haney's back. "Next time ya drive through the woods at night," Crazy Eyes advised him in the art of getaway driving, "outen yer lights. That way it's harder to locate you, even if someone can hear yer truck."

Reaching their campsite, Crazy Eyes informed Haney, "You be stayin' here as our guest in our humble abode, at least 'til morning. Then we gonna decide what ta do wit' ya. Now sit." When Haney sat down, Tattoo took more binder twine from the truck and securely tied his legs. Then he stuffed his mouth with a dirty cloth and tied another across it, making sure he wouldn't scream. Haney and Tattoo slept in the lean-to. Crazy Eyes kept watch with the gun, at least for the first four hours.

A mile to the north, over the wooded hill and just inside the White Oak

Valley, sat the Whelan farm. Another mile to the south, over that same wooded hill and deep into a different bend of the valley, stood the Haney homestead. In the middle on a secluded stretch of dense wooded hilltop sat Larry Haney, tied and gagged.

High above them from on the top of a tree a great horned owl screeched loudly. Crazy Eyes instinctively fired erratically. Needless to say, he missed. He had used his fifth bullet. Only one more remained.

Chapter 22

The rain fell heavily on the dark, gray slate, shingled roof of the farmhouse. Lightning bolted and thunder rumbled across the hills, keeping Pepper awake. The young lad slipped his pajama top on over his tee shirt and quietly tip-toed down the stairs to the kitchen. Walking across the kitchen floor to the opposite side, he stopped to check on Crab Cake, making sure the dog was okay in the violent thunderstorm. "No need ta be scared," he told his dog. "Everything's gonna be okay."

Crab Cake's eyes were already open. The dog wagged his tail as if he understood the words of encouragement his master had just offered. Pepper walked across the kitchen to check the back door. It was locked. Then, on second thought, he unlocked the door, opened it and stepped outside on the back covered porch. Slowly and cautiously, Crab Cake joined him.

The driving rain created a fine mist that washed up against Crab Cake and the face of Pepper. It felt good. The two stood there for the longest time watching the lightning, listening to the thunder, with Pepper wiping his face occasionally from the mist. Crab Cake stayed right by his side, never moving until Pepper decided he had seen enough. In time, the two entered the farmhouse kitchen much too late to see a vehicle in the glow of the lightning flashes, cross near the top fencerow high above the potato field, with its lights off.

Pepper walked Crab Cake back to where he was lying. Sitting down next to his dog, he patted him gently on the head. Periodically a flash of lightning would break the darkness and the accompanying crack of thunder broke the quiet of night. Soon, Crab Cake's eyes closed sending him deep into sleep. Within minutes, Pepper joined him, both lying on a blanket on the kitchen floor. Outside the storm raged on.

"Turn right at the end o' the hedgerow," Tattoo directed. "Take that lane ta the main dirt road. Keep the lights off. We'll pace ourselves. Long as it ain't lightning no one's gonna see us."

"Sure am glad ya thought o' this, Tattoo," Crazy Eyes said. "'Stead o' sleepin in that wet lean-to, why with this here nice, warm, gray Dodge truck we can exscape in this storm and no body'll be the wiser. An' long as this local yokel's wit' us here," Crazy Eyes reminded his partner, pointing to Larry Haney tied up and sitting between them, "we gots us our tickets ta freedom. We juss gonna foller this field road ta the main road and then we's home free."

At the edge of the fencerow, Crazy Eyes turned and started down the narrow field road, its ground already soft from the week's soaking rainwater. The field road ran adjacent to the back of Whelan's barn. From the house it was not visible. Near the bottom a soft depression in the field road made trucking difficult. Everyone familiar with the mushy spot would gun their vehicles in plenty of time to prevent getting stuck.

Larry Haney, sitting between the two and not about to warn his captors, knew the depression was slowly approaching. Because Crazy Eyes was unfamiliar and driving without headlights, he drove slowly. As he hit the depression, the truck slowed, and then came to an abrupt halt. Crazy Eyes hit the accelerator but the only thing happening was the continual spinning of the rear wheels.

"Try backin' up in r'verse," Tattoo instructed him. "Then shift back ta second. Rock the truck. See if that helps give us some m'mentum."

Crazy Eyes did as he was told but to no avail. "Ya got us into this mess, idiot," he charged Tattoo. "Now get us out. An' be quick 'bout it," he yelled.

Out of the truck jumped Tattoo. "Don't juss gun it," he told his partner, "keep arockin' it. I'll get behind 'n' push. Rock it back 'n' forth slowly. When ya think ya got 'nough m'mentum, then gun it."

But every effort the two made only resulted in the truck making deeper ruts and slowly sinking farther and farther down into the soft earth. Crazy Eyes was becoming furious. It seemed like every time they'd get a break, something weird would happen that would set them back. They needed a streak of luck if they were going to escape from what they considered to be this strange hold White Oak Valley and its unreceptive people had on them.

"C'mon. Tattoo," he said, "let's hop in the barn an' git dry. We gonna take this character along juss in case he tries ta exscape," he added, pointing to Larry.

Abandoning the truck, now stuck deeper than ever in the muddy ruts it created, the three ran for the barn door of the upper rear level. Once inside they climbed high on a hay loft near the far side. In doing so, it gave them the advantage of watching for any cars that may perchance happen upon the farm. Tattoo, noticing the soft cooing of fifty or so barn pigeons, watched out the opening in the wooden vertical side slats. Crazy Eyes ordered Larry to lie down. Then, with the gun still in his hand, he rested it on his chest and closed his eyes, hoping to catch forty winks. Tattoo stood guard as the rain continued.

It was really too dark for the two felons to recognize they were at the very same place they held four hostages Monday evening, escaping a dragnet of Pennsylvania State Policemen through the basement of the farmhouse as they left near dusk. This time they had approached the farm from behind the barn, completely out of view of the house. Larry Haney knew, but he had no intentions of sharing that secret with them.

Crab Cake sat up. He licked Pepper's face, waking him. "Yeah, boy," Pepper said to his dog. "I heard it, too. Sounds like wheels spinnin', like sumpin's stuck." Crab Cake whined softly as if he understood.

Jack Whelan descended the stairs, appearing in the kitchen. "What are you doing up?" he asked Pepper. Then seeing him on the blanket with Crab Cake, he didn't bother waiting for an answer. "You heard it, too?" he asked his son. "Sounds like a vehicle's stuck."

Returning to his upstairs bedroom, Pepper followed his dad. Reaching high above the shelf of a closed door closet where no one but he could reach, Jack inserted a key and unlocked a small door. Slowly and carefully he removed a wooden case. Using a different key, he unlocked the lid. Lifting it, he removed a small caliber hand gun. Checking the gun closely, he made sure the safety latch was in the '*on*' position. From a cardboard box inside the wooden case he grabbed a handful of ammunition and returned the box to its shelf. "In times like this," he told Pepper, "it's always best to be prepared."

Downstairs again, Jack opened the back kitchen door, looking out first and then stepping onto the porch. Pepper and Crab Cake joined him. Reaching inside the pantry door he grabbed two black rubber raincoats and a flashlight. The veteran soldier put one on and handed the other to Pepper. Slowly and cautiously, the two walked out toward the barn, using the illumination of distant lightning to see. Jack decided to use the flashlight only if absolutely necessary.

Looking around they saw nothing. No vehicle anywhere. The lane was free of vehicles. There were none on the road and nothing along the fencerows. "Must've been our imagination, Jack said to his son. "Let's get in out of the rain. C'mon, Crab Cake."

Suddenly the Border Collie took off. Slower than usual, of course, but nevertheless up the back lane that winds behind the barn he slowly ran. "Crab Cake, get back here," called Pepper. But in suspicious times like this, Crab Cake had a mind of his own. "He's too weak to go running in the rain, Dad. C'mon, help me catch him."

167

The dog led them to the top hill along the rear of the barn. For a second he stopped, looked at the barn door and then ran up into the field. Pepper and Jack followed. Crab Cake made a right along the fencerow. On the other side was the field road used by farm equipment to get from one field to another. And in that field road, stuck deep in a muddy depression was Larry Haney's gray Dodge pickup truck.

Jack walked over and touched the hood. It was still warm. Because the open exhaust usually cools down faster, he walked behind and checked the exhaust pipe. That was still warm, too.

"Whadaya think, Dad?" asked his son. "Looks like Larry Haney's truck."

"It is his truck, Pepper," Jack answered, cautiously looking over the truck, "it is. He must've gotten stuck out here and decided to walk home over that muddy field. Poor guy. Must be soaked by now. If he'd have rapped on the door, I would've been glad to give him a ride. It's a shame, Pepper," he said, shaking his head. "And after all he's done for us. Even left his keys in the ignition," he added, pulling them out and slipping them into his pocket. "I'll take them over in the morning. That truck's not going anywhere tonight," he told his son, the two fighting the stiff wind that was driving the rain. "C'mon, Pepper. Let's get in. We're getting soaked to the gills."

From out of the storm a loud bang... bang... bang caught their attention. Looking down toward the barn they saw nothing. Slowly they walked back along the hedge row until they came to the opening that led to the back of the barn. The banging had stopped. "Call Crab Cake and let's get some sleep," Jack said. "Larry can depend on my help in the morning." And they started down the rear barn hill toward the lane.

Once again, a bang... bang... bang. This time, stopping quickly in their tracks, they turned around and spotted the culprit. The rear barn door, unlocked, was opening and closing from the force of the wind, banging against the outer siding of the barn. "Thought that door was locked," Jack said, and walking over toward it, he ordered Pepper to stay where he was.

Crab Cake growled. "What is it, boy?" asked Pepper. "Sumpin' wrong?" Crab Cake growled again, this time a little louder. "Dad, be careful," Pepper called out. "Crab Cake's 'spicious."

With extra caution, Jack opened the door slowly, shining the light inside the second floor of the barn. Stepping in, he looked around. The only thing he saw were pigeons cooing and bales upon bales of straw and hay stacked on top of each other. In the middle section some farm implements were still parked. Shining the light up on the stacked bales, he saw nothing but hay. On the other side, he did the same. There was nothing within his view except bales of straw.

Satisfied that all was well, Jack left closing the door behind him, and this time he locked it from the outside. Then Crab Cake, Pepper and he walked slowly down to the house in the pouring rain, looking this way and that, watching carefully for anything that might be out of order.

Taking off their raincoats and hanging them in the pantry, they also removed their shoes and set them on the pantry floor. Pepper took a towel and wiped Crab Cake dry before letting him in the house. Inside the warm kitchen Jack moved the tea kettle over the heat in preparation for hot tea, a cup for Pepper and one for him. Then he returned his gun to its upstairs closet hideaway before coming back down and pouring tea for both him and Pepper.

"Something isn't right, Dad," he said, looking at his father and reaching for the honey to sweeten his hot tea. "I feel funny saying this, but I sense it. I just can't put my finger on it."

"Don't ever feel funny about what you feel, son," Jack told him as he finished pouring hot water into his cup. "I feel the same way. Think about what we saw and then think about what we should have seen." It seemed to Pepper as if his father knew what was wrong, but rather than tell, he wanted him to figure it out for himself.

They sat at the kitchen table, sipping hot tea, Pepper on the end of the long bench against the kitchen's eastern wall and Jack on a chair at the head of the large table. Both were staring out the front window thinking. Periodically a far away bolt of lightning would cast a soft illumination over the valley, lighting up the road from the Barnes farm all the way down to the woods. It was close to 2 a.m.

"Son, you've got to get up in a few hours to start your chores," Jack said. "Call me before you do. But for now, you better get some sleep." It was too late. Pepper had already nodded off under the table on the long bench. Jack took his half empty cup, along with Pepper's and emptied them down the sink drain. In them he poured water and left them there.

Crab Cake moved from under the table and was snoozing lightly on his floor blanket. Suddenly Pepper shot up. "Dad," he called in excitement. Jack turned around startled at his son's sudden alertness. "Muddy as it was, we shoulda seen foot prints leadin' away! There was no footprints goin' from the truck across the field toward Haney's house. The only footprints I saw were those from the truck headin' down toward the barn!"

"Yes, son, you're right," his father said, softly. Then looking at Pepper with a sense of deep pride, he told his son, "Ya have the makings of a great detective, Pepper. That's what I meant when I said, 'Think about what we should have seen.' Ya learn fast, son. Congratulations!"

Chapter 23

Crazy Eyes and Larry Haney were the only ones listening. Still, Tattoo said to no one in particular, "It's a good thing we found that trap door." He had a strange habit of periodically blurting out whatever was on his mind, regardless of whether anyone was within earshot. "That saved us from being discovered wit' this guy, huh, Crazy Eyes?"

"Take these long boards," Crazy Eyes ordered, ignoring Tattoo's idle chatter and pointing to a pile of one by sixes stacked neatly against the one inside wall of the barn, "an' place 'em unner the wheels. We gonna get that truck outta that ditch an' then we gonna be outta here. I wanna be clear o' this place 'fore sunrise."

Tattoo piled eight boards on his shoulders and with Larry and Crazy Eyes following, the three headed up the hill behind the barn to the stuck pickup truck. Carefully, Tattoo placed a board under the front side of the two back tires, jamming them securely against the tire treads. He did the same with a board under the front side of each front tire, also jamming them against the tire tread. He followed that with boards to the back side of all four tires.

"Now get in an' start the truck. Rock it 'tween r' verse and second an' don't race the injine," Crazy Eyes instructed. "You," he said, pointing to Larry who was still gagged and bound, "Git in the back an' gimme some weight. Sit right over that there rear axle. Okay, Tattoo," he ordered, "start 'er up."

"Need keys ta do that, Buddy," he said, holding his open hand out the rolled down window in anticipation of Crazy Eyes handing him the truck's ignition keys. "Gimme the keys."

"They already in the ignition, ya goofball," Crazy Eyes shot back. "All ya gotta do is look. Now quit yer clowning 'round an' help git us outta here afore I lose it an' really start up on ya." Crazy Eyes waited and waited but still no attempt to start the truck was made. "Ya gonna start the truck now, or we gonna sit here an' wait 'til the cops show up so we can feel sorry for all the hard work they do and juss give ourselves up?"

"They's not here," Tattoo yelled back. "I tole ya before, there ain't no keys in the ignition. Look in yer pockets, Buddy."

Both hands went into Crazy Eyes' pockets, but there were no keys there to be found. Storming to the front, he yelled like a maniac, "Them keys was in the ignition. I left 'em there. What happened to 'em, huh?" He directed this question to no one in particular. "You," he said to Larry. "Ya got the keys?" Larry just shook his head no. "Ya got 'nudder set?" Again, Larry shook his head no.

"Okay, Tattoo," Crazy Eyes exclaimed. He was ready to admit the situation had him frustrated, but still not ready to give up. "Hot-wire it," he ordered Tattoo.

"Hot-wire it? Whatta ya talking 'bout, hot-wire it?" Tattoo responded, somewhat surprised. "I'm notta mechanic. I ain't got no idea how ta hot-wire a truck, Crazy Eyes," he told his comrade. "In fact, I don't know a hot-wire from a cold cable. Looks like yer on yer own this time, partner. This one's outta my league."

Crazy Eyes looked around. "You," he said, pointing to Larry who was still sitting in the rear of the truck, "hot-wire this truck." He pulled Larry from the bed of the truck, pushing him in the mud to the front cab. All Larry could do was shrug his shoulders and shake his head, indicating he, too, knew absolutely nothing about the art of hot-wiring. Actually, Larry did know, but as long as the truck was stuck, the crooks couldn't leave, which meant the chances of him being freed and the two hoodlums being caught were so much greater.

"Why don't you hot-wire it?" Tattoo finally said to Crazy Eyes. "Ya seem to know so much 'bout it. Go ahead, you do it."

Crazy Eyes ignored Tattoo. He also knew nothing about hot-wiring, but this time he wasn't about to become the butt of Tattoo's laughter again, not after the horse riding episode.

Suddenly it dawned on Crazy Eyes. "Those two birds in that house. That father an' son duo. They's the ones that took the keys," he said. "They's the only ones near the truck who coulda done it. C'mon. We've gotta git them keys back."

"Son," Jack said to Pepper. "Take a flashlight, go through the basement door, walk along the creek through the meadow to Patterson's and ask to use the phone to call the police." Then as an afterthought, he added, "Pepper, only use the flashlight if it's absolutely necessary. I don't want anyone seeing you. And you'd better take Crab Cake with you."

"What 'bout you, Dad?" asked Pepper. "Whatta ya gonna do?"

"I'll be here watching the outside and protecting the family," he told his oldest son. "I'm not about to take a chance leaving them alone again. They've already gone through enough trauma to last a lifetime." Then he turned off all the inside house lights.

After watching Pepper and Crab Cake walk through the meadow toward Patterson's and into the darkness of night, Jack locked the back kitchen door, checked the cellar door and the front porch door before climbing the steps to the second floor bedrooms. Checking the one room, the girls were fast asleep. In the other room, both boys were deep into their world of dreams. Doris stirred as Jack entered their bedroom. Opening her eyes, she mumbled something about why he was up this early.

"Shhh," Jack told her, putting his finger vertically across his closed lips. "Don't panic, Honey. We might have company tonight." Having said that, and knowing she'd insist he tell her everything, he related what happened earlier between Pepper, Crab Cake and him.

"They might be in the barn," he said. "They can't escape. I have the keys to Haney's truck. I suspect they're holding him captive."

"What about Pepper?" asked his wife. "What happened to my son and his dog?"

"They're on their way to Patterson's to call for help. I watched as they entered the woods. They'll be fine," said Jack. "At least they're out of any potential danger."

Jack picked up a chair and set it by the window overlooking the yard. Sitting down and watching the area of the barn, he opened his wooden case, retrieved his gun again, loaded it and set it on a table close by. Noticing his wife stare at the loaded weapon, he said in a soft calming voice, "It's only a precaution, Honey. It's simply here for protection. Trust me. No one in this house will be hurt."

The wind picked up and the moon played peek-a-boo with the ominous clouds as they covered the skies once again. Soon the rains returned. Lightning lit up the night sky and thunder boomed its warning across the valley. "Pepper must be there by now," Jack told his wife, more as an assurance that their son wasn't caught in the storm.

In a thunderclap, accompanying a brilliant flash of lightning which turned the pitch darkness of night into the brightness of mid-day, Jack saw something that caught his eye. There, just inside the garage, near its side corn cribs, stood the images of three men.

A second glow from an equally bright flash revealed Larry Haney with his hands behind his back and a gag in his mouth. He was standing between, what seemed to Jack to be, two unwelcomed characters. One had his hand on Haney's upper arm. The other had his hand hidden in Haney's side.

Jack suspected Haney was being held at gunpoint. Even though he had never seen them in person, he also suspected the two characters were the same two who eluded authorities earlier in the week, Crazy Eyes and Tattoo.

Thinking of helping Larry Haney, numerous plans flashed through his mind. But first he must make sure his family was safe.

The small summer house sat to the east of the big farmhouse. Almost all the farms in the area had them. They were used mainly in the summer to can or cold pack freshly grown produce in the truck gardens for the families' winter use. Both processes needed a good hot fire and by using the summer house, it prevented the bigger farmhouse, where everyone lived, from heating up so much during the hot summer months.

Inside, on the south wall was a mammoth stone fireplace, the kind used in the olden days. It was big enough for an average adult to stand in. The downstairs had one room, the kitchen. On the east wall was a window overlooking the meadow used as a ball field. There were also windows on the north and west sides. Pull down blinds and curtains adorned the three windows.

The second floor also had one room. It was used for storage and it also had three windows, one each on the north, east and west sides. Doris used it mostly to store her Ball quart jars used for canning and the brass screw rings that held the rubber sealed lids securely onto the jars. When not in use, the summer house was always kept locked.

Outside, by the brook that originated from the spring within the basement of the big farm house, stood a huge fireplace. It also was constructed of stone and nearly as large as the one inside. This was used for outdoor gatherings such as family corn roasts and other cookouts. So cold was the water coming from the underground spring that it was put to good use. It cooled drinks and other foods that required colder temperatures.

Twenty feet of lawn separated the entrance to the summer house from the basement door of the farmhouse. A concrete sidewalk joined the two. A small, ground level porch made from concrete greeted all who entered the summer kitchen.

Looking out the east bedroom window, Jack quickly decided that's where the family would hide… at least until the trouble subsided. "Honey," he directed his wife, "wake the kids gently. Try not to alarm them. Don't turn on any lights and bring them all into the bedroom."

Doris woke up the girls first. "Sarah, Paula, wake up," she said, gently shaking them so as not to startle them from a deep sleep. Paula opened her eyes first, followed by Sarah. Looking straight at their mother, they said nothing. "Shhh," Doris ordered, "go into our bedroom quickly and be quiet."

Into the other bedroom she went, shaking Ty and David just as gently. Because this room was closer to the garage, she used extra precaution so as not to make any noise. Directing the boys to do the same, she followed them into her dark bedroom where Jack, Sarah and Paula were waiting.

"I need the utmost cooperation from each and every one of you," Jack began. "We have a situation here that could get blown out of proportion if we don't take measures to prevent it. That's why I want you four and your mother to hide in the top floor of the summer house and be absolutely quiet."

Jack explained to the children what had happened, where Pepper and Crab Cake were and what he saw by the garage corn cribs just recently. "I suspect they're going to try and break in here to get the truck keys," Jack said. "We have to try and help Larry Haney. After what he did for us, we owe it to him. Now, quickly put on your coats and shoes, quietly go downstairs and wait by the cellar door for your mother and me," he ordered.

"Take this flashlight, Honey," he said to Doris slipping it into her coat pocket. "Use it only if necessary. We don't want to tip off these clowns that the family is hidden in the summer house. Oh, one more thing, Honey. Here's the key to the summer house door. Don't forget to lock that door *after* you get inside," he calmly told her, emphasizing the word, after. Then he took his wife in his arms and held her tightly, kissing her gently on the lips.

"Please, Jack," she said, "be careful. I don't know what I'd do if anything tragic happens where I'd end up losing you. You're my whole life." And she held onto him tightly, returning his kiss.

Unexpectedly, a knock was heard on the back door. "Shhh," Jack said, holding his hand across his wife's mouth. "Quickly everyone, follow me quietly." The two parents, followed by their four children, descended the dark stairs to the first floor kitchen, unlocked the cellar door and with Doris in the lead, stepped down into the basement. From there they quietly opened the back door leading outside and cautiously crossed in the pouring rain to the summer house porch. Once inside, Doris locked the door and led her charges upstairs.

Through the walls they heard another rap, this time louder than before. And then there was silence.

Chapter 24

With the loaded gun behind his back and the safety off, Jack turned on the kitchen and porch lights and opened the door. To his surprise, there stood Larry Haney, untied, ungagged and all alone. "Larry, c'mon in," Jack said loudly and yawning for show, just in case the two hoodlums were watching.

Once inside, Jack locked the door, set the gun's safety and put the gun down on the table as he told Larry how he took the keys out of the truck's ignition. "They had me all tied up an' then they gagged me," Larry whispered. "One's inside the pantry now, waiting to spring on ya if I don't come out. The udder one's headin' around back, downstairs 'tween the cellar door an' the summer house," he told Jack, talking as low as he could.

Jack immediately thought of his wife and children whom he just sent to the summer house through the basement door. But since he himself saw them enter the summer house, he knew they made it before being seen. "Larry, I'm going to need your help," Jack said. "Are you willing?"

"Don't want no harm ta come ta anyone in yer family, Jack," he said, "but I'm particularly concerned 'bout my mom an' dad. I'm half afraid if I don't cooperate wit' them two hoodlums, they might harm my parents."

"Larry, here's the keys," Jack said, handing him the set to the truck. "I want you to leave, calmly. If they ask what we spoke about, just say you told me you came back to get the keys and that you thanked me for keeping them until I got back. Tell them you told me you were going to get the truck out of the mud."

"What 'bout you, Jack?" Larry asked. "These guys ain't no ones to mess with, I'm tellin' ya!"

"Look," said Jack, "in a little while it'll be time to start the farm chores. You should be up at the truck. They'll probably be pushing while they have you behind the wheel, so you won't be tied up and gagged. Give me ten minutes. When you hear me walking toward the barn, let them know I'm starting the morning farm chores. Then go with them, as they'll probably leave the truck and come around to abduct me."

"What if we get the truck out and they start drivin' away? Larry asked.

"Not a chance, Larry," Jack answered, "not a chance. Your truck's stuck too deep into the mud. The only thing that's gonna get that truck out is your Ford tractor. That or the Farmall."

"You're takin' a mighty big chance, Jack," insisted Larry. "What 'bout Doris an' the kids? Ain't they gonna be in danger?"

"Trust me, Larry. Help is on the way this very minute as we talk," Jack said to calm the younger man. "The family is safely hiding. No one but me knows where they are. It's best that way, Larry, but believe me. They are safe."

Jack unlocked the back door, opened it and, as Larry stepped off the back porch, said loudly to give the hoodlums a false sense of security, "Good luck, Larry. If you need any more help, just let me know." Jack figured if the two felons think he doesn't suspect anything, there's a good chance they just might let down their guard.

Immediately after Larry left, Jack turned out the lights and quickly locked the door. Then from inside the darkened kitchen he watched out the front window near the sink as Larry slowly walked toward the barn. The two hoodlums could not be seen, but Jack knew they were following his friend from a distance.

"Ya sure ya called the Pennsylvania State Police, Mr. Patterson?" Pepper questioned. "I wanna make sure we get these guys tonight so's things can get back ta normal."

Pete Patterson looked at Thursy's friend and assured him he spoke directly with the State Police. "They're on their way, Pepper," he said. "In the meantime, let's all three quietly walk up to the house and see if we can be of any assistance to your mom and dad."

Pete Patterson was a stocky man, not fat, but solid. He had been a marine and like his neighbor Jack Whelan, had also fought in the Second World War, seeing front line action during the war's waning days with the Normandy invasion. He still maintained his side arms and other weapons and was considered by the Army as a skilled marksman.

During the fall hunting season, he enjoyed the sport and hunted both deer and bear in Potter County near the New York state line. Small game, such as rabbits, pheasants and squirrels, he hunted locally. Out of view from the boys, he discretely slipped his sidearm into his jacket pocket before leaving.

Then Pepper, Thursy and Pete Patterson took off in the rain up Sawmill Road toward Pepper's house. Crab Cake followed. When they reached the end of the woods, they climbed the wooded hilltop, just inside the tree line to avoid being seen. At the top of the hill, they crossed over the fence row and continued down the hill walking as close to the brush as was possible.

Halfway down they stopped to case the area, making sure they weren't walking into a trap. It was at this point that Pepper took hold of Crab Cake, telling him to be as quiet as possible. Then he picked up the dog and carried him the rest of the way. When they reached the end of the corn field where the lane ends, they stopped again, watching carefully for any signs of activity or disturbance.

"Looks good, so far," Pete Patterson whispered to the boys. "You see that building to the left?" he asked, pointing to a chicken coop. "Let's make it to there and stop again."

Crab Cake growled lowly, a deep guttural growl that only Pepper could feel because he was holding him. "No, no, boy," he ordered. "Stay quiet. Don't make a sound, Crab Cake."

The back door opened and the three saw Jack walk out toward the barn with a flashlight in one hand and a stainless steel milk pail in the other. They watch curiously as they heard all the noise he made walking toward the barn. When he reached it, Pepper thought he made an unusual amount of racket opening the barn doors. Then they saw the inside light come on.

Slowly they made their way closer to the house. When they reached the old stone smokehouse, they waited again, making sure no one was watching. "You boys and the dog stay here," Pete Patterson ordered. "I'm going to make my way to the barn to make sure everything with Jack is on the up and up." Then he left them and slowly moved onward to the lower part of the barn.

Crazy Eyes and Tattoo immediately stopped pushing the truck. "Turn off the injine," they ordered Larry, who was sitting behind the wheel. "An' stay quiet."

"It's okay," Larry whispered to the two criminals, feigning cooperation. "He thinks I'm up here getting my truck out. He doesn't know you two are holding me captive." The last thing Larry wanted was to have the two criminals capture Jack and hold him, too. For that reason it was important they didn't suspect that Jack was aware of their little game.

"Okay. You," Crazy Eyes said, pointing to Larry, "get outta the truck an' push. Yer bigger'n Tattoo 'n' me. You git b'hind the wheel," he told Tattoo, "an' work 'em gears. Don't gun it. Juss make shore ya get in a nice an' easy rhythm an' rock this here truck. I'ma push on the back left. You," he said again, ordering Larry, "push on the back right. An' don't try 'scaping. This gun's loaded an' on my right side."

Tattoo started the truck again, slipped it into second gear and hit the accelerator. In doing so, he suddenly sent the two back boards shooting out from behind the truck and throwing mud everywhere. Crazy Eyes and Larry continued pushing from behind while spitting out a spray of wet, soggy earth the spinning tires had kicked up. Tattoo shifted into reverse, hit the gas and the truck moved backward a foot or two.

This procedure went on for some time until a chunk of soft mud hit Crazy Eyes smack in his good eye, causing him to slip. Watching him fall flat on his face in the mud hole made by the spinning tires, Larry immediately took off. Dropping backward out of sight from the cab, he swiftly ran toward the back side of the barn. With one hoodlum laying face down covered from head to feet in a thick layer of sloppy, loose mud and the other behind the wheel with his mind on shifting gears and watching straight ahead, in the darkness of the night, neither saw the escape.

Picking himself up, Crazy Eyes was furious. Opening his eyes, he tried looking at Tattoo but only made matters worse by allowing more mud to seep into his eyes. "You," he hollered, thinking Larry was standing next to him, "gimme sumpin' ta wipe this mud off with."

By this time Tattoo was out of the truck and laughing like a hyena at Crazy Eyes. "Here," he said, handing him a dirty cloth that he found on the front seat of the truck, "lemme help ya."

Tattoo opened the dirty cloth and started wiping his partner's face, but was abruptly interrupted when Crazy Eyes angrily grabbed it out of his hands and quickly wiped it himself. Looking to his right, he instantly realized Larry Haney was no where to be seen. "Ya seen what ya did, ya numbskull," Crazy Eyes charged. "I tole ya notta race the injine an' spin them wheels. Now we ain't got no hostage. An' I'll guarantee ya he ain't gonna be going home ta clean up."

Both now understood the gravity of their situation. And both suspected that Larry Haney tipped off Jack when he went to the door for the keys. "This guy that lives here is the same one who brought all those cops on us the udder day," Tattoo said to his partner, as if it suddenly dawned on him.

"You know, Tattoo," Crazy Eyes began, "for the life of me I'll never unnerstand why you always hafta tell me the obvious like it was some late breaking news story that no one had ever heard before. Ya think I'm blind? I know that. Now get in the truck and let's see if we can get it outta that blasted mud hole."

But so deep were tires stuck in the hole that the truck was of no use to them. Their only hope was to get away quickly before any authorities arrived. After all, the cops knew where the house was. They were there just five days earlier.

Then it dawned on Tattoo. "Crazy Eyes? The car! The farmer's car," he said referring to Jack Whelan. "All we need ta do is ta git the keys. That should be a piece o' cake. He probably carries 'em wit' him alla time, an' he's in the barn now, milkin' the cows."

"Well," exclaimed his partner, "yer finally earnin' yer keep. Notta bad idea, Tattoo, notta bad idea. But this time, let's plan it right." And sitting on the bed of the pickup, they laid out their plans.

Tattoo was to go around the front, into the barnyard through the wide gate and into the lower part of the barn where the milking was taking place. If all went according to plans, Jack would be sitting on a low three-legged milking stool with a bucket between his legs and his head tilted down watching milk squirt into the bucket as he milked the cow. The advantage of surprise would allow Tattoo to sneak up, club him over the head and take the keys.

Crazy Eyes would head for the back of the barn and quietly sneak into the upper part through the narrow door. He would remain up there, lying down on the floor at the top of the steps. With the lights on downstairs, he'd be watching everything Tattoo was doing in the barn's lower part. If Tattoo ran into trouble, Crazy Eyes would be his backup.

Tattoo left for the lower front part and Crazy Eyes checked his gun before he departed the truck for the upper barn. As the rain started falling heavier once more, Crazy Eyes reached his destination first. He quickly opened the upper rear barn door and entered. With his gun in his hand, he slowly moseyed over to the doorway. Lying down, he spotted the glow from the lower barn lights, but the cows were out of view. Tattoo had not yet entered.

"Drop the gun and stay where you are," a voice over him said. Crazy Eyes felt the cold metal barrel of a pistol jab him in the back of the head. "Now!" the voice commanded. "Don't even think about cute tricks." Jack Whelan had snuck up into the second floor of the barn by way of the steps long before the crooks had laid out their plans and there he waited, hiding in the hay loft. He finally had Crazy Eyes right where he wanted him.

"When your partner comes through that downstairs barn door," Jack ordered, "tell him to come up the steps. If there's any warning on your part that I'm in here, they'll be picking lead out of your body at the county morgue."

They were the last words Jack Whelan remembered saying. A sudden thud on his head dropped him like a heavy sack of wet oats.

When Tattoo couldn't get the locked gate to the front barnyard open, he quickly came around the back to the upper floor. Entering the barn by way of the second floor's back door and seeing Crazy Eyes at the mercy of Jack Whelan, he picked up a two by four and used it like a baseball bat.

Jack Whelan lay motionless, sprawled out on the floor in the upper section of the barn. His fully loaded gun was now in the hands of criminals.

Chapter 25

With the rain falling faster, Pepper, Thursy and Crab Cake were getting soaked standing out in the open behind the old stone smokehouse. "C'mon, Thursy," Pepper said, "let's make a beeline for the garage." Holding tightly onto Crab Cake, Pepper joined Thursy in running as quietly and as fast as their legs allowed. The trio headed straight for the garage with a good view of both the lower and upper entrances to the barn.

The building used to park the family car was part garage, part corn crib. Both short ends of the building were open. The lengthy sides consisted of corn cribs about five feet wide and were used to store corn for animal feed during the long, bleak winters. In the back of the building, two farm implements, a disc and a harrow, were stored. Because the family parked the car in the empty front space, it was always referred to as a garage.

Upon reaching the open ended garage, they saw Pete Patterson standing near the front, waiting for the rain to let up. "Dad," Thursy spoke first, "I thought you were gonna see if Mr. Whelan was okay."

"The barn gate's locked," Thursy's dad answered. Then more to Thursy than to Pepper, he continued in a scolding tone, "I thought I told you to stay behind the smokehouse. Why did you disobey my orders? Why are you here?"

"There's a key on the inside ledge above the gate," Pepper volunteered. "An' it was my idea, Mr. Patterson," he admitted. "It started ta rain an' I didn't want Thursy getting soaked just 'cause there's problems at our house.

"Okay, kids," said Mr. Patterson, calmly, "now this time do exactly what I ask of you. Stay put. Do *not* move from this garage. Do you understand?" he asked, and then added, "There's been a change of plans. It may be better if I get into the barn through the back door of the upper floor."

After both boys watched Pete Patterson climb the hill around the back of the barn and enter through the same door Tattoo had entered just minutes earlier, Thursy sat down on the seat of the rusty disc to rest. Pepper, spotting the old weathered harrow and still holding Crab Cake, did the same. Quietly, like unseen clandestine sentries, they kept the barn's front and back entranceways under a tight surveillance.

Looking up, Thursy noticed the second floor of the garage. Toward the front was a small window on the gable with outside shutters facing the barn.

"What's up there?" he asked Pepper.

"Nuttin', really," answered his buddy, "juss some old boards piled up. Dad uses 'em for repairing things 'round the farm." Suddenly Pepper realized the advantage of being up there instead of where they were. "C'mon, Thursy," he said. "Let's climb up there. We'll be able ta see a lot better."

"Better not, Pepper," Thursy said, trying to stop him. "We'll get ourselves in a mess of trouble again. My dad made us promise not to move from here."

"Technically we're not, Thursy. We're still here," his friend answered. "Your dad'll be proud of us 'cause all we're doing is switching our location from a dangerous downstairs position out in front where everyone can see us to undercover in the safety of the second floor where no one can. C'mon. You go first and I'll hand you Crab Cake."

With the boys carrying Crab Cake, they slowly made their way up the inside of the near empty corn crib to the second floor of the garage. Once they were situated, they sat and watched. Downstairs, where they were before, it was possible for someone to reach the back door of the upstairs barn level without being seen. Now no one would be able to enter or leave without Thursy, Pepper or Crab Cake's eagle eyes spotting them.

Handing Jack's loaded gun to Tattoo, Crazy Eyes looked at him gratefully and thanked him. "Here," he said, "hang onto this. In our sitchiashun two guns is better'n one. Now help me wit' this guy, partner. Let's get 'im downstairs."

With Crazy Eyes holding Jack under the shoulders and Tattoo holding his legs, they stumbled down the steps to the lower floor of the barn. Still holding him, they dragged his unconscious body to the far end of the first floor, past the stalls where the cows were kept and sat him up against the whitewashed stone barn wall.

Directly above them on the upper floor of the barn was row after row of stacked bales of straw. Except for the area where the steps descended, stacked in the same manner on the opposite side were bales of hay. In the middle of the upper floor Jack stored farm equipment. The second floor itself consisted of rough cut, solid oak two by tens, loosely laid so an eighth to a quarter inch of space separated the boards. This was done purposely to allow for air circulation during the hot summer months, thus preventing fires caused by spontaneous combustion that destroyed so many of the old wooden barns in the area.

Anyone lying on the floor of the upper part could see the lower floor between the boards. All barns were built the same and all farm children discovered this very early in their young lives whenever they'd play hide and seek while their parents did farm chores in and around the barn.

When they reached the far end of the first floor, they left Jack's motionless body slump to the floor. Standing over him, Tattoo, again emphasizing that he wanted nothing to do with anymore killings, asked Crazy Eyes what they were going to do with him.

"Relax, partner," Crazy Eyes said, putting his hand on Tattoo's shoulder, "right now, he's our hostage. When he wakes up, we gonna get his car keys. He's gonna be our brand new ticket ta freedom," he added, "and when we reach the promised land, that there eastern shore, he's gonna hafta figure out fer himself how ta git home when we let 'im go."

Crazy Eyes took a bucket of water from the cow's stall and threw it on Jack's face. "Wake up, Buster," he ordered Jack. "C'mon, c'mon," he insisted. "You weren't hit that hard." But Jack Whelan just lay there, slumping against the barn wall and motionless.

"Ya don't think we did him in, do ya, Crazy Eyes?" asked Tattoo. "I tole ya I don't want nuttin more ta do wit' any killings."

"Well, then, why'd you hit him so hard, partner?" Crazy Eyes shot back. "Don't look at me wit' that stupid stare on yer face. I didn't club him over the head with a two by four. 'Sides, if I tole ya wunst, I tole ya a hunnert times to clip 'em upside the head, not ona top."

Tattoo went to the second cow's stall, picked up another bucket of water and just like Crazy Eyes did moments before, drenched Jack with the cold water. Still he lay there motionless. Now Tattoo was concerned. So was Crazy Eyes. Tattoo leaned down against Jack, putting his ear against his chest. When he did, Jack opened his eyes ever so slightly and being that Crazy Eyes was intensely watching Tattoo, he never saw Jack grab his partner and the gun out of his right hand.

Crazy Eyes backed away, running for cover at the far end of the barn. Behind a wooden divider he hid for protection, and taking the same gun he stole from the warden, he aimed and quickly fired in the direction of the two struggling men. The bullet, going astray, missed Jack by a foot. Holding Tattoo with his left arm under his neck, Jack returned the gun fire with his sidearm, only hitting the wooden divider which Crazy Eyes was using for protection.

Suddenly Crazy Eyes saw a window of opportunity. Standing straight up were Jack and Tattoo. The criminal was still trying to escape from Jack's hold. Jack was struggling more with trying to subdue Tattoo than what he was concentrating on Crazy Eyes. A clear shot straight into the left side of Jack's upper abdomen was possible. Quickly, Crazy Eyes raised his pistol and took deadly aim. Jack Whelan's heart was dead center in his gun's site.

Holding the revolver steady with both hands, Crazy Eyes slowly pulled the trigger. Jack looked straight down the barrel of the gun. In slow motion he saw the trigger being squeezed. Jack knew he had made a mistake. His own gun was in his right hand by his side. He had no chance of stopping him with a shot. His only chance might have been to dodge to the right or left. But it was too late. He saw Crazy Eyes complete the pull of the trigger. As the man's life flashed right before his eyes, he heard, "Click!"

The gun misfired was his first thought. Either that or he's out of ammunition. Jack had no way of knowing that Crazy Eyes had only one shot left when he fired at him and Tattoo only moments earlier. And in the excitement of the moment, Crazy Eyes had forgotten the correct count of bullets that had been fired.

But as Jack watched in the drama of the moment, Tattoo, finally got the upper hand and with his leg, locked it inside Jack's, tripping him to the ground. "Crazy Eyes," called Tattoo, "I got him. Give me a hand." And his partner in crime immediately ran to his side, thanking Tattoo once more for saving the moment. With Tattoo holding the gun on Jack, Crazy Eyes searched his pockets for the car keys. It didn't take him long. Once they were found, he started ordering, "Now you gonna be taking a ride wit' us," Crazy Eyes told Jack, pushing him back against the far wall where he lay before. "For me an' Tattoo, it's gonna be a one way ticket ta freedom. But for you, because youse been such a thorn in our side, it's gonna be juss a one way ticket."

A chute used to drop hay from the top floor to the cow's stall stood above each of the eight downstairs stalls. Five cows were kept in the barn. The milk they gave was used for the family's needs, including churning butter and making cheeses. The leftover skim milk from skimming the cream was usually fed to the hogs and cats that hung around the farms in the area. Farmers had always kept cats around the barn to keep rodents away from the feed.

No one but Jack Whelan saw Pete Patterson descend the hay chute at the other end. Jack was facing that end. The two criminals, with their backs to it, were facing Jack and watching him very carefully. "Ya make one wrong move an' truss me, mister, you are his... to... ry." Holding the loaded gun on Jack, Tattoo emphasized each syllable for effect.

Jack really didn't need the criminal's dramatic overtures to know they meant business. He opened both hands, spread them out as a sign of peace and shrugged, indicating they had the upper hand and he'd do whatever they wanted. "We gonna juss wait here for awhile," said Crazy Eyes. "Juss 'fore dawn breaks, you gonna be drivin' us outta here. Where ya got the car?"

Instantly, a rush of fear for Thursy, Pepper and Crab Cake rushed through Pete Patterson as he heard Jack answer, "It's in the garage. I always keep it in the garage at night."

Still facing Jack, the two crooks never heard Pete creep up along the inside of the cow stalls and move to within three feet of them.

"Boys," said Jack, in an attempt to prevent any more violence, "suppose I ask you to just turn over the gun to me and we can end this charade by holding you until the cops come."

"Ha, ha, ha, ha, ha." Tattoo was laughing so hard tears began rolling down his cheeks. Crazy Eyes was staring at Jack as if he just took a leave of his senses. "Whatsa matta wit' you, mister?" Tattoo asked. "Whatta weird sense o' humor you farmers got," he added, not waiting for an answer.

"But juss ta play yer silly game, and hear whatever goofy answer you may have, why would I wanna go 'head an' do a stupid thing like that?" he asked. "Ya blind or ya just fo'gettin'? It ain't you that gots a gun pointin' at me, it me that gots it pointin' at you."

"Maybe so," said Jack, pointing to the rear of Tattoo, "but it's he, that one special person you can not see, who now has a gun pointing at your back."

Never bothering to ask who 'he' was, Tattoo, still laughing, answered, "Naw! Ya gotta try sumpin' more original than that. You not gonna find us two hardened jail birds fallin' for that ol' line. Soon's my head's turned 'round ta look, WHAMO! Ya jump me juss like ya did earlier when I thought ya was dead," Tattoo charged. "We's not so dumb that we'd fall for it twict in one night."

"Regardless of how low your degree of intelligence is, you had better drop your gun anyway," Pete said, moving out of the shadows with his own sidearm in his hand. "You see, this time he wasn't ferhoodling you," he explained to the two crooks as Jack grabbed his gun back. "You two world travelers really ought to listen to him more often when he speaks. He really does know what he's talking about."

"Who the Sam Hill are you?" asked Crazy Eyes, looking depressed and hoping Tattoo would once more do something to get them out of their sudden predicament. "An' juss where in the name of a good, home, pan fried chicken dinner did ya come from?" Whenever Crazy Eyes felt he was cornered, his questions and answers were usually laced with colorful verbiage.

"For you two," answered Jack, "you don't need to know who he is. All you need to remember is that by the time this is over, you two guys will wish you'd never met him. He's the last person you'd ever want to tangle with, fellows. So if I were you, I'd behave myself and do exactly what he says." Then turning back and facing the dangerous duo, he added, "Otherwise, it'll be a one way ticket for both of you. And trust me when I tell you it won't be to freedom."

"Now, gentlemen," said Pete, "there's binder twine upstairs. We're going to slowly and cautiously climb the steps to the second floor of the barn. When we get there, you'll both be tied up." He had no way of knowing Crazy Eyes still had the roll he had taken out of Larry Haney's truck stashed away in his big pocket. And Haney was no where to be seen.

"Then we're going down to the farmhouse and wait for the police whom, I suspect, are already on their way," added Jack, while looking at Pete for confirmation. Pete just nodded his head affirmatively. "And by the way," he said, looking straight at Tattoo, "I'll take back my car keys now."

"This is how we're gonna be climbing those steps," said Pete. "I'll go first. You will follow," he said, pointing to Crazy Eyes. "Then you'll follow him," he said to Tattoo. "Jack, you'll bring up the rear. I want you to remember that both he and I will have a loaded weapon pointing at you at all times. So any shenanigans from either one of you, I'll guarantee they'll be the last shenanigans you'll ever pull." And like a U.S. Marine Drill Instructor, he ordered, "Okay, move 'em out."

Resembling a Marine battalion, Pete took the lead, walking to the ladder and climbing the steeply pitched steps first, followed by Crazy Eyes, Tattoo and then Jack. When they reached the halfway point, Jack finally put his foot on the bottom step and started his ascent. Just as Pete reached the top, Tattoo bumped Crazy Eyes ever so slightly. These two crooks had been together long enough to know when to make their move and when not to. They've eluded more captures than any two criminals in the state's history. That's why they were still free.

Crazy Eyes knew the bump was no accident and instantly fell forward, tripping Pete on the top steps. As he did, Pete's gun dropped out of his hand and fell between two hay bales, deep down into the bottom of the stack. Using his added weight to his advantage, Crazy Eyes immediately tackled him, holding him down against the top barn floor and rendering him useless.

Like the finely rehearsed choreography of a skilled dance team, when his partner fell forward, Tattoo pushed backward against the handrail, throwing Jack off the steps and onto his back. With Tattoo landing on top, Jack struggled to take control of the skirmish as both dove for the dropped gun. Both reached it simultaneously and manhandling the loaded weapon, they thrashed about wildly on the floor, each trying to claim it as their own.

In the split of a second, a shot rang out. With his front splattered in blood, Tattoo, struggling to release himself from the grip of his opponent, slowly raised himself. Exhausted from the ordeal, he finally stood up, albeit wobbly, then bent over and reaching inside Jack Whelan's pocket, he removed the car keys. Quickly, he climbed the ladder, joining his criminal partner and their hostage, Pete Patterson, and leaving the severely wounded husband of Doris Whelan, and father of their five children, behind.

A stream of bright red blood spurted from Jack's upper body, pooling on the barn floor by his side. Jack Whelan lay motionless, his life now in the hands of fate.

Chapter 26

Doris Whelan shuddered with fright upon hearing the gunfire. David, Ty, Paula and Sarah questioned their mother. "Can't really tell what's going on from up here," she said, trying not to show even the slightest hint of worry on her face. "Could've been someone in the fields shooting at a groundhog. Ya know how our neighbor farmers around here are always shooting at the groundhogs, trying to stop 'em from eating the crops, don't ya?"

Deep within her she feared the worst, but nevertheless assured her children there was nothing to worry about. "Your father is fine. He's a very careful man," she said, "and he's always been extra cautious with a firearm. Besides, it's hard to believe anyone could ever get the drop on him. Not with all his special training he's had in the Second War."

Then she heard the third shot and her imagination ran rampant. Even the four children were unconvinced their father was fine. Hiding in the second floor of the summer house with four kids and not knowing what was happening was torturous. It was, to say the least, wear and tear on her worn out nerves. Should she send one of the girls out to get an update? They were older and therefore more mature than the boys was her reasoning. Where would she tell her to go? How would she instruct her to protect herself? What if she failed to return?

Perhaps she should go herself and leave the children under the supervision of the oldest, Sarah. But what would happen to the children if her husband was shot and she put her own life in danger? She could very well be risking the orphaning of five beautiful children. So many, many questions. So few, few answers.

No, she decided. The best way to handle this situation is just to wait it out. Do what she promised Jack she'd do, keep the children safely hidden. *'Tis better to be safe than sorry!* she thought, using an age old cliché. *Besides, Pepper and Crab Cake already went for help. By now the police must be on their way.*

"Patience, dear children," she told them, "have patience. Everything will be fine if we just remain patient. Perhaps it might be better if we all put our faith to work by saying a fervent prayer that your father remains out of harm's way."

191

"And don't forget Pepper and Crab Cake, Mom," said Ty. "Those shots could've been meant for my big brother and his dog."

Rubbing the lad on the head and pulling him next to her, Doris agreed. "Let's include Pepper and Crab Cake in those prayers, and anyone else you might be able to think of that could be helping your dad." The five went silent as they bowed their heads in prayer.

From high in the upper floor of the corn crib sided garage, the boys heard the first two shots ring out and a look of worry swept their faces. They knew if they didn't see their fathers exiting the barn soon, it could only mean one thing, they were hurt, and quite possibly dead. Ten minutes, which seemed like ten hours to the boys, passed. Then the third shot rang out. Now they started debating whether to disobey Pete's orders and go help or listen to him and stay put. Crab Cake, still in the arms of Pepper, whined.

From out of the woods, Pepper thought he saw some figures walking. From Sawmill Road, down from the Barnes farm, Thursy imagined the same. They looked eastward over the hill and noticed the dim glow from the dawn starting to break. But also aware that images can quite easily play tricks on your eyesight, especially in the valley with the breaking of dawn, they said nothing to each other.

Suddenly the back door to the barn sprang open. First out was Thursy's father, followed by Crazy Eyes with a gun in Pete's back. Soon they saw Tattoo emerge. Waiting and waiting for Jack, their hopes were dashed when Tattoo closed the barn door.

"Thursy, we gotta get into the barn. I think my dad might be hurt," Pepper said.

"But they got *my* dad," Thursy countered, emphasizing 'my.' "I can't leave here without helping my father. That wouldn't be right, Pepper," he added, almost pleading with him to understand.

"Okay. Here, hang on to Crab Cake," Pepper said. "I'm gonna go inta the barn the front way. I gotta find *my* dad."

Quickly, Pepper climbed down from the upper loft. From behind the Ford he snuck out the rear between the disc and harrow. Cautiously, he walked toward the front, staying out of sight by continuing his short trek along the outside of the one filled corn crib. Looking both ways, he crossed the lane and approached the gate. There he reached up to an outside barn ledge near the front and retrieved a key. Unlocking the gate, Pepper entered, closed the gate, locked it and returned the key to where only the family knew its secret spot.

As he did, he saw the backsides of Crazy Eyes, Tattoo and Pete Patterson enter the garage. Pepper slowly opened the barn door and entered. He looked about. There were the five cows in their stalls mooing, waiting to be fed, watered and milked. He glanced toward the far end wall and saw only a cat kept in the barn to control mice.

Cautiously walking toward the steps, the young lad spotted feet. After breathlessly running toward the fallen figure, he reached the body lying face down and turned it over. His father lay quiet. This time he was not feigning. "Dad, it's Pepper," he said, holding back tears. "Stay still, Dad. I'm gonna go get some help."

Looking down he saw a pool of blood by his father's right arm. Then he realized his head was up against the stone barn wall. He reached for a bucket and poured cold water in it. Dipping his hand into the water, the boy gently patted his father's face and head with the refreshing liquid. Jack opened his eyes slightly and then closed them. Pepper dipped his hand into the water again, generously rubbing a handful on his father's face.

This time Jack's eyes stayed open. "Pepper, son," he called out slowly and then moaned. "Ooh! I've got a terrible headache!" Trying to sit up, he noticed the stone wall. "Must've hit my head on it during the struggle."

Looking down on the floor, he saw the pool of blood at which Pepper was staring. "Dad, lie still," his son directed. "I think you've been hit. There's blood everywhere."

"Just winged me, Pepper," his dad explained, examining his right arm near the shoulder. "Got me below the shoulder in the upper arm. I had the safety latch on but somehow it must've been released accidentally during the scuffle. Hitting my head on the stone wall felt worse. Boy could I use an aspirin!"

"Dad, lie still. I'm gonna go get help," Pepper told him again. He reached in his back pocket and removed a large, clean, red printed handkerchief, the kind cowboys used to use on their western drives. With a loose knot, he tied the kerchief around his father's upper arm and above the wound. Inserting a small wooden peg he found in the barn to use as a tourniquet, he quickly slipped it under the kerchief. Then the young lad twisted it until it was tight.

Placing Jack's hand on the tourniquet, he instructed his father to do the same. "Hold it tight, an' then release it. Keep doing that, Dad. Lie still an' remain here 'til I get back. An' don't move." It felt strange ordering his own father around. "I'll be right back."

From high on the western hill above the rear side of the barn were five neighbors. They joined forces after Larry Haney moved swiftly from farm to farm asking for help. Tom Carmichael called Roy Haney, who rounded up neighbors in his area. Whenever a neighbor had problems, it became everyone in the valley's problem. It was a common occurrence for them to band together in an effort to help others. And each always looked out for the other. On the hill, ready to descend to the barn area were Chet Cline and his brother, Patrick. There were also Floyd Brouse, Tom Carmichael and Delano Heiney.

Approaching the house from the northeast end of Sawmill Road were Larry Haney and Lucas Barnes. Lucas's brother, Leonard, also joined the group of men, as well as Elwood Gampee, who lived across the road from the Barnes farm. Lastly there was Pinkus Mueller, the German farmer noted for his acres upon acres of early sweet corn.

Approaching from out of the south woods and across the freshly plowed field were Larry Haney's father, Roy, Pete Patterson's oldest son, George, Nelson Wertz, Clyde Fenstermaker, a retired farmer who annually grew wheat, barley, corn and oats and Paul Heiney, who worked for a local ice manufacturing company in York.

Bringing up the rear and far behind the rest of the gang was Amos Springler. Every now and then he'd stop, reach into his back pocket, pull out a small flask and take a nip. Slowly following by his side was Ol' Shep.

In the garage, Thursy and Crab Cake watched from above as Crazy Eyes and Tattoo opened the door of the black Ford sedan. If he could only surprise them, it'd give his dad a chance to overpower the two. But how could he get down without being seen?

Looking behind him at the far right corner of the upper loft, he noticed another opening, much like the one they used to climb up. "Crab Cake, you stay here," he whispered so low only the dog could hear him. Crab Cake answered by licking his face.

Thursy quietly tiptoed across the wooden second floor to the far end of the loft. He stuck his head down, looking first in the direction of the automobile and then behind him at the back of the disc and harrow. When he was convinced no one was watching, he slowly and very quietly descended the side's open slats of the half-empty corn crib.

Dropping to the ground, he hid behind the farm implements. A two prong pitchfork was resting against the corn crib. Next to that was a wide shovel with a long handle. Suddenly from behind the sour cherry tree, which grew next to the outer part of the garage's upper corn crib, came Pepper. "Dad's been shot. He's okay fer now. I put a tourniquet on his arm. But I gotta go get him some help," he whispered softly to Thursy.

"Can't get away ta help ya, now," Thursy said. "They got *my* dad in there," he added, pointing to the front part of the garage where the Ford sedan was parked, "an' they're ready ta take off with him in your car."

"Let's work our way up ta the front," said Pepper. "Stay b'hind the disc an' harrow, buddy. Long as they keep looking forward, they never gonna be able ta spot us in the rear."

Crazy Eyes sat in the front behind the steering wheel. Pete Patterson sat in the middle. Next to him, holding a gun on his side, about heart level, was Tattoo. "No trouble from ya, mister," Tattoo said to Pete, loud enough that the boys heard, "an' you gonna go free when we get outta here. Udderwise, like yer friend lying over there dying," he said, pointing to the barn with the gun, "yer hours enjoying the good life could come to a screeching halt. It's all up ta you."

"And even if he 'spects that youse thinking about any shenanigans," Crazy Eyes reminded Pete, "I already give him permission to shoot ya 'xactly where the gun is pointed. But then again, that gun just might go off accidentally on purpose, since he got a reputation known far an' wide fer havin' such itchy fingers." And then he let loose with a devious, high pitched and penetrating cackle.

Thursy gulped upon hearing what the two crooks had to say to his father. Pepper, in an attempt to calm his friend, patted his shoulder, putting his pointer finger to his lips and mouthing the word, "Shhh!" With sign language that said you take the left, he pointed to Thursy first and the left side second. Indicating he himself would be moving in on the right side, he silently pointed to his pattern for Thursy's benefit.

They both left their hiding spot at the same moment. Pointing for Thursy to approach first, Pepper waited for a second, and then he himself moved in from the right.

Sitting in the middle of the old Ford's front seat, Pete had the advantage. The two crooks had not had a chance to adjust the car mirrors for their benefit. Glancing in the rear view and then the side mirrors, Pete noticed the advancement of his son, Thursy, and Jack's son, Pepper. Neither of the boys knew who had the gun or that only one gun was in their possession.

Suddenly, Thursy sneezed. When he did, both Crazy Eyes and Tattoo looked behind them and to the left. As they did, Tattoo inadvertently moved the gun from Pete's side, where it had been positioned. Pete immediately took advantage of his good fortune and let loose with a mighty right elbow into the abdomen of Tattoo. Crazy Eyes saw what was happening and grabbed Pete in a head lock. Thursy, running to the left side, saw his dad in the headlock and jumped Crazy Eyes. "That's my dad," he shouted. "Let him go." And he was all over the criminal, beating him mercilessly on top the head.

Pepper approached from the right and surprised Tattoo. He grabbed him around the head and tried to wrestle him out of the car, but Tattoo was just too big for the small lad. Still, frustrated to the point where he dropped his gun, he cried out, "God, Crazy Eyes, how many more of these pests are there out there?" Pepper picked up the gun and pointed it at the two, but Tattoo, seeing that the safety lock was still on, slapped the lad and grabbed the firearm right out of his hands.

Instantly, the boy's mind flashed back to his father, who was still lying on the barn floor expecting his son to fetch help. Only instead, he finds himself trapped by the criminals themselves because of his own foolishness. He got himself into this mess. Now somehow he had to find a way to get himself out. If not for his own sake, then at least for his father's.

Chapter 27

"The safety catch was still on," Pete Patterson said to Pepper. "Your dad must've put it on in the barn, hoping no one would get hurt, but somehow in the struggle with these hoodlums, it must have accidentally been released and that's probably how your dad was shot. These two criminals must have put it back on."

"I put it back on so no one else would get hurt," Tattoo proudly volunteered to Crazy Eyes, who by this time was shooting darts at his partner. "I juss wanted ta use it ta put some fear inta these guys," he added in a low voice, "not ta kill anyone."

Upon hearing Tattoo's explanation, Pete commented facetiously, "Well, that was mighty thoughtful of you. I'm sure the court will take this into consideration when it sentences you." Then turning back to Pepper, he asked seriously, "How's your dad?"

Pepper told Pete about the tourniquet he put on his father's upper arm and about how his dad hit his head on the stone barn wall during the struggle. "He needs help real bad," Pepper told Pete. "He lost lotsa blood."

"Let's make a deal," Pete Patterson said to Crazy Eyes and Tattoo, but mostly to Tattoo. "By your own admission, you don't want any more killings and we don't want to lose Pepper's father. Let us go free so we can help his dad, and we won't bother you anymore. You'll be free to take the car and go without any restrictions or any complications."

Laughing harder than before, Tattoo took Pete's face in his one hand, turned it toward himself and looked straight into his eyes. "Hero boy," he said, "you ain't in no position to offer us no deals. We gots the gun. You ain't got no gun. An' since we gots the gun and you ain't got no gun, you do what we say. Vishtay?"

Then it dawned on Pepper, the safety catch was still on. Even after Tattoo admitted he had set it so no one would get killed, he still had forgotten to release it. Without thinking, Pepper grabbed Tattoo around the neck and, catching him off guard, caused him to lose his balance, dropping him out of the right side of the truck and onto the ground. Picking up the two pronged fork, he held it next to his neck and said, "Drop the gun, or I'll shove this pitchfork straight through you neck."

Tattoo could see he meant it. Dropping his gun, Pepper continued holding the pitchfork just below his chin, while giving the gun a kick out of harm's way. But instead, his kick sent the weapon sliding under the car and out the other side. It happened so fast, Pete had very little time to react. Sitting in the middle of the front seat, next to Crazy Eyes, this time he was at a disadvantage.

After seeing the gun go sliding under the car, Crazy Eyes immediately rushed out of the car and retrieved it. With the pointer fingers of both hands held tightly on the trigger, he pointed the loaded pistol dead ahead as he crossed over the front of the truck and aimed it square on Pepper. Still standing over Tattoo, Pepper breathed a deep sigh and said a silent prayer.

Taking off the safety catch in full view of everyone, Crazy Eyes fired a shot into the air, warning, "We all know that the safety catch is off. Now, folks, we gonna get back to the business at hand in a moment before getting outta here. But first I had 'nough of this little pipsqueak. He's been nothing but a thorn in my side ever since he showed up at that fishing hole last Monday," he said. "We know you saw what we did to the warden. An' because you couldn't keep yer nose outta our bidniz ya gonna hafta pay the price.

"'Cause ya ain't never gonna interfere wit' what me an' him does no more, ya young upstart. Ya days is numbered," he threatened. "Better yet, ya minutes is numbered. Say your prayers, trouble maker," he said to Pepper. "You gonna meet yer Maker!" And slowly he started squeezing the trigger.

For a few seconds, with all the commotion, Thursy's whereabouts had been forgotten. From the left rear side he slowly crept up to the opened left door and reaching into the wheel, he hit the horn, sending out a sudden blare while instantly he whistled loudly. For a brief moment the blaring sound of the car's horn rattled Crazy Eyes so badly he almost forgot the job at hand was that of wiping out Pepper.

During that sudden distraction, no one but Pepper heard the low deep growl from high above. No one but Pepper saw Crab Cake leap the instant he heard Thursy whistle. As the blare of the horn startled Crazy Eyes, he turned, only to find he was face to face with an armful of growling fur, two angry eyes and a set of gnashing teeth concentrated on his gun hand.

Barking ferociously and with teeth flashing their pearly whites that said he was nothing to tangle with, Crab Cake made his move. It was one that had let them know he was not going to sit idly by, recuperating from a snake bite, while they had their way with his master.

His jump was bullseye perfect. Crazy Eyes attempted to maintain his stance but the sudden appearance of the Border Collie was more than he expected. With canine teeth sunk deep into his right arm, backward he stumbled in pain, a growling dog hanging on to him as if his upper limb was a freshly grilled steak bone.

"Hold him, Crab Cake," ordered Pepper, keeping Tattoo at bay with the pitchfork. While still weak for his serpent experience earlier in the week, Crab Cake's adrenaline was flowing freely. To say the least, he was having the time of his life. The dog's wagging tail left no doubt in anyone's mind.

Pete Patterson jumped out of the truck and rushed to the hero dog. "Hold him down good, Crab Cake," he said, "Good boy! Now I'll take the gun." The dog had Crazy Eyes' wrist in his jaws and pushed back toward the ground. Crazy Eyes was writhing in pain. The gun, while still in the felon's hand, was, nevertheless, barely in his control. Pete leaned over and assisted Crab Cake by holding the hoodlum down with his foot, and then he reached for the gun, freeing the outlaw of the dangerous weapon.

"Thursy," called Pete, "hand me that roll of binder twine hanging on the corn crib." The son did as his father asked. "Now hold the gun on this guy," he said, referring to Crazy Eyes and handing the revolver to Thursy. "If he as much as wiggles without being told, son, shoot him right between the eyes. You have my permission." The hoodlum knew he was serious.

Not a muscle of Crazy Eyes moved as Pete took both his hands and tied them securely behind his back. Then he tied both legs together in the same fashion. After finishing with Crazy Eyes, Pete turned his attention to Tattoo, still being held by Pepper with a pitchfork. He performed the same tie-up on him as he has done with his crooked partner.

Facing them together on the ground, Pete finished his tying task by securely tying their tied feet together. When he was finished, they sat facing each other, hands tied behind their backs, feet tied together and then tied to each other. Even if they did manage to stand up, they wouldn't be able to walk.

Pepper rested the pitchfork against the side of the corncrib and rushed back to the barn. There he found his father lying in the same spot where he left him, barely conscious.

"Dad, hang on, Mr. Patterson's on his way." And he tightened the tourniquet a little more to slow the bleeding.

The sound of the warning shot brought five neighbors running at top speed from over the western hill. The same amount ran swiftly from Sawmill Road's north end. From the south came five plus Amos Springler, stumbling slowly behind the others. As Pete Patterson walked out to greet them, they mentioned about the gunfire they had heard. Looking past Pete, they saw the two crooks bound together with binder twine.

"What about Jack Whelan?" asked Larry Haney. And motioning toward the barn, Pete led them to the lower floor where the injured man lay.

Six men picked up Jack, one lifting from under each shoulder, one under each side and one under each leg. Together, they carried him to the car and sat him upright in the middle. Larry Haney got behind the wheel. Joining him on the right was Lucas Barnes. The three started down the lane for the York Hospital. Speed was of the essence. Jack Whelan had now lost consciousness.

"Mom and the rest," said Pepper, "they must still be in the house." Pete, Thursy, Pepper and Crab Cake started for the big farm house when they saw Doris come out of the small summer house with Sarah, Paula, Ty and David following. They had been peeking out from behind the pulled window blinds and knew all was okay again.

"Doris," Pete began, "Jack was hit. He's on his way to the York hospital now. He should be okay, Doris. Jack's a strong fighter. I'll drive you and Pepper there." Leaving to get his car, he told her, "Stay here. I'll be right back."

At the hospital, Pepper waited with his worried mother, his new best friend, Thursy, and Pete Patterson in the waiting room just outside the operating area. Since hospitals had rules prohibiting animals, Crab Cake was locked inside the car in the hospital's parking lot with both side windows cracked about an inch. He was lying down on the front seat and taking a snooze until the others returned.

The family was waiting for word from the doctors. The huge double doors to the surgery area swung open as Doctor Hutchinson entered the waiting room. "Mrs. Whelan?" the doctor asked, looking at Doris. "I'm Doctor Hugh Hutchinson. Sit down, please."

Doris suspected the worst when she heard him tell her to be seated. "Your husband's lost a lot of blood, but he's going to make it. I think he should remain here for a few days so we can observe his progress."

"What happened, Doctor?" Doris asked. "The kids and I were hiding inside the summer house."

"Well, in the scuffle, Mrs. Whelan," the doctor answered, "it's my understanding that your husband took a bullet in the arm below the right shoulder. It hit an artery but looks like it just missed a major nerve. It also looks like he tore his rotator cuff during a scuffle. At any rate, Mrs. Whelan," the doctor added, "he's lost a lot of blood and needs round the clock professional care until he's out of danger."

Then he turned to Pepper. "I understand it was you who put the tourniquet on you father's arm, son," the doctor said, holding out his hand to shake it with Pepper's. "Congratulations. If he isn't already now, your father's going to be mighty proud of you when he comes to," he continued. "You see, son, he's lost an awful lot of blood. And as a doctor, I feel relatively sure the actions you took by putting the tourniquet on him saved his life."

"May I see him?" Doris asked, her eyes misting, holding back sobs, legs weakening and hands trembling as she looked hopefully at the doctor. "May I at least just hold his hand?"

"Certainly, Mrs. Whelan," Doctor Hutchinson said. "But right now he's still under sedation. I'll instruct the recovery room nurse to allow you in as soon as he comes to," the doctor said, patting her on the hands as a sign of reassurance.

Pepper's mother thanked the doctor and then returned to the lounge area, waiting for word her husband was awake. For Doris, it had been a trying week. She never did have the strength to cope with emergencies like her husband. Consequently, she recognized her weaknesses and hoping in time she'd learn how to strengthen them, she relied more on him than she felt she should have.

But that never bothered Jack. The more Doris did rely on him, the more he'd graciously respond, "These are lessons for our sons to learn. When they grow up, they'll need to know how a husband should treat a good wife." Then he'd hold her in his arms and kiss her gently.

Pete returned from somewhere within the hospital holding two cups of hot coffee. "Drink this," he told Doris, "you'll feel somewhat better."

"I really don't know how to thank you for risking your life in this mess which involved only us," she said to Pete Patterson. "I want you to know how much we appreciate all you've done."

"No need to thank me, Doris," he answered. "Jack would've done the same for me had it been my family. Beside, it did not involve just your family. Larry Haney was involved, the warden, my son, Amos Springler, Chet Cline, Crab Cake and before the whole story comes out, don't be surprised if those two subversives didn't endanger the lives of a lot more good people in the area," he added.

"The most important thing," Pete said, "is that they're finally captured, they're in custody, sitting in the county jail as we speak at this very moment and hopefully, they'll be put away in a prison far from here for many years to come. Most importantly, those two crooks may not know it, but they did teach us a very valuable lesson on what it means to help each other in a time of need. We can all sleep better knowing that if danger comes to any of us in the future, there are others nearby who will be watching, and if needed, willing to help."

Chapter 28

The following week found Crab Cake slowly returning to his old spunky self. Pepper's dog had been recuperating nicely and was starting to feel his oats. His energy level continued to rise and periodically he'd give a half hearted chase down the fence row near the garden after a ground hog. He certainly wasn't as fast as he had been and for some unexplained reason, Pepper sensed that the wood chucks knew it. But he was getting there and in time, he'd be back to full strength challenging all who dared to enter his territory.

It wasn't until the following Friday when the York Hospital finally released Jack Whelan. Once again, Pete Patterson volunteered to drive Doris in to pick up her husband. Naturally, Pepper, Thursy and Crab Cake rode along. As before, the dog stayed in the car with the windows cracked for air. This time, instead of snoozing, Crab Cake watched intently all who walked by, releasing a warning bark to anyone who ventured near the Patterson vehicle.

On the way home, Jack Whelan, with his right arm in a sling, thanked Pete Patterson for all he had done in helping his family. Pepper and Thursy had become much friendlier since that Sunday two weeks ago before the opening day of trout season. The events of that week were mainly responsible for their sudden bonding. No longer was Thursy considered by others at Hametown School as an outsider. Everyone wanted to hear firsthand about his adventures, even the girls. Thursy was in his glory. Naturally, he was enjoying it.

Crab Cake was the first to hop out of the car upon arriving at the Whelan farm early that Friday afternoon. He barked once, announcing their arrival. Pete walked to the automobile's right side to help Jack if it was needed. Doris, Pepper and Thursy were the last to exit from the back seat.

Inside, daughters Sarah and Paula had warm pastries, lemonade, ice tea, cocoa and hot coffee ready in celebration of their father's homecoming. Each gave a special and longing hug to their dad, followed by sons Ty and little David, shortly after entering the farmhouse kitchen. Jack was still somewhat weak from loss of blood, but he was young enough to bounce back quickly. More than anything, he needed the love of his family, good home cooking and plenty of rest in his own bedroom and on his own bed.

Pepper and Thursy accepted a cup of hot chocolate and a slice of warm Dutch apple cobbler before joining Crab Cake on the back porch. "Sure would like ta try 'gain for Ol' Uncle Louie," Pepper said to Thursy. "Heard the other day at school that no one's caught him so far." He paused to take a bite of his cobbler, then added casually as if it was expected, "Ya wanna go with me?" It was the first time Pepper had ever invited Thursy. Up until then, it was always Thursy inviting himself.

Recognizing the importance of the moment, the young lad looked at Pepper and humbly said, "Thanks, buddy. Asking me ta go with ya means an awful lot. I'd love to join ya. Maybe this time we could juss fish," he said, laughing heartily.

Pepper, sipping his hot cocoa while grabbing the humorous meaning of Thursy's words, let out a belly laugh, too. Crab Cake, looking at the two and as if he also understood the meaning of the joke, wagged his tail. Then the Border Collie laid his head down on Pepper's lap and sighed. Pepper responded by patting his dog affectionately on the head.

"Time to go, son," Pete Patterson said to Thursy as he left the kitchen and walked out on the back porch. "Gotta finish cleaning that swimming pool. That's a big day you've got ahead of ya."

"Dad," Thursy started slowly and humbly, "Pepper's going fishing tomorrow and asked me ta join him. I thought if it was okay with you, maybe I could finish the pool on Sunday."

Pete Patterson studied his son's face. He saw in him a pleading he hadn't seen before. It was more than a beg. Without Thursy saying it, it remained a simple request to his father that said this was important.

"If he can join me fishin', Mr. Patterson," Pepper interjected on Thursy's behalf, "I'd shore be glad ta help him Sunday in finishing the pool."

That was a deal too good to pass up. Pepper knew it, Thursy knew it, and most importantly, Pete Patterson knew it. Even Crab Cake seemed to know it as he looked up at Pete and gave one friendly bark. "Okay, you two. You've got me," Pete responded, answering Thursy's plea, "but that pool had better be finished by Sunday evening, son, whether Pepper helps you or not. It's not his responsibility, it's yours."

The two boys shook hands. As Pete and his son got ready to back out of the driveway, Pepper cupped his hands around his mouth to yell that he'd meet Thursy at his house about seven in the morning after he had finished his morning chores. "I'll be waitin' for ya," Thursy yelled back. And within a few minutes they drove down the lane, turned right onto Sawmill Road and disappeared into the woods that led to their home.

The following morning, after he had finished his morning farm chores,

Pepper picked up his fishing gear on the back porch and started down the field toward the fence row that led to the woods. From there he walked the dirt road to Thursy's house. Fresh bait in the form of earthworms had been dug in his mother's garden after Thursy and his father had left the day before. Crab Cake followed closely.

The morning dew evaporated and the fog lifted swiftly as the sun slowly rose, spreading its rays of brightness and warmth from beneath the horizon of the eastern hills. The few scattered clouds in the sky dispersed and throughout the meadow a robin's song could be heard calling its mate. Other birds gathered small pieces of dried grass here and there as they busied themselves with the business of nest construction.

Along the way a rabbit darted about, and squirrels chattering with one another announced to all that spring had finally sprung. Crab Cake, making an effort at chasing a pheasant, soon realized he still wasn't up to full strength and gave up after a short run. A squirrel teased him needlessly as the dog snubbed the bushy tailed animal and continued following closely behind Pepper.

Upon seeing a groundhog, Crab Cake never gave a second look. He knew he wasn't in its league. At least not yet. Another day sometime soon and he'd have some fun, but today, he'd be content just to follow along.

Thursy was waiting by the stone fence that separates the dirt road from his front yard. He had two poles leaning back over his one shoulder; he was holding onto its handles with his one hand. In the other he held the handle of his tackle box and a new fishing net, one big and strong enough to hold Ol' Uncle Louie.

His bait was in a metal can with holes for circulating air and was attached to his belt around his waist. He carried with him a brown bag packed with sandwiches, mostly peanut butter and jelly and across his shoulder a strap connected to his dad's old metal quart army canteen. It was filled and sweetened with freshly brewed ice tea.

Earlier in the week Thursy had walked down to the secret fishing hole on Rehmeyer's Run alone to retrieve the fishing gear the two lads had left behind when the downpour chased them into the cave the week before.

"Two poles?" asked Pepper, eyeing his buddy's equipment curiously. "Boy, Thursy, you mean business today. Guess I ain't got much of a chance catching Ol' Uncle Louie," he said, laughing. He noticed one of the poles still had a price tag on, indicating it was new and had never been used.

"It's a new one from my dad," said Thursy. "I thought you'd like my old one as a way of saying thanks for inviting me along yesterday, and also for offering ta help with the pool." Surprised, Pepper graciously accepted Thursy's gesture of gratitude and thanked him for the gift. His newly established friend wasn't so bad after all. Even though it was used, it was still a good one. Most importantly, for Pepper, it was his first real fishing rod and reel.

"Dad said that Crazy Eyes and Tattoo had ta be separated in that jail where they're being held," Thursy told Pepper. It made him feel quite important that he was the bearer of this late breaking news. "Dad said they kept blaming each other fer gitting caught until the guards got so sick o' hearing 'em argue, they juss up an' put 'em in two different cells far apart from each other."

"My dad," continued Pepper with the conversation, "said that they're facing up ta 75 years in prison for attempted murder of the warden and armed robbery and attempted murder of that old couple before they met us. Those people that lived near York Springs. Guess those two crooked hombres won't be doing no fishing for Ol' Uncle Louie for a long, long time."

"Ya ever hear anything about some hidden loot that seems ta be missing, Pepper?" Thursy asked his friend.

"Here an' there I did, but never could make heads nor tails outta it. Figure it's juss sumpin' that got started wit' the local folks when they heard 'bout those two criminals on the loose," Pepper answered. "You know how everyone talks so much about what little they know."

Reaching the White Oak School Road, they continued until they approached Amos Springer's house. Old Amos was sitting on his porch swing moving back and forth oh so slightly. "Hi, Mr. Springler." Pepper waved as they approached the house. "How's Ol' Shep doing?"

"He'll outlive you an' me." The retired barn painter waved back as his words rang out loud and clear. It was much too early for him to be inebriated. At seven-thirty in the morning he barely had time for more than three beers. "Going after that big trout?" he asked. And then assuming the answer would be yes, he chuckled and quickly added, "Good luck! You'll need it if ya 'spect ta catch Ol' Uncle Louie." Lifting a cold brown bottle of an off brand brew to his lips, he added, "Gonna have nice weather fer a change today. No rain in the forecast."

The boys waved back as they continued on their way. Turning left at the 'Y' in the road, Pepper, Thursy and Crab Cake soon reached the bridge crossing Rehmeyer's Run. What a difference almost two weeks meant. Gone were the crowds lined up along the banks shoulder to shoulder. Gone were the game wardens checking everyone for their fishing license. And most importantly, gone were the two criminals who had terrorized the local community and their trout loving fishermen. Only the landing of Ol' Uncle

Louie remained on the uppermost portions of the boys' minds.

"C'mon, Thursy, let's see if the 'secret' fishing hole's available," Pepper suggested. And before you could say Ol' Uncle Louie, the two boys and dog were headed upstream and rounding the bend, checking out their favorite fishing spot.

The banks were void of anglers, save for one kindly looking fisherman on the opposite side who was snoozing as the boys and Crab Cake approached. With his line in the water, he had his floppy hat pulled down over his eyes. A metal thermos bottle sat by his side with an empty cup, probably filled earlier with hot coffee, turned upside down. He made neither a sound nor did he move an inch. His line sagged lazily in the calm waters of the deep pool.

"Uh, pardon me, Mister," Pepper addressed him. "You don't mind if my friend an' me fish from this side, do ya?"

Crab Cake stood by Pepper and, neither growling nor barking, watched the lifeless man closely.

Lifting his hat from over his eyes, the grandfatherly figure looked calmly at Pepper, Thursy and Crab Cake. "Come to catch that elusive trout?" he asked, a twinkle in his eye as if he knew something about Ol' Uncle Louie that the boys didn't. "Well, don't be too disappointed if ya don't. The Great Angler in the Sky's been saving him for me," he chuckled. Then as an afterthought, he added, "But don't let that stop you, fellas. Help yourself. This creek here's big enough for us all."

Pepper thanked him and the two boys wasted no time in getting their poles ready. Pepper set his bamboo pole aside and baited the hook on the line of the used rod Thursy had just given him. Suddenly, Crab Cake spotted a chipmunk and being smaller than most of the game he's spotted the last couple of weeks, barked loudly and decided to give chase. "No, no, Crab Cake," Pepper admonished. "You stay here. And no barking, you understand?"

Man, what a bummer. Here was one he could finally chase and now he's not allowed. With his head hung low and his tail tightly tucked between his back legs, the Border Collie turned and slowly crept back to where Pepper was sitting. How he would have enjoyed chasing that chipmunk. "Lay down an' be quiet," Pepper kindly ordered his dog. "No more shenanigans, Crab Cake. We're here ta catch Ol' Uncle Louie. That means ya muss stay quiet. Understand?" Crab Cake wagged his tail and lay down next to Pepper.

"Gonna try me a smaller hook," Thursy said to no one in particular. "Then I'll load it up wit' fresh worm. That's a meal in itself, Pepper. They ain't gonna be able to resist a breakfast like that."

Pepper noticed the old man's pole bending as he tried reeling in the line. "Did ya hear Larry Haney had ta use the tractor ta get his truck outta the mud?" Pepper said, holding small talk with Thursy. "Also heard he might be buying a newer one soon. If he does, Dad said he might buy his old truck. Said he'd teach my mom ta drive an' leave the car there fer her durin' the day."

The old man was still trying to reel in his line. The pole was bent as far as it could go without breaking. "It's a good thing ya got your chores done in time," Thursy told him. "We got down here pretty early 'fore the place gets too crowded." He leaned back on his one elbow and watched his line.

"Oh, Ty's helping me," Pepper said. "Dad decided that after being as brave as Ty was the past couple 'o weeks, he's earned the right to a little responsibility. So I'm training him ta take over my morning chores come September." Then to the old man across the creek he said, "Looks like ya got a big un on the line, Mister."

"Not really, son," the old man answered. "Hook's just caught on something. Not a root. I felt it move. Feels like something real heavy," he said, and then as his line broke, he finished, "like I snagged it on something metal." The old man put new tackle on his line, baited his new hook and threw it in again, this time upstream from where he lost his last hook.

"My dad said this may be the last year for Hametown's one room schoolhouse," Thursy continued the conversation, informing Pepper. "Everyone up ta the sixth grade's gonna be transferred to Shrewsbury School in September. From the seventh grade on they'll be going to the new high school they just built. They're calling it Susquehannock, after the local Indian Tribe."

With neither of them recognizing it as such, the conversation was turning into a challenge between the two as to whose dad told them the latest and most important information that would be affecting their young lives. This went on back and forth until a jerk on Pepper's line grabbed their attention.

"Shhh! Hold on a minute, Thursy," Pepper said. "I might be getting' sumpin'." He sat up quickly and took the rod more firmly in his hands. Another small jerk on the line and Pepper whispered, "C'mon. Quit playing an' run wit' it." But this time nothing more happened and the boys went back to their meaningless conversation.

Ten minutes had passed since Pepper last had a bite. Then, from out of the blue, his line went tight. The tip of his rod suddenly bent in an arc. Pepper stood up and set the hook. The fish took the bait and ran. Crab Cake was up like a flash, his head cocked to one side, watching Pepper diligently. Suddenly, in the bright morning sun, the stillness of the water was broken by a mighty rainbow trout. His wet shiny sides glistened in the sun, brilliantly intensifying his deep gorgeous rainbow colors.

"Thursy! Get yer net ready," Pepper ordered. "I think I got him. All I gotta do is work him toward the bank. Get ready, Thursy." Back and forth the rainbow went with the line. "C'mon, Thursy, get the net," Pepper called.

But Thursy was too busy to hear what his pal was asking. His line was also tight. With his new rod bent in an arc, he set the hook and soon a trout, bigger and prettier than the one Pepper had on his line, broke out from beneath the water into the air, its tail bent and showing off its beautiful rainbow colors on each side for all to see.

"The net, Pepper. Grab the net and stand by the bank," Thursy asked his friend, not realizing Pepper was in the same predicament as he was. "I'll work him this way. You be ready for him with the net."

With both boys concentrating on their respective catches, Crab Cake watched as two humongous trout simultaneously broke from their watery domain and flashed their brilliant sides in the morning sun. It was then the boys finally realized what was happening. Both had hooked a huge trout. Only one could be Ol' Uncle Louie. Or could it?

So preoccupied were they with their hooked rainbows that neither saw the old angler's line on the other side shoot straight down. Tightening his grip on the handle, the elderly gentleman set the hook. From far right to his far left the tightened line swiftly traveled. His rod was arched as far as it could bend without breaking. The third time his line ran past him, the top of the water broke with a monster rainbow trout leaping high into the air and falling back into the water with a mighty splash.

Both boys saw the huge rainbow in the morning sun. Both boys knew it was bigger than the ones on their lines. And in the back of both minds, both boys knew it was none other than Ol' Uncle Louie!

Chapter 29

The old man's trout was bigger, far bigger than Thursy's and almost twice as big as the one on Pepper's line. Its wet, seemingly iridescent sides glistened with the colors of the rainbow and its tail flashed wildly back and forth with each bend of its body. With every break of the water it showed great determination to spit the hook. After all, it didn't get to be as big as it was by quickly giving in.

It was a sight to behold. Both boys stood up, their mouths hanging open, gawking at the humongous fish. Crab Cake stood up too, ready to let loose a ferocious bark. "No, Crab Cake. Don't ya dare bark," Pepper warned him. Crab Cake cocked his head and stared at Pepper. Figuring he couldn't have any fun around Pepper and Thursy, he jumped up on a small ledge overlooking the stream and, rather than stand there and allow himself to be scolded, decided to just lie back, watch and bask in the rays of the early Spring's warm morning sun.

Again the rainbow broke the water line and leaped high into the air, its colors glistening more brilliantly than before. Pepper and Thursy continued watching in awe, both secretly wishing it had taken the bait on their line instead of the old man's.

In the excitement of the moment, the two boys had forgotten about their own catches, leaving their lines go limp. By the time they remembered, both of their fish had spit their respective hooks and were gone. Now with nothing to land, they laid down their poles and watched. "Is it Ol' Uncle Louie?" Pepper asked, knowing it was but hoping the elderly gentleman might disagree.

"Well, if it ain't, son," the old angler answered, "it's the biggest rainbow trout I've ever seen in all the years I've been fishing for 'em. That, son, has been for a long, long time, and I've caught a many of 'em," he added, holding tight to his rod and turning the reel's handle to bring the huge fish closer to shore. The last thing the old man wanted was to break the line. He skillfully wound the handle of the reel, drawing the great fish closer to the bank. Then he'd give him some line and let him run, hoping to tire him out. Each episode brought the trout closer to the grandfatherly figure on the opposite side who may have just hooked a living legend.

"I hope ya land him," Pepper said, but deep in his heart he was struggling

211

with mixed feelings. If it had to be caught by someone else, there's probably no one better to reap its rewards than the decent old fisherman on the bank across from them.

If the elderly angler does land Ol' Uncle Louie, the challenge to catch the huge elusive trout will end, and with it, much of the fun of fishing Rehmeyers Run. If somehow he fails, hope still remains alive. And within that hope lies the dream of catching him that brings all fishermen back to that stream, time and time again.

By Pepper's watch, twenty-three minutes had elapsed since the fish took the bait. Still there was no indication the old man had taken control of the situation. The mighty fish was putting up a tremendous battle, one that was tugging at the heartstrings of both boys, as they found themselves secretly and subconsciously rooting for Ol' Uncle Louie. After all, they thought, with that much resolve, it'd be a shame if he lost.

Now the old man himself seemed to be tiring, and both boys wondered if they should cross over and offer him their assistance. But discretion, being the better part of valor, lost out to good common fishing sense. After all, no fisherman would want to say he needed help to '*land the big one*'! No, they were better off where they were, staying out of the way and just watching. That way, if he should lose the fish, there'd be no one else to blame it on but himself.

Once more the enormous rainbow trout shot out of the water, mouth wide open, fins straight out and tail slapping from side to side as if it were an airplane readying for take off. On its descent, however, it inadvertently landed closer to shore and once there, the old man took advantage of his good fortune by quickly reeling in the slack line. Now the fish was no more than ten feet from the far bank. As the two lads watched, they witnessed the great fish slowly tiring. The old man was winning this battle. Ol' Uncle Louie was about to be caught.

Holding the rod in his left hand and grabbing his huge net's long wooden handle with his right, he whipped the net through the air above the waters, opening its woven fabric basket. Watching the struggling fish near the top of the water, the old man lowered the net into the water and under the fish. Each time he tried to land the fish, the rainbow trout did a dive and eluded the net. More than once the old man tried to net him, and each time the great fish escaped.

Now the elderly gentleman dropped the net on the ground next to himself and decided he'd try bringing it closer with his reel. Slowly he wound the handle, making sure there was not too much pressure on the line. And slowly the great fish moved against its will closer to shore. Finally, the old man had him right where he wanted him. Ol' Uncle Louie was wallowing near the bank in no more than six inches of water. His minutes were numbered. The old man knew it, the boys knew it and above the bank on an outcropping of rock which formed a ledge, basking in the morning sun and staying out of trouble, Crab Cake seemed to know it.

As the fish finally came to rest against the earthen bank, the old fisherman removed all slack from his line. Now, from the tip of his rod to the mouth of the fish was no more than four feet of distance. Down he bent onto one knee. Holding the rod in one hand, with his other hand he reached into the shallow water and grabbed the fish under his gill. Lifting it out of the water and onto the bank, he raised it up to chest level.

Other than a token flash of his tail and the normal gasping in air that all fish do when they're removed from water, the huge rainbow trout gave little resistance. Reaching deep into his mouth with a pair of needle point pliers, the old man gently removed the hook and holding the great fish up high in front of the boys, he admired the vivid sparkling colors on its sides.

All were preoccupied admiring the beauty of Ol' Uncle Louie that no one either saw or heard the strange noise on the ledge above. Crab Cake did. Recognizing the slithering serpent as it hissed its way closer from the far side of the ledge and aiming its deadly fangs toward the canine's wagging tail, he learned his lesson from two weeks before and quickly backed up. As the deadly copperhead moved toward the warm spot where the dog was resting, Crab Cake never looked behind as he continued moving back.

One step farther and he'd be in the water. Instead, the old man shouted to the boys to be aware of the possible danger that lurked overhead. "A snake's on the ledge above you near your dog," he warned them. "Better be careful," he added. "They can be nasty with their bite."

"Crab Cake! Jump!" shouted Pepper. "C'mon Crab Cake. Jump now." Then Pepper remembered, and gave a mighty shrill whistle that ran the length of the valley.

All three watched as the Border Collie decided he wanted no more to do with copperheads and gave up his warm sunny spot on the ledge to his slithering enemy. As the old fisherman held the prize rainbow trout up high for the boys to admire, the dog jumped backward, landing in the deepest part of the fishing hole. Laughing at the whole scene, the old man lowered his arm while watching Crab Cake do the doggie paddle toward him.

This was hardly a laughing matter and Crab Cake knew it. How'd the old man like to be in his situation, ready to be bitten by a poisonous snake? Crab Cake knew what it was like. This old man needed a lesson in compassion. Walking toward the old fisherman, he reached within a foot of him before suddenly letting loose with all the water that was soaked in his long flowing fur. Shaking wildly, Crab Cake drenched the old man as if to say, "Take that! That'll teach you to laugh at me."

Caught completely be surprise, the old fisherman gasped for air as the shaken ice cold spring water of Rehmeyer's Run caught him by surprise. In the process of being drenched with the icy water, he inadvertently released his grip on the great rainbow trout, dropping him back into the shallow water below. Having been giving a reprieve on life by the unlikeliest of creatures, a dog, Ol' Uncle Louie made the most of his good fortune by gasping the oxygen rich spring waters swiftly into his gills.

As the old fisherman wiped the water from his eyes with his hands and then reached down into the water to grab the fish again, Crab Cake let loose with another barrage. By now the mighty rainbow had enough oxygen to revive itself and slowly made its way from shore into the deeper waters of Rehmeyer's Run. As he did, he moved toward the bottom until his brightly colored sides could no longer be seen in the clear, cold mountain water.

On shore the old man did an about face, showing a side of himself the lads had not seen. He let loose a volley of angry words denouncing Crab Cake and all who bring their dogs fishing. And then realizing the entire episode of the dog spraying him was unrehearsed and losing Ol' Uncle Louie was probably nothing more than an Act of God, he simmered down, apologizing for his sudden and uncharacteristic outburst.

The boys felt better, accepted his apology and assured him that better luck would greet him the next time out. "There may not be a next time," the old man answered. "I just may hang up my rod for good. After all, how many anglers can say they've actually landed and held in their hands for all to see, Ol' Uncle Louie? I have," he said, answering his own question. "And to prove it, I have two witnesses. That's a big enough trophy for any fisherman's lifetime." And then looking down at Crab Cake he laughed and corrected himself, "Better make that three witnesses!" he added. Crab Cake, wagging his tail, barked his approval.

"Maybe catching Ol' Uncle Louie is not to be," Pepper suggested, winding in his line from his lost trout.

"You could be right, son," the old man said. "Perhaps he was put here just to test the fishing skills of all anglers. And to teach them they don't always win. For me, I think my day is finished. I'm going home and bask in the memory of landing the biggest trout I've ever seen. And to think, with the help of a dog, it got loose. This is one fish story no one's gonna believe!" he said, shaking his head and laughing at the irony of the situation. "Seems like it's never the little ones that get away." He picked up his pole, net and tackle box, left his unused bait for the boys, bid them good day and hurried up over the hill toward the road.

"Funny," Thursy said to Pepper. "I ain't never seen that guy before. Who is he?

"I don't know, Thursy. I thought maybe you knew him. I ain't never seen him before either," Pepper answered. "An' who knows? Maybe we won't ever see him again. He never did say his name."

Deciding they too had had enough excitement for one day, Pepper and Thursy headed for home to work on the pool. Suggested Pepper to Thursy, "If we work on it today an' git done with it, we'll have tomorrow ta play ball. If you could join us, we'd love to have ya,"

"Thanks," Thursy said, suddenly remembering this was the second time in two days he received a Whelan invitation from Pepper. "I'll be there," he said, excitingly. "Let's get home. There's a pool to clean."

As Thursy, Pepper and Crab Cake wandered up the road toward home, occasionally stopping to see how far they could kick stones that lay on the road in front of them, they talked about the next six Saturdays and once school was out the entire summer when they'd be able to cast their lines every day into Rehmeyer's Run in their quest of catching the elusive monster rainbow trout, known to all as Ol' Uncle Louie.

Crab Cake, moseying along with them, spotted a rabbit darting out of the brush up ahead and wanting in the worst way to give chase, had second thoughts. He, too, had had enough excitement for the day. When his full strength returned he'd have plenty of time to chase whatever it was he desired. After all, he was still alive, and for that he was grateful. Beside, the warm months of summer were still ahead of him.

Somewhere out there, locked up in a prison, Crazy Eyes and Tattoo were still arguing. Somewhere out there, deep in the waters of a local trout stream, stolen loot remained to be found. And somewhere out there in a creek known as Rehmeyer's Run, deep in the hill country of Pennsylvania's southern York County, Ol' Uncle Louie was beckoning Pepper, Thursy, Crab Cake and all freshwater anglers to come try their luck once again.

After all, that $100 prize was still waiting!

Printed in the United States
22205LVS00004BA/70-510